Adelaide Ristori

Adelaide Ristori

Studies and Memoirs

Adelaide Ristori

Adelaide Ristori
Studies and Memoirs

ISBN/EAN: 9783337008963

Printed in Europe, USA, Canada, Australia, Japan

Cover: Foto ©Raphael Reischuk / pixelio.de

More available books at **www.hansebooks.com**

Famous Women.

ADELAIDE RISTORI.

Already published:

GEORGE ELIOT. By Miss Blind.

EMILY BRONTË. By Miss Robinson.

GEORGE SAND. By Miss Thomas.

MARY LAMB. By Mrs. Gilchrist.

MARGARET FULLER. By Julia Ward Howe.

MARIA EDGEWORTH. By Miss Zimmern.

ELIZABETH FRY. By Mrs. E. R. Pitman.

THE COUNTESS OF ALBANY. By Vernon Lee.

MARY WOLLSTONECRAFT. By Mrs. E. R. Pennell.

HARRIET MARTINEAU. By Mrs. F. Fenwick Miller.

RACHEL. By Mrs. Nina H. Kennard.

MADAME ROLAND. By Mathilde Blind.

SUSANNA WESLEY. By Eliza Clarke.

MARGARET OF ANGOULÊME. By Miss Robinson.

MRS. SIDDONS. By Mrs. Nina H. Kennard.

MADAME DE STAËL. By Bella Duffy.

HANNAH MORE. By Charlotte M. Yonge.

ADELAIDE RISTORI. An Autobiography.

ÀDELAIDE RISTORI.

STUDIES AND MEMOIRS.

An Autobiography.

BOSTON:
ROBERTS BROTHERS.
1888.

UNIVERSITY PRESS:

JOHN WILSON AND SON, CAMBRIDGE.

PREFACE.

———◦∘◦———

"LIFE is a journey,'' they say. Certainly this proverb could be applied to me. My existence has been wholly passed in long journeys, and I have carried on my art in all countries.

Under every sky I have personated the immortal heroines of immortal masterpieces, and I have seen the powerful accents of human passion thrill with intense emotion the most different peoples.

I have brought into this task, often very heavy, my whole art conscience ; I have sought even to live the actual life of the personages I represented ; I have studied the manners of their times ; I have gone back to historical sources, which enabled me to reconstitute faithfully their personality, sometimes gentle, sometimes terrible, always grand.

The applause bestowed upon me has rewarded my honest efforts; but I must say again that I have experienced the most lively pleasure when I succeeded in identifying myself sufficiently with the

(v)

characters of the tragedies which I was playing; when I felt myself inspired by the great breath which animated them, and my whole soul vibrated to the passions I was to interpret. I have often left the stage, after extreme tension of nerves, half dead with fatigue and emotion, but always happy.

CONTENTS.

——◦◦——

ADELAIDE RISTORI.

CHAPTER I.

CHILDHOOD AND DEBUT IN ITALY.

BORN a member of an artistic family, it was natural that I should be dedicated to the dramatic art, and this being, as it were, my natural destiny, it is not surprising that my parents should have accustomed me to the footlights even from my birth. For I was not yet three months old when, a child being wanted in a little farce called *The New Year's Gift*, the manager availed himself of the services of the latest addition to his company, and I, poor baby, with my mother's consent, made my first appearance in public.

The subject of the comedy was extremely simple and common-place. A young lady having been forbidden by her father to marry the lover to whom she was passionately attached, wedded him clandestinely, and in due time had a son.

Not having the courage to communicate this terrible fact to her inexorable parent, the young mother decided to confide in an old man, who was a dependent of the house, and who had helped her in other difficulties. He sympathised greatly with the troubles of the two delinquents, promised to assist them to obtain the paternal pardon, and for that purpose decided on a singular stratagem.

It was the custom then, as it is now, to give presents at the beginning of the New Year. In country districts the proprietors of estates and owners of houses are considered as the principal people of the neighborhood, and their tenants are in the habit of then offering to their master the best of their fruits, their largest fowls, and their finest eggs. So the worthy servant in the comedy determined to place the poor child in a large covered basket among the fruit and poultry (taking, of course, every precaution that it was neither crushed nor suffocated), and sent it by a peasant to his master.

The stage was duly prepared for the arrival of the customary offerings. All the family and the guests who had been dining with the master of the house collected round the basket as soon as it was brought in, ready to admire its contents, and in the background appeared the comic countenance of the good servant, who rubbed his hands with a smiling and self-satisfied air as he waited patiently for the success of his stratagem.

At last his master opened the basket. With real satisfaction he began to take out and examine the various gifts. First the fowls, then the eggs, then the fruit; but it seemed as though the excessive fragrance of this latter had affected me, for before there was time to lift me from the basket I began to shriek in lusty tones. Imagine the amazement produced by such an appearance on the stage!

The grandfather, in his surprise, took an involuntary step backward, while his good old servant, without much ceremony, lifted me from the basket and placed me in his arms. The spectators stood with their mouths open, the husband and wife tried to justify themselves ; but my cries increased so much in intensity, and gave such evident proof of my good lungs, that I was hastily carried off to my mother's chamber, where I found what alone would quiet me at that moment.

The public, of course, went into a fit of laughter especially as it seems that my voice was then so loud and shrill as completely to drown the actors' words.

Whenever my mother related this incident to me— and Heaven knows she was never weary of repeating it—she always laughed until the tears came into her eyes.

On another occasion, when I was about three years of age, a play called *Bianca and Fernando*, by Avelloni, was put upon the stage. The time was the Middle Ages, and I had to take the part of the little boy belonging to the widowed mistress of the castle, who was passionately beloved by a noble knight. But another great personage in the neighborhood, to whose care her dying husband had confided his wife, and who possessed the supreme power in that country, was also in love with the lady, and desirous of gaining her hand.

There was one scene in the play in which this latter nobleman, seeing himself constantly repulsed by the widow, and finding she was determined to unite herself to the man of her heart, cost what it might,

resolved to raise such a tumult as would frighten her
into compliance with his wishes. The partisans of
both combatants were ready to come to blows, when
the lady thrust herself between them to try and avert
the conflict. Thereupon the tyrant seized the child
who had been left alone for a moment, and threatened
to murder him unless the mother did as he desired.

Then ensued a general panic. It was in vain they
tried to snatch me from his arms. The cries of my
poor mother ascended to heaven. The tumult and
noise terrified me. I began to cry, to fight about in
my captor's grasp, to pull his beard with my little
hands, and scratch his face in my attempts to free
myself. And with such success that at last he let
me slip from his arms, and I scampered away as
fast as my legs would carry me, screaming at the top
of my voice, "Mamma! mamma! he is hurting me!"
and eluding all the efforts of the actors to catch me,
while they exclaimed, "Stop! stop! It is a joke!
it is nothing!"

I was speedily behind the scenes, where I threw
myself into the arms of my mother, and clung to her
in spite of all the efforts of those who came in search
of me to continue the act. Alas! they were obliged
to drop the curtain amid universal laughter.

Seeing myself such a favorite with the public,
although a little girl, I had already acquired a good
share of the cunning of the stage, and, understanding
that I bore an important part in our little company,
I had begun to take the tone and airs of a grown-up
woman.

I remember it was then the custom for the most

fluent and easy-mannered of the company to come before the curtain in the interval before the last act and announce the play for the following evening to the public, indicating also which actor or actress would sustain the principal character in it; and, according to the interest the public took in the player announced, there would be either a murmur of approbation or a hearty applause. The members of the company crowded with curiosity to the curtain to listen to this manifestation of the public. I naturally had also my little ambitious curiosity, and when it was announced that the little comedy ending the performance would be the particular task of the little Ristori, the public burst into loud applause. They all then came round me with jesting compliments, whilst I walked off behind the scenes with my hands in my apron pockets, shaking my head and shrugging my shoulders, saying with pretended annoyance, "What a bore! Always making me act!" while I was secretly exulting in my heart.

What would those who love to prophesy the future life of children from the observation of their early tendencies have said of me after this last escapade just recorded? Why, that the stage would have been hateful to me, that I should never have been able to sustain any tragic parts or endure to see a sword or dagger brandished in the air. And, instead of that, I devoted myself to tragedy, and the sword and dagger became the familiar weapons of my craft.

When I was but four and a half years old I was already made to act little farces in which I took the principal character, and I should not like to be accused of impudence if, in deference to the truth, I record in these memoirs the no inconsiderable profit which my manager drew from this my early appearance on the stage.

I remember that at the age of ten I was entrusted by preference with the minor parts of servants, and my manager made me rehearse several times such a small matter as carrying in and laying down a letter, so that I should not appear to do it in either too familiar or too prim a manner.

At twelve I was selected for the parts of children; and shortly after, my rapid growth enabling them to dress me as a little woman, they entrusted me with the small parts of *soubrettes*. They seem to have taken it into their heads that I was only adapted for that kind of *rôle*.

But at thirteen I had developed so much in person, that I was occasionally allowed to play as second lady, a most monstrous thing certainly, but one that could not well be avoided in small companies. When I was fourteen I joined the company of the famous actor and manager, Moncalvo, to take the parts of young first ladies, and act sometimes as prima donna, in turn with another actress, and it was then that I undertook, for the first time, the character of Francesca da Rimini, in the play by Silvio Pellico, which I performed in the city of Novara in Piedmont.

The result of my attempts was so satisfactory that when I was sixteen, I was offered the important post of permanent first lady on very advantageous terms. But my excellent father, who was gifted with plenty of good sense, did not allow himself to be tempted by these offers. He considered that by thus prematurely overtasking my energies, I should probably lose my health, and stop my progress in my art, and he therefore declined the proposal, preferring for me the more modest part of an "ingénue," which was offered me in the Royal Theatrical Company in the service of the King of Sardinia, and which then passed several months of the year at Turin. This company was directed by the manager, Gaetano Bazzi, the most intelligent and able manager of that day. He ruled his company with a firm hand, and though severe in some things, yet he succeeded in turning out very good artists.

Prominent among the members of this brilliant company were those luminaries of the Italian stage, Vestris, the Marchionni, Romagnoli, Righetti, and many others, whose names are as famous in dramatic art as are those of Pasta, Malibran, Rubini, and Tamburini on the operatic stage.

My engagement as "ingénue" was for four years, but at the end of the first I played the parts of the leading young ladies, and during the two last I was the actual first lady. Thus my gradual progress step by step led to this splendid result, for which I had also to thank my careful education so well directed by my excellent teacher, the esteemed actress, Carlotta Marchionni, who vied with the manager, Gaetano Bazzi, in kindness towards me.

At that period my artistic education began in earnest. Then it was I acquired that knowledge which placed me in a condition to discern the qualities which make the true artist.

My power of giving expression to the stronger and fiercer passions gradually increased, though my natural disposition led me to prefer those of a more gentle and tender kind. I carefully observed and studied them, in order to learn how best to blend the contrasts between them into one harmonious whole; a most minute, difficult, and sometimes tedious task, but one of the greatest importance and necessity. The transitions in a part in which two extremely opposite passions are called into play are, to it, what the chiaro oscuro is to a picture; they unite and amalgamate its various portions, and thus give a truthful representation without allowing the artifice to appear.

To succeed in this you must make a study of the best actors, and if you are endowed by nature with artistic genius you must be careful not to circumscribe it by servile imitation, but rather to try and accumulate rich stores of scenic erudition, which may be given out to the public stamped with the hall-mark of original and creative individuality.

There are some people who fancy that the accidents of good birth, and an excellent education are enough to enable them to tread the stage with the same ease and freedom that they would enter a ball-room, and they do not hesitate to appear there in the full belief that they can acquit themselves as well as an actor who has grown upon it. This is a great mistake. One of the principal difficulties they encounter at the very outset is that of not knowing how to walk upon the stage, which by the sensible incline of its construction makes the steps of a novice very unsteady.

I may cite myself as an example of this difficulty. Although I had been dedicated to the theatre from my earliest infancy, and instructed, day by day, with the greatest care by my paternal grandmother, yet, even at the age of fifteen, my movements had not acquired that freedom and naturalness necessary to render me perfectly at home on the stage, and I still felt a slight nervousness.

No less important is the study of elocution in order to speak distinctly.

The diction ought to be clear, distinct, not too slow, well understood, in order not to fall into any mannerisms, but at the same time deliberate enough to allow the audience to grasp the meaning of every word, and there must not be any suspicion of stammering.

When my artistic training began, elocution was a point to which the greatest importance was attached, as enabling a judgment to be formed of the value of an actress. The public was then a very severe critic; in our days this same public has grown less exacting, less particular, and does not pride itself too much on forming an actress by correcting her faults. According to my ideas the present system is not just, for it is certainly not by excessive indulgence, or by simply considering the good qualities without attempting to correct the bad ones, that real artists are made.

It is my decided conviction that no one who desires to devote his life to the stage ought to begin his studies by assuming parts of great importance, whether in Comedy, Drama, or Tragedy. The task is too great for a beginner, and may in some way

damage his future, either by leaving him overwhelmed with discouragement in consequence of the
difficulties he has encountered, or by filling him
with excessive vanity, because of the consideration
with which his attempt has been received, and which
will probably cause him to neglect the study essential to further success. By confining himself, on the
contrary, to small parts, whether they are congenial
or not, he will render himself familiar with the stage,
and acquire a correct and natural way of acting ;
and he may rest assured that by taking pains to
render these correctly, he will be preparing for better
things, and his study will be more accurate.

But to return to my subject. In the year 1840 my
position as a *prima donna* was completely established,
and, thanks to the favor of Fortune, I saw myself
rapidly arrive at the summit of my ambition, struggling, meanwhile, with courage against every obstacle
that interposed to prevent the full accomplishment of
my successful and very happy career. I never felt
any fatigue, and such was my passion for the stage,
that when my manager chanced to give me a quiet
evening, in order not to overdo my strength, and
perhaps, also, a little with the malicious design of
making the public miss me, I felt quite like a fish out
of water. It was in vain I meant to devote these
leisure evenings to the study of a new and difficult
part. I applied myself to it with the greatest ardor,
but when the hour struck for the play to begin I was
seized with such restlessness, that nothing sufficed to
calm me. I seemed to hear the first chords of the
orchestra, the impatient murmur of the audience, the

intoxicating sounds of applause. I walked up and down my room with rapid steps, seeking to distract my mind; I tried to repeat from memory some of the passages in the play I had been studying. It was all of no use. I could apply myself to nothing; and at last I hastily entered my mother's chamber, saying:

"Shall we go for an hour to the theatre?"

"Well, let us go, then," she answered, "if you cannot keep away from it for one evening."

Immediately we put on our cloaks and hats, and went. As soon as we reached the theatre, my spirits rose, and I began to think of all sorts of practical jokes to play upon my fellow actors. I remember that on one of these occasions they were performing *Le Memorie del Diavolo,* and a number of masks were required in one part of the comedy. The whim seized me to appear on the stage under a mask, and surprise the first actor. It was in vain they attempted to dissuade me from this childish trick. Then, entering my room to put on a domino, and to cover half my face with a tiny black mask, was the work of a minute; and so dressed, I went on the stage among the Figurantes.

When midnight struck, it was necessary for us all to unmask; and what an ugly face the first actor made at me, as soon as he discovered who I was! But though I had difficulty in stifling my laughter, I remained immovable, and quite undisturbed by the affair; and the audience, becoming aware of the true state of the case, burst into hearty applause. Then, seeing how badly my companion took this little pleasantry, I withdrew from sight among the crowd of silent characters that filled the stage, and, hiding myself behind them, laughingly asked pardon for my folly of my good comrade, a pardon that was readily granted me.

But my humor was not always gay. Sometimes I fell a victim to an inexplicable melancholy, which weighed on my heart like lead, and filled my mind with dark thoughts. I believe that this strange inequality of temperament might be entirely attributed to the excessive emotion I experienced in performing my most impassioned parts. For I so entirely identified myself with the characters I represented that, in the end, my health began to suffer, and one evening, when I had been acting in *Adrienne Lecouvreur*, the curtain had scarcely fallen after the last act, when the great tension of nerves and mind and body I had undergone during that final scene of passion and delirum brought on a kind of nervous attack, and an affection of the brain which deprived me of consciousness for a good quarter of an hour.

Sometimes, similar causes brought on a fit of spleen which quite overpowered me. On such occasions, I wandered by choice in the cemetery of the city. There I remained for long periods, reading the inscriptions.on the various gravestones, and I would return home full of sadness, feeling as though I had myself been one of the sufferers in these sad cases. Thus also it was my custom when I arrived in a city hitherto unknown to me, after I had visited the picture and sculpture galleries, to obtain permission to inspect the lunatic asylums; for if I did not go to the cemetery, it was there that the nightmare which for the moment possessed me, impelled me to wander. Mad girls were those who attracted my deepest sympathy; their sad, tranquil lunacy allowed me to penetrate into their cells without danger of any kind, and I was able to stay long with them, to gain their affection and confidence. Gradually however, as years rolled on, I outgrew these eccentricities; my nerves began to acquire the temper of steel; I learned to confine my romantic ideas within reasonable limits, and I applied myself with redoubled energy to the study of my art.

In consequence of the dramatic conditions existing in Italy, especially in those days, it was not usual for engagements to last longer than thirty or forty nights in one city. It was an extremely rare thing for them to last two months, and this constant change of public had the greatest advantages.

It was not necessary to possess a very varied répertoire, and the public had not time to grow accustomed to the actors, to the detriment of their enthusiasm. And what a power does that living and continued fascination of the public exercise over an artistically creative mind! Thus, then, I had always a fresh public before me, which I moved at my will, and which, thanks to the powerful magnetic influence that so readily established itself between us (and this was most essential in my case) communicated to me that electric impulse which alone forms an artist, and without which every study bears the impress of mediocrity.

In this manner my early youth passed away.

My love of study never diminished. With the progress of years, I went on completing my education. That nature had called me to art, I felt within me from the feverish desire which impelled me to see and study all that gradually came before me in my artistic peregrinations. Music, painting and sculpture always had for me a fascinating attraction. I remember one evening at Florence, fatigued by continual performances, I was longing for a day of rest, but my desire was not shared by the Lessee of the Cocomero, now the Nicolini Theatre, Signor Somigli, who was not disposed to put the padlock on the money-box by interrupting the performances of the *Pia dei Tolomei*, which was having an immense run. But I had a right to one day's rest. When, behold! the cunning lessee called in to his aid a brother of his who, recollecting a certain lively desire of mine which might, he thought, serve as a bait, came to me saying: " Play to-morrow evening, and you will get a very handsome present."

" I want rest, and I don't know what to do with your present," I answered.

" Well," he added, " if you only knew! Come, I know you want the beautiful drawing of the façade of our famous San Miniato al Monte, which you so much admired in my sitting-room. If you consent to play to-morrow, you shall have it."

It is true that I had been wishing for it for some time, and they, who were not ignorant of the fact, laid the trap for me. I could not resist ; and so it came to pass that the lessee had another full house, and that I played another full evening for a drawing !

This return which my memory makes to a past embracing so large a part of my existence leads me back to that time, and I feel once more the firm resolution, which never failed me in youth and womanhood, to follow the sacred precepts of my illustrious mistress, Carlotta Marchionni.

Once upon the stage, not even for one moment did my consideration for the public ever diminish.

Whether the audience was large or small, intelligent or the reverse, mattered nothing to me. The possibility that it might contain one educated and cultivated person, able justly to decide upon, and appreciate my artistic merit, was enough to make me attend to the minutest details of the part I was playing. I would not omit a single gesture, a single idea. The simple, familiar style of the French school was then greatly in vogue, and was so much preferred to our way of acting, that in many actors it became quite wearisome. Therefore, without entirely forsaking my habitual method, which, thank Heaven, had not the above-mentioned defect, I endeavored to blend the two styles together, for I felt that, if progress was to be made in everything, even the drama must undergo certain changes. This sentiment did not, however, make me a servile imitator. Neither in drama nor in tragedy was I ever lacking in that Italian fire which is inherent among us, for it is our nature to experience passion in all its intensity, and not to be circumscribed in our expression of it by any academic rules. Indeed, if the impetus of passion is taken away from an Italian "artist"—the true coloring in fact—he sinks at once into a weak and insufferable actor.

For my part, I always endeavored to act in as natural a manner as possible. The public highly approved my careful study, as well as the efforts I made to render myself really worthy of their favor. In short, my countrymen were profuse to the utmost of their power in their demonstrations of affection and approval. Their appreciation penetrated to my inmost heart. It was delicious to me to be thus understood ; to feel that I could move human souls at my will, and excite their gentlest as well as their strongest passion.

I hope the reader will pardon me such language, remembering that the actor lives upon the fame won by much severe study and hard conflict; and how the mere consciousness of having attained the desired goal is sufficient in itself to re-light the fires of early enthusiasm.

When, at the age of eighteen years, I for the first time acted the part of Mary Stuart, in Schiller's play, how much did that great, profound and most difficult study cost me ; how hard and thorny was the road I had to traverse to obtain the object of my desires ! The reader will be surprised when he peruses my analytical account of that part, to find the circumstances which attended my assumption of it.

The time came when my art no longer sufficed to satisfy the desires of my soul. The passion I always had for children was not only innate in me, but was developed in an extraordinary degree ; and it seemed to me that in them was to be found the realization of true felicity on earth. Maternal instinct was even so strong in me that I revolted from playing the parts in which it was overlooked. I shall have occasion, in regard to this, to relate how I had always refused to play Medea in the various tragedies she had inspired, and in consequence of what circumstances I at last consented to undertake Legouvé's magnificent *Medea*, because in this last tragedy the mother's crime is caused by her maternal affection itself.

For all that, I considered the duties of marriage incompatible with my art ; but Fate had in store for me a partner of congenial spirit, who shared my worship for the fine arts, and who, far from repressing my ardor, urged and stimulated me to pursue my way with increased energy.

After a series of strange and romantic incidents, which have been narrated by many of my biographers, I was united in marriage to the Marchese Giuliano Capranica Del Grillo. Many painful circumstances obliged us to be frequently separated during the earlier years of our wedded life.

I had the inexpressible happiness of becoming the mother of four children, two of whom were cruelly torn from us by an early death. We were almost insane with grief ; but the two surviving children, Giorgio and Bianca, were destined to fill the void left in our hearts by the loss of their poor brothers. We never separated from them. We kept them always with us, and they were the source to us of great happiness.

By degrees I began to perceive that the sweet influences of maternal affection gained such hold upon me that imperceptibly my enthusiasm for art diminished gradually in intensity, and its sway over me became less powerful.

This abnormal state of mind, joined to certain secondary causes, decided me to retire from the stage as soon as my three years contract with the Royal Sardinian Company had expired. Chief among these reasons was the fact that, although the *répertoire* of the Company was most varied, well chosen and rich in the productions of our best and most celebrated authors, such as Alfieri, Goldoni, Niccolini, Monti, Pellico, Carlo Marenco, Nota, Giacometti, Ferrari, Gherardi del Testa, Leopoldo Marenco, son of the renowned author of *Pia dei Tolemei*, Fonti, Castelvecchio and many others all worthy of notice, yet it was impossible to fight against the growing rivalry of the lyric stage. The muse of melody seemed alone in favor with the public.

In order to provide for the expenses of the Opera, the managers, or directors, or theatrical academies spent enormous sums, and the prices of admission were, of course, in proportion. A great performance was an event. Everything was sacrificed to it, and it was necessary to make herculean efforts to prevent poor dramatic art from being left altogether in the background.

During the early years of my career, the preference of the public for the works of French writers, which were at the height of fashion then, was such that, in order to be certain of a full audience for several consecutive evenings, it was enough to announce a play of Scribe, Legouvé, Melsville, Dumas, &c. in the bills. It was not that the productions of our native genius had no chance of finding favor with the public, who appreciated their literary merit, the spontaneity of the dialogue, and the purity of the language. But, with very few exceptions, all the applause was reserved for French pieces.

Besides, it should be remembered that the censorship then exercised in Austria and the Papal States had a great share in the decay of our native productions. Thus patriotic subjects were absolutely forbidden. Morality was expressed in the most fantastic way. In consequence our native dramas were reduced to a mass of absurdities when they escaped being utterly silly and without any interest whatever.

I will give a few examples of the absurd changes made by the ecclesiastical censorship in these years.

It was forbidden to an actor to utter the name of *God*, or to use the word *Angel* or *Devil*. Actors were forbidden to take on the stage the names of Gregory while Gregory XVI. was Pontiff, and of John and Pius during the pontificate of John Mastai, Pius IX. The word "fatherland" *(patria)* was likewise prohibited as a blasphemy!

One day a certain play was submitted to the Censor, in which the principal character, who was dumb, returned to his native land after a long exile. The book of the piece contained certain directions which were to be reproduced in dumb show. Among them was the following: "Here the actor must convey to his audience the joy he feels in once more seeing his own country." Well, actually, the word *patria* (fatherland) was erased by the Censor, and *paese* (country) substituted, as though the change of words could be indicated to the public by gestures!

On another occasion, when Macbeth was given at Rome, and one of the three witches says in the second scene of the first act:

> "Here I have a pilot's thumb,
>   Wrecked as homeward he did come,"

the Censor cancelled the lines.

"Why?" asked the manager of the company.

"Because," was the answer, "the public will probably find an allusion in them to the vessel of St. Peter which is in danger of being submerged by the wickedness of the times."

What can be said in defence of such absurdities?

Nor did the operas fare any better than the plays. In Verdi's *Luisa Miller* the following words occur in the tenor's beautiful song:

> "Ed ella in suono angelico
>   Amo te, sol, dicea."

Unfortunately the expression *suono angelico* (angelic note) offended the Censor's delicate sensibility, and he substituted *suono armonico* (harmonious note). This so excited the hilarity of the public, that a wit amused himself by writing under the name of the Via di Porta Angelica—a street near St. Peter's— the words, Via di Porta Armonica.

When Bellini's *Norma* was to be given in Rome, the Censor would only allow it with the following stipulations: First, that the opera was to be called *The Forest of Irminsul*, to avoid using the word "Norma"—literally "guide" in Italian—which constantly occurs in books of devotion; then, that

Norma's sons were to become her brothers; further, that she was condemned to death for having shown favor to the enemy; and that in the famous finale, where she is about to mount the funeral pyre, instead of committing her children to the care of her father Oroveso, it is he whom she must recommend to the Druids.

In Verona the memory is still green of that Veronese, and imperial Censor, who, in a piece of poetry which was to be recited, changed the words "Beautiful sky of Italy" into "Beautiful sky of Lombardy Venetia!" Can anything exceed this? How could the Italian stage prosper amidst such a state of things? How could it move the public to enthusiasm? And, wanting prosperity and enthusiasm, it was a body without a soul.

I felt, as it were, paralyzed under the insupportable yoke which restrained my movements and suppressed half the words. And it was not enough to know that the public had for me a sincere and unalterable affection, a constant and lively sympathy. I was by this time accustomed to identify myself with the personage I represented, to live for those few hours the artistic life of the work by me interpreted, and when this was either misunderstood or ruthlessly mutilated, no longer raised up the same enthusiasm, nor drew forth those electric currents which thrill and carry away the artist. I felt myself falling from the sublime height of my aspirations. The applause lavished on me personally seemed cold, and left in my heart a kind of encroaching sadness.

Thus it was that at Turin, at the epoch above men-

tioned, in 1855, I suddenly made up my mind to retire from the stage. It seemed to me that, in the
quiet of domestic life, I should realize my most
golden dreams.

But these discouragements, these projects, were of
short duration. That the sacred fire was not totally
extinguished within me was proved by my after journeys round the world.

But, at the same time, one idea incessantly occupied my mind. This was to vindicate, before leaving
the stage, the artistic worth of my country in foreign
lands, to show that, in spite of all, Italy was not the
land of the dead. But how was I to do this? All
of a sudden I made up my mind to go to France.

CHAPTER II.

I WAS aware that an Italian Company, directed by the well-known actors Carolina Internari and Luigi Taddei, had been in Paris in 1830, and that their experiences were anything but encouraging. But the speculation was rendered so unfortunate by many exceptional circumstances! The revolution of July had ruined them. Their patroness, the Duchess de Berry, had had to fly with Charles X. and the poor Italian players had been reduced to such straits that a benefit performance had to be given to raise the funds for their return journey.

But in 1855 circumstances looked much more propitious. France was in a flourishing condition ; the great Exhibition had attracted many strangers to Paris. It was a well-known thing that the Italian emigrants, the greater part of whom did honor to our country, had met with the warmest of welcomes in France. The Venetians gathered round Manin as round the banner of their future redeemer, were a subject of constant admiration. And not less an object of interest were all the other Italian exiles. Everything seemed to promise success to my attempt.

I spoke about it to my husband, who approved of it. We thought that the Royal Sardinian Theatrical Company would worthily uphold the dignity of Italian art. 23

The chief members of the company at that time were the now famous Ernesto Rossi, Gaetano Gattinelli, Bellotti Bon, Mesdames Cuttini, Mancini, and Righetti, Boccomini, Gleck, and many others. It was far from my desire to attempt to vie with the French actors, who have no rivals in the perfection of their acting in Comedy, but I was anxious to show those people who cried up the merits of French players to the detriment of those of our nation, that, in a certain measure, we could compete with the French on the Field of Comedy, and equal them, at least, in Drama and Tragedy; that in Italy we still knew what was true art, and could express it in a worthy and dignified manner.

I expounded these views to my eminent and intimate friend, the Commendatore Alessandro Malvano, on whose clear intelligence and judgment I felt I could rely. He thought my project excellent. Encouraged by his approval, I went at once to Righetti, our manager. He was thunderstruck when he heard me, called my ideas chimerical, and ended by opposing the realization of my plan in every point. He set himself to enumerate all the risks to be encountered, the most possible losses, and probable want of artistic success. But here Malvano interfered, declaring himself to be so firmly persuaded of the good result of the affair, that he was willing to assume the entire responsibility.

"The loss shall be mine; the gain yours," he concluded. These words of Malvano made our Manager a little more favorably disposed towards my proposal. I then suggested to him that, as I wanted to have a share in the profits (in case there should be any), besides my regular salary, I was also prepared, in case of loss, to share it with him. At last I succeeded to persuade him, and the matter was finally arranged.

The necessary negotiations were concluded; our departure was fixed for the 1st of May, 1855, while the 22d of May was named as the date of our first appearance, and the *répertoire* was chosen.

Our chief care was to select such pieces as should allow no room for comparison with the French actors; for we knew that Tragedy was the field in which we could best measure ourselves with them, and in Italian dramas we feared no rivals.

So we chose for the first evening Silvio Pellico's tragedy of *Francesca da Rimini*, and a one-act comedy by the Roman author Giraud, called the *Gelosi fortunati*. In this latter piece, I took the part of a young wife very much in love with, and extremely jealous of, her husband. It seemed to us that this transition from Tragedy to Comedy ought to make an impression upon the French public.

Before setting out on my journey I provided myself with several introductory letters; among the rest, with some for the famous critic, Jules Janin, and our lamented Pierangelo Fiorentino, who afterwards so greatly assisted our interests. We left Italy with hearts full of hope. Our journey was pleasant and successful. We traversed the superb and picturesque road for the first time, and our admiration was excited by its grand Alpine scenery.

A small party of friends accompanied us on our

journey, whose enthusiasm for the dramatic art, and
hereditary ties of friendship with the Royal Sardinian
Theatrical Company had induced them to share our
doubts and fears, and be witnesses of the triumph
they hoped was in store for us at Paris. They
undertook this journey with the greatest delight.

We reached Paris towards evening, and I found
my apartment ready prepared for me. It was on
the second floor of No. 36 Rue Richelieu, near the
fountain to Molière.

Every time since that I have passed before this
house, the sight of it has awakened the tenderest
recollections within me.

The members of the company found quarters in
two modest hotels situated near the Italian Theatre.
My husband and I and our friends lost no time in
turning out to see the much-talked-of Boulevards.

We sat outside the Café Veron. I cannot express
the mingled impression of wonder and terror which
overcame me in the midst of this crowd, where not a
single word of my native language reached my ear.
I seemed to understand for the first time the boldness
of my enterprise. The idea of having hoped, even
for a single moment, that I, a stranger, should be
appreciated by this public, unacquainted with the
reputation which I might have gained on the other
side of the Alps, appeared to me decidedly absurd.
My imagination began to work ; an unspeakable
discouragement took possession of me, and I went
home a prey to profound sadness.

We returned home without speaking a single word.
I dared not hint at the doubts which oppressed me,

either to my husband or friends, and, as it may be easily imagined, I passed a most restless and agitated night. During the following days, however, the more material occupations of preparing for our first performance somewhat distracted my mind, and the assurances of friends who had been living for some time as exiles in Paris, further encouraged me. Alas! the greater number of these will never read my Memoirs. Manin, Montanelli, Musolino, Carini, then Director of the *Revue Franco-Italienne*, later on, a general in our army—Dall' Ongaro, Ballanti, Pierangelo Fiorentino, Dr. Maestri, Federici, Toffoli, eminent colleague of Tommaseo, Sirtori, are no more! The reader must allow me to lay on their graves the wreath of friendship. We were very anxious, in common with our young friends from Turin, to be present at some French theatrical performance. Above all, we desired to see the great tragedian, Rachel, who had filled the world with her fame.

To our great disappointment, we were told that she was not acting in Paris just then, having taken her formal farewell previous to repairing to the United States, and that the public were very angry with her on this account.

Not being able, therefore, to see Rachel, the chief object of our curiosity, we limited our desires to attending a play at the Comedie Française so highly renowned for the perfection of its acting and its *mise-en-scène*, considered the first in Europe.

We had no time to lose. Our representations were to begin on the 22d, and it was already the 17th. Seeing announced in the bills, that Mlle.

Augustine Brohan, especially known for her talent and vivacity in comedy, was to play that very evening in one of our favorite pieces, *Le Caprice*, by Alfred Musset, we were all most anxious to go and hear her.

Being quite taken up with our own approaching performance, we had not given a thought as to the probable necessity of taking tickets beforehand, and presented ourselves at the ticket office only a little before the beginning of the play.

"A box, if you please," demanded one of our party.

"A box?" answered the office-keeper; for what day?"

"For this evening."

"For this evening!" replied the astonished official; "you should have thought about it long ago!" But apparently our evident disappointment awakened his compassion, for he generously offered us tickets for the gallery.

My husband hesitated. Our young friends, with their habitual good humor, were quite ready to accept. For my part, I was not much flattered at the idea of such an entry into the house of Molière, but we had no choice. We deliberated a moment, and then ascended laughingly the five flights to install ourselves triumphantly *among the gods!*

From our exalted situation we could applaud freely and enthusiastically. The exquisite acting of Mlle. Augustine Brohan gave us all great pleasure, and I never forgot it.

Before commencing my performances, I delivered my letter of introduction to M. Jules Janin, and as he was a great friend of Rachel's I ventured to ask him a favor I ardently desired, namely, to make me personally known to such a celebrity, and, at the same time, as a sister in her art, to ask her support in my difficult experiment.

Rachel was at her country house. I determined to write to her, but was dissuaded by M. Janin and others, who assured me that she was daily expected back in the city ; that they would invite me to meet her, and thus I should have every opportunity of speaking to her.

I took their advice, but my impatience to be acquainted with her was such that I did not cease to importune M. Janin to allow me to write to her. And they succeeded also in dissuading me from this intention. Given, the nervous, impressionable temper of Mlle. Rachel, such a step on my part would effect a result diametrically opposite to that purposed by me. To write without the previous formality of a presentation, would be almost to treat as an equal one who justly believed herself to hold an exceptional and privileged position. It might appear like a forcing of her will, or as giving her a lesson of courtesy in doing that which the laws of hospitality ought to have suggested to her as the mistress of the house towards a stranger who was crossing her threshold. I yielded to these arguments, although they appeared to me too subtle and far-fetched. But I had good reason afterwards to repent of my pliability. I was cruelly punished for consenting for the first time not to act according to my own instinct.

On the appointed evening the series of our repre-

sentations began with the play already decided upon.
The impression produced on the French public was
very satisfactory for our *amour propre*. The press
was entirely favorable, and we had the approbation
of the greater number of the most renowned critics.
The famous scene in the third act, in which Paolo
and Francesca each in turn reveal their love, excited
much applause, and *her* death, although lacking in
remarkable effects or great difficulties, inspired Alexandre Dumas with an article most flattering to me.

The impartial critics of journalism, prominent
among whom were Alexandre Dumas—afterwards
my great friend—Theophile Gautier, Pierangelo Fiorentino, Jules Janin, Jules de Premoray, Paul de St.
Victor, Leon Gozlan, Méry, Theodore Anne, and
many others, also gave us kindly notice. Some few
who were devoted to Rachel, timidly and half inau-
dibly granted me some aptitude for acting tragedy,
and in particular those very special dispositions
which the great French actress possessed in a lesser
degree, and of which she made less account—for
example, the faculty of touching the tender and com-
passionate feelings. But they absolutely denied in
me the force, the energy, the vigor necessary for
interpreting successfully the violent passions proper
to the tragic poem, in fact, those qualities which had
most largely contributed to the triumph of Rachel
and to her fame ; they denied me that too classic
elasticity of movement and posture, that "step of
a goddess," which the great actress possessed in a
supreme degree when she crossed the stage draped
in peplum.

I might have bowed my head to this judgment, and believed that nature and study had refused me those very gifts for which the indulgence and affection of my countrymen had most frequently lavished applause and praise upon me. But the sentence thus hastily pronounced appeared to me questionable. To speak of *energy*, *force*, *violence*, in relation to the gentle, pathetic character of Francesca da Rimini was an absurdity which revealed the deliberate purpose of making naughty comparisons at whatsoever cost; and to make them unhesitatingly without giving time for consideration or comparison, or for the public to manifest freely their own opinion. Thus, if I had been self-conceited, that condemnation would have served rather to awaken my pride than to arouse in me the honest sentiment of diffidence.

But pride was not, in truth, my besetting sin, and this early opposition alarmed me at least in so far as I perceived how ill my real intentions in appearing upon the Parisian stage were interpreted by some.

"I never had the presumption," I said to my most intimate friends and most severe critics, "to come to Paris to compete with your sublime artist. My aim is a more modest one; and, permit me to add, a more generous one." I wish to show that in Italy also the dramatic art, once our boast and our glory, still exists, and is cultivated with affection and passion. As for me, personally, let them criticise me with the utmost severity; but before pronouncing judgment upon me let them wait at least until I have given proof, in all the various parts of my repertory, of the full measure of my powers. And if they persist—as

they have a right to do—in making comparisons I do
not desire, but which it is impossible for me to avoid,
let them show their impartiality and clearness of
judgment by delaying their sentence until they have
seen me in some part which may give them reasonable
ground for such a verdict.

Thus, for example, *Myrrha* may be compared with
Phædra (a minute comparison of them is given in two
of the chief analytical studies in these pages).

Our third performance on the 26th of May included
the *Curioso Accidente* and *La Locandiera*, by Goldoni.
These plays were well received, though comedy in a
foreign language is most difficult to understand.

It was then proposed to give the *Myrrha* of Alfieri,
without, however (from want of sufficient time), those
special announcements that generally excite the curiosity of the public in all countries ; yet the theatre
was more crowded than on the preceding evening,
and the entire press assisted at the representation.
This tragedy, written in pure and severe Italian style,
and with many distinctly Greek forms, gave me an
opportunity of showing my artistic feeling, the profound psychological study I had bestowed on the part,
and the ability of our Italian school to unite national
spontaneity to Greek plasticity, detaching itself entirely from academical conventionalisms, not because
academical conventionalisms are devoid of anything
praiseworthy, but because we argue that in the whirl
and fury of the passions, it is not possible to give full
attention to the greater or lesser elevation of the arms
or hands. Provided the gestures are noble and not
discordant with the sentiments expressed, the actor

must be left to his own impulse. Constraint and conventionalism, in my opinion, obscure the truth.

One of the living examples of this realistic school, and one also of its brightest ornaments, is my illustrious companion in art, Tommaso Salvini, with whom I had the good fortune to share the labors of the stage for several years, as I also shared them with Ernesto Rossi. Salvini was, and is, justly admired ; for his rare dramatic qualities have nothing conventional about them, but are characterized by that spontaneity which is the truest and most convincing revelation of art.

The richness of *pose*, of which Salvini makes use, is in him a natural gift, brought to perfection by his close study of nature which the teachings of no school could have produced or fostered in him. In a word Tommaso Salvini is to me the living incarnation of Italian inspiration.

But to return to *Myrrha.* I must say that the success of this tragedy surpassed all our expectations. After the fourth act—a most majestic conception of the great author's—the audience seemed almost beside itself with delight.

The Foyer was crowded with the most distinguished persons in literature and art. Alexandre Dumas kissed my mantle and my hands ; Janin, Legouvé, Henri Martin, Scribe, Theophile Gautier, and many dramatic artists (I do not speak of the enthusiasm of my compatriots, because it was indescribable) could not find words to express their emotion. During the fifth act, where the great scene occurs between Myrrha and her father, which Ernesto Rossi gave

3

with a talent that was unique rather than rare, the public never ceased to applaud. The success of this tragedy at Paris more than compensated me for the immense trouble which the interpretation of such a very difficult character did cost me in order to succeed in representing it suitably. From the analysis of this play, given in the second part of this volume, the reader will be able to judge how difficult and intricate had been my task.

That evening, those who had not shown themselves very favorably to us after hearing *Francesca da Rimini*, were constrained to share in the common approval. In order to afford an opportunity to the other clever members of the company to display their powers, it was necessary to bring forward pieces more especially suited to them. So, on the 31st of May, the *Burbero Benefico*, by Goldoni, was played, followed by the *Niente di Male*, by F. A. Bon. On the 2nd of June, *La Suonatrice d'Arpa*, by David Chiossoni, and *Mio Cugino*, by Angelo Brofferio, were given.

On the day when the *Burbero Benefico* was performed I learnt, to my surprise, that Rachel had not only returned from the country, but had bespoken a box for that evening at the theatre. I was extremely annoyed at this. If, after all the noise aroused by the papers, it was the intention of the great French actress to come and judge for herself, she had made a bad selection of the piece which was to furnish her with the elements for estimating me.

The *Burbero Benefico* is certainly one of Goldoni's best comedies, but in it the part of the first actress is absolutely sacrificed and left in the shade in order to throw into fuller relief the very original personality of the principal character. I could not, in the *Burbero Benefico*, display my artistic qualities, such as they were, nor put forth to the full extent my dramatic powers in representing the creation of a great poet, with the needful amount of truth and dignity due to an historical personage. Rachel's resolve again placed me in another dilemma. She having, unknown to me, and without even mentioning it to our mutual friends, sent to take a box at our theatre, plainly showed her determination to keep aloof from me, and almost to remain *incognito*. Could I—ought I to come forward and present myself to her ; offer her a box, and thus, not only prevent her from effecting her design, but further, in a certain way, have the air of depriving her of her full liberty of judging me in her own fashion ?

It was, at the same time, a question of delicacy and propriety mingled with a question of artistic *amour propre*. If I was to have invited Rachel to one of my performances, I should frankly have preferred for her to judge me in *Myrrha, Francesca da Rimini*, or *Mary Stuart ;* but I did not wish either to appear proud in abstaining from entering into relations with her, or importunate in meeting her half way and forcing her to be civil to me while she seemed rather to avoid me, or at least first form her opinion of me as actress before receiving me as a guest.

I spoke of it to the Janins, who, not knowing anything precisely, dissuaded me from making any move, advising me rather to wait for the opportunity of a repetition of *Myrrha* to send Rachel a box with a card of invitation from me. Meantime they offered to plan a meeting between us at their house on the excuse of a dinner.

But this meeting never took place ; whether the Janins forgot to arrange the dinner, or—as it seems to me more likely—Rachel declined to accept the invitation, I never heard more of it.

Meanwhile, we were not too well satisfied with the pecuniary result of our speculation, and Signor Righetti, my manager, did not spare me his lamentations and reproaches, and roundly asserted that I should be responsible for his forthcoming ruin.

We busied ourselves in trying to find some way of escape from the present very gloomy outlook. Our friends tried to reassure us, to encourage us, and boldly asserted that if we were fortunate enough to follow up the great success we had achieved with *Myrrha*, we should easily carry the public along with us.

On Tuesday, June 5th, we repeated *Myrrha*. After the enthusiastic criticisms on the previous performance in the newspapers, people came in crowds to see it, and our success surpassed every anticipation. Indeed, from that evening *Myrrha* was all the rage. Our artistic and financial success was assured. The tragedy was repeated until it had to be removed to make way for *Mary Stuart*.

The Press was as unanimous in its verdict as the Public. But I regretted that in praising me a certain bitterness was mingled against Rachel. There was no doubt that this most significant change in the attitude of the Press had been brought about in some degree by the accusation that she had responded with ingratitude to the great affection the public had always shown her, adoring her as a Muse, and as its special favorite. Whether the accusation was right or wrong I could not judge, but, as matters were in such a state, it was certainly not expedient for me to invite her to come and hear me. Had I done so, it might have been supposed that I wanted her to be a witness of my triumph. I blushed at the mere thought! And I abstained from offering any such invitation, and in this had the approval of my friends, Janin, Ary-Scheffer, and others, whose advice I sought.

Meanwhile the intimates of Rachel, alarmed at the magnitude of my success, made every effort to neutralize it, fearing it might eclipse the brightness of the great actress's crown.

When, through an unexpected return of Rachel to the stage, I had the privilege of seeing her on the evening of June 6th in the character of *Camilla* in the *Horatii*, I was still more confirmed in that conviction. A box was kindly sent me for this play through the courtesy of M. Arsène Houssaye, at that time Director of the Comedie Française, in his name and that of the whole Company, to be present at that solemn performance which coincided with the anniversary of Corneille. The moment Rachel appeared on the stage I understood the potency of her fascination. I seemed to behold before me a Roman statue: her bearing was majestic; her step royal;

the draping of her mantle, the folds of her tunic, everything was studied with wonderful artistic talent.

Perhaps critique might have been able to find a little fault with the unchanging arrangement of the folds, which never fell out of order.

As a woman, it was easy for me to understand the reason for that arrangement: Rachel was extremely thin, and used every pains to conceal it. But with what marvellous skill she did so ! She knew thoroughly how to modulate her voice—at times it was magical. At the wondrous culminating point of the imprecation flung at Rome and the Romans, such accents of hate and fury rushed from her heart that the whole audience shuddered at them.

I had ratified without hesitation the enthusiasm, the judgment borne by all Europe to the eminent qualities which won Rachel her glorious renown. She had not only the genius of the stage, enthusiasm, mobility of feature, variety and nobleness of *pose*— she was able to incarnate herself in her *rôle*, and keep it up from the beginning to the end of the piece without neglecting the smallest detail ; giving all her great effects skilfully, and the most minute scrupulously. Now it is in fulfilling these requirements, and on this sole condition, that one can be proclaimed a great artist.

I heard and saw only her, and I paid her the tribute of the most frantic applause ! How fully I appreciated the judgment of the critics when they ascertained that there were no such points of contrast between us two, which could be used to our mutual injury. She was the tragic genius of France, and we followed two widely different paths. We had two different modes of expression; she could excite the greatest enthusiasm in her transports, so beautiful was her diction, so statuesque her *pose*. In the most passionate situation, however, her expression was regulated by the rules imposed by the traditional French school, yet the power of her voice, the fascination of her look were such, that she compelled admiration and applause. We, on the contrary, do not believe that in culminating moments of passion this self-possession is possible. When a person is overtaken by unexpected sorrow, or sudden joy, is it not the natural instinct to move the hand to the head, and as a necessary consequence must not the hair be disarranged?

The Italian school of acting, then, holds that one of the chief objects of the stage is to represent nature in a living and truthful manner.

After all, what most troubled me, was the knowledge that these numerous and faithful admirers of Rachel had influenced her against me; but that whatever efforts my friends and her acquaintances made to draw us together, in accordance with my intense desire, none seemed likely to succeed.

Unfortunately, in these cases, there are always zealous people, so-called friends, who are ready to foment disagreements by a variety of injurious misrepresentations. It was a pleasure to these to impress upon Rachel's mind that I had spoken disrespectfully of her. Others, again, came and reported to me that Rachel, in a fit of artistic jealousy, had used malicious expressions concerning me. They

tried to make me believe that, desirous to be present
at a performance of *Myrrha*, and yet anxious to
escape recognition, and avoid the observations and
comments of the curious, she seated herself closely
muffled up at the back of a box; that after the fourth
act, which contains some of my most important
scenes, and in the midst of the public applause, she,
not being able any longer to control herself, tore to
pieces the book of words she held in her hand,
and, exclaiming, "*Cette femme me fait mal; je n'en
peux plus!*" left the theatre, in spite of all the persuasions of those who were with her. I never
believed such gossip and I should have wished to
hint to the friends of the great artist the way to calm
her, proving to her that her immense merit placed her
above the instability of public opinion, and that in
spite of the reality of my success this could in no
way diminish the power of her genius.

My performances excited increasing interest and
enthusiasm and I became a great favorite with the
public. The burst of applause which saluted my
appearance on the stage was not so grateful to me as
the deep silence which followed upon it. How much
that silence of the audience is fertile of inspiration, how
it penetrates in the soul of the artist, how the creative
fire which exists in art transports and transforms
him! When it was my good fortune to represent
subjects of supreme importance before an audience
who worshipped art with true devotion, and were
ready and able to identify themselves with the passions reproduced upon the stage—to count, as I may
say, the heart-throbs of the character which moved

them, by their own—all this intoxicated me, made me feel as though I were endowed with superhuman powers; enabled me by a sudden inspiration to improvise effects which I had never studied, but which were truer and more vigorous than those I had before conceived ; while above and beyond all was a predominating feeling of legitimate pride at knowing that there yet lay dormant within me unrevealed and fertile germs of art.

Mary Stuart, by Schiller, translated into splendid Italian verses by Andrea Maffei, was the last of my most successful performances in Paris. This tragedy was played alternately with *Pia de' Tolomei*, but I cannot say that the latter excited as much enthusiasm in the French public as *Myrrha* and *Mary Stuart*, although I remember that it was successful in producing a considerable impression ; for the adventures of the unfortunate Sienese lady were so thrilling and pitiful that they diverted the attention from the more emotional parts of the play. It was, however, received with much interest by literary men, because the subject is one immortalized by Dante, by whose verses the tragedy is inspired.

Our renowned tragic author, Carlo Marenco, has certainly known how to raise the action in the last act to the highest grade of sentiment, and so to arrange that the most terrible final idea of the play embraces in itself, in one grand emotion, all the development of the subject.

The critics have been severe in analyzing the preceding acts, but there is no doubt that this last act

was enough to be obliged to give the tribute of a tear
to her who said :

> Ricordati di me, che son la Pia
> Siena mi fe, disfecemi Maremma.

I made a special study of the death of Pia, in the
fifth act, as I desired to reproduce faithfully the
dying agony and the last gasps for life of a young
woman imprisoned by order of an unjustly cruel
husband, in the pestiferous Maremma Marshes.
This end caused me serious thought. But how to
represent upon the stage with perfect truth, in full
realism, as it would now be said, the mournful picture of a slow agony, without having recourse to the
imagination ?

While thus irresolute, a really extraordinary chance
caused me to witness the last moments of a poor girl
who was dying of *perniciosa* (violent malaria fever).
This afflicting scene made such a deep impression
upon my memory, that although I succeeded in faithfully reproducing that heart-rending close, identifying
myself, so to say, with the dying victim, I was de-
pressed at every representation with the vividness of
that painful remembrance.

At this point it might be said that the Italian drama
had entered into Parisian habits. The partisans of
Rachel were inconsolable. The attacks against me
continued incessantly. It was then, to my great surprise, that I one day received from some of them an
invitation to supper where I was at last to meet the
great artist in the house of a literary man—a bachelor.
My husband, after having read the list of guests, did
not think himself justified in allowing me to accept

the invitation given in this way. We found a plausible pretext for excusing ourselves.

Time went on, and I was no longer thinking of the
possibility of a meeting with Rachel, when one
morning Mdme. Ode, the famous dressmaker of the
Empress Eugenie, was announced to me. She had
to speak to me on a subject of importance. I fancied
it was about some dresses of mine, but she said
immediately:

"You know, certainly, how much Mlle. Rachel
has been hurt by the attacks of which she is the
victim, and to which you served as a pretext. But
you do not know, perhaps, that there has been an
attempt to embitter her against you by reporting that
you did not speak of her with the consideration which
she rightly believes her due."

"It is not true!" I answered sharply, "and I hope
Mlle. Rachel has not given any more credence to
those mischievous insinuations than I did when I
heard reported some very unkind criticisms she was
said to have uttered about me! I went to hear her
in the *Horatii*, and I expressed all the enthusiasm
she aroused in me. I commissioned some intimate
friends to make known to her my admiration, as well
as my keen desire to meet her; but all their attempts
to bring us together were fruitless. Let us say no
more about it."

"And if I were to tell you, Madame, that Mlle.
Rachel has made known to me her wish to see you?"

"If that is true, let her come to me, then, and I
will receive her as such a celebrity is entitled to be
received."

But, as Mdme. Ode seemed not willing to take in the sense of my proposal, but, on the contrary, made me to understand that the first advances should come from me, I thought it best to answer:

"I do not think I ought now to renew the expression of my desire to know her, which was communicated to her by my friends on my arrival in Paris, when I was most anxious to obtain the support of the great actress in the serious undertaking I had embarked in—now it is too late!"

"But, if Mlle. Rachel were to send you a box to hear her, would you accept it?"

"With delight! and I would give up any engagement I might have already, in order not to deprive myself of such a treat."

So the next day I received a letter, enclosing a box-ticket for the Comedie Française, on which was written "*A Madame Ristori, sa camarade Rachel*"— a letter which I have carefully preserved.

I was in my place on the evening mentioned before the play began. It was *Phædre*. Not only was I most anxious to see Rachel in this masterpiece of Racine's, but it was also one of the favorite parts of my own *répertoire*, and had been the object of most serious study with me.

Although I perceived that the spectators were interested in the manifestations of my approval, yet I did not lavish it upon everything Rachel did. I found her person statuesque, and her first entrance on the stage magnificent, but the prostration she showed seemed to me excessive; all the more so because she neglected to make clearly apparent how greatly this prostration was due only to moral depression, which disappears when its cause is removed, allowing the physical powers to resume their full vigor.

Grand and powerful was the scene in the second act with *Hippolyte*, in which she reveals her passion ; but I found, contrary to her habitual acting, too much realism in the impetuosity of its execution. In the fourth act Rachel was really sublime, and the admiration and irresistible emotions she excited in me were so great that I was most powerfully moved, and yet, hearty as was my applause, I felt it but half expressed the enthusiasm which possessed me. When the curtain fell, in the fullness of my enthusiasm I wrote hurriedly on one of my visiting cards a few words, which I sent to Rachel in her dressing-room. The sending of this card was the last intercourse I ever had with her.

Towards the end of my stay in Paris, I received repeated and most pressing offers to dedicate myself exclusively to the French theatre, but nothing would ever have induced me to renounce my Italian career. To all such proposals I gave an unqualified refusal, alleging, as a pretext, the great difficulty of acquiring the necessary purity of language and perfection of accent.

It was then that the minister, Fould, repeated a similar request in the name of the Emperor, offering me a year's sojourn in Paris at the expense of the State, in order that I might qualify myself, under the best masters, for occupying the post which Rachel was going to leave free at the Comedie Française. I held firm in declining the honor offered me, not without thanking the Minister, and adding that I thought the great actress would not be able to do without the applause of her public, and that this would be always glad to see her again on the stage. However, my refusal in no way prejudiced me with M. Fould, who with much courtesy granted me the favor I requested him, in allowing me for three consecutive years the use of the Salle Ventadour for the purpose of giving a series of Italian dramatic representations. Thus I not only had the great satisfaction of succeeding in my original design, which was to render our art esteemed in foreign countries, but I went beyond it in opening up a new field for the exercise of Italian artistic ability, not only in Europe, but, as will afterwards be seen, in America as well, where it did honor to our country.

It was with much regret that I left Paris, where I had had the good fortune to become acquainted with the men and women most celebrated in literature and art. I may especially mention Lamartine, George Sand, Guizot, Mignet, Henri Martin, Ary Sheffler, Halevy, Janin, Legouvé, Scribe, Patin, Theophile Gautier, Sarcey, Eduard Plouvier, Reigner, Samson, Roqueplan, Theodore Anne, Mlle. Georges, Madame Allan, Augustine and Madeleine Brohan, besides many others whom it would take too long to enumerate. I had to say "Good-bye" to all these—to bid farewell to the excellent Alexandre Dumas, who used to came to us daily, when we had the benefit of his inexhaustible wit and humor. How many hours we spent together! It was indeed delightful to hear him tell story after story with his prodigious eloquence.

He would tell us anecdotes of travel, and events in his own life, reminiscences of past days which he has scattered throughout his books. We were only too charmed to listen to him, and took good care never to interrupt him. It seems to me that I hear him still when he related that, in the early days of his admiration for me, one evening as he came out from a representation of *Myrrha*, and was striding along the Passage Choiseul, he met a great friend of his.

"What do you think of her?" he asked.

"Of whom?"

"Of Ristori. Have you not been at the theatre?"

"I have never heard her."

"And are you not ashamed of yourself to say so?" And with this he crushed his friend with an avalanche of eulogistic epithets upon me. "I will never speak to you again if you do not go to see her!"

A few days after, meeting his friend again at the corner of the Rue de Berlin, with his head still full of the same subject—

"Well, what play have you seen her in?"

"Let me alone; one has not always six francs in one's pocket, nor am I reduced to the condition of a *claqueur*."

"Then you would rather I lent you six francs?"

"No, thank you. I will go when I can."

"You can return me the money at your convenience."

'But no, no, no."

Then Dumas, who would not let him alone, persisted: "I am determined you shall go and see

Ristori." He drew his purse out of his pocket. "Look here," he said, "I shall lay the six francs down here; if you wont have them, the first comer may." And he laid the money on a street-bourne, such as were still standing in Paris at that time.

"Do pray leave me in peace," replied the friend; and both of them went away in opposite directions.

Meanwhile the six francs remained where Dumas had placed them; but the friend had hardly turned the corner of the street when he stopped, saying to himself, "But when all is said and done, six francs are not a fortune. I can return them to him. And if I leave the money there some one would be sure to come by and say, 'Some fool has placed this here; let me take it;'" and, supported by this logical conclusion, he turned back. To his intense surprise, when he reached the spot he came upon Dumas face to face, who in his turn had concluded that if his fool of a friend would not have his money he had better take it back himself. Thus meeting each other, they burst into a fit of laughter, and the obstinate friend promised that he would certainly come and see me. Dumas always laughed immoderately when he related this adventure, which he declared he would by and by write under the title of *The Two Millionaires.*

Another day Dumas boasted at our house that he could cook and season *maccaroni alla Napoletana* as well as an Italian cook, and when he heard our exclamations of incredulity he dared us to put his skill to the test.

We were then living at the Hotel de Bade, Boulevard des Italiens, which was filled with foreigners.

The report spread in the hotel of what Dumas was going to do. The windows were full of people watching the author of the *Trois Mousquetaires*, arrayed in white jacket and apron, a cook's cap to match on his curly head, a saucepan in hand, and his jovial face showing at the moment that he had quite forgotten the triumphs obtained by the adventures of Athos, Porthos, and Aramis, in his eagerness to achieve successfully the dressing of a dish of *maccaroni*.

With this pleasant reminiscence I conclude the narrative of our first sojourn in France. I was heartily sorry to leave this country after having received there, I may venture to say, the baptism of fame. The French had proved to me that for them there is no foreign boundary in the domains of art, and I shall ever preserve in the depths of my heart a sentiment of deep gratitude for the generous reception they gave the stranger.

4

CHAPTER III.

AFTERWARDS we went into Belgium, not without having given some representations on the journey through the north of France; then we proceeded to Dresden and Berlin, obtaining a great success everywhere.

In November I returned to my own dear country, and there finished my original contract, giving various representations at Milan and Turin, and then making a brief stay at Verona, Udine, and Trieste, on my way to Vienna.

When they saw me again, the Italian public did not know how to thank me sufficiently for having rendered Italian art known and esteemed in foreign lands.

I was invited to Vienna to give twelve performances at the Karnthnarthor, the old Imperial Theatre.

My first appearance in the Austrian capital took place on the 4th February 1856. Alfieri's *Myrrha* was my first performance, and I could not possibly have wished for a more enthusiastic welcome than that which I received from the Viennese public.

The theatre was crowded at every one of my performances, and I was frequently honored by the presence of the Court. In preparing for the first representation of *Mary Stuart* I experienced the

(50)

greatest agitation, for I knew what comparisons I had to sustain, and what publicity and importance attached to that evening. My nerves were shaken, and a certain agitation took possession of me.

At my customary hour I repaired to the theatre, and went to my dressing-room in the perfect possession of all my usual health, and with scarcely concealed nervousness I began to dress. The excessive heat of the stoves, of which the theatre was full, began to tell upon me ; the blood mounted to my head, and affected my voice. My heart beat fast in fear of some serious consequences; by degrees my voice grew husky until I almost lost it entirely! I was in despair! Without hesitation or reflection I threw up the window, which looked upon a bastion of the city, and heedless of the cold usual to the season—it was now the 17th of February—or of the possible evil consequences such an imprudence might entail upon me, I unfastened the body of my dress and I exposed myself to that icy temperature, hoping that the reaction it would produce within me would be sufficient to restore my voice and enable me to undertake my part in the tragedy.

The doctor, surprising me at the window, asked me if I had lost my senses.

" My voice, Doctor !" I cried. " For mercy's sake give me back my voice ! "

He replied that if I had the courage to use a very strong gargle which had been employed advantageously in similar cases by famous vocalists, he could restore me at least as much voice as would enable me to go through the play.

"Give me poison if it will do any good!" I cried. I knew that the remedy suggested was not poison, but it did taste quite bad enough to have been such.

I did not, indeed, fully recover my voice, but an announcement was made to the audience, asking them to excuse any deficiency on my part in the representation of *Mary Stuart*, and I was more successful than I could have hoped.

This anecdote will serve to show how great was my consideration for the public, and what a strong hold the feeling of duty had upon me.

Indeed, I cannot describe the influence the public exercised over me. Since childhood, a sentiment of mingled respect and awe towards my audience had been inculcated in me, and the feeling had grown with my growth. I made it a special study, therefore, to allow no unforeseen circumstances to disconcert me, so that the public should not be disappointed on account of the performance not being as good as we could make it. And I was called upon to put one of these fundamental maxims into use, on one of the evenings when I appeared as *Judith* in the Biblical tragedy written expressly for me by my friend and favorite author, the lamented Paolo Giacometti.

In the culminating scene of the play, when I have cut off the head of Holophernes, his favorite slave, Azraele, discovering the murder of her lover, hurls herself in her fury upon me, and I seize hold of her and throw her to the ground, thus terminating the act with great effect. A very short time before she ought to have made her entry, they informed me from the wings, with much perturbation, that the actress had been seized with convulsions, and would not be able to finish the act. I replied in an instant, "One of you put on her dress, throw a veil over your head, and come to me." My order was obeyed with the rapidity of lightning ; but the poor girl who assumed the part did not know how to move, nor how to speak, as she had no idea of the words she ought to say !

But I was not dismayed. I induced her to advance towards me as though to kill me, when I seized her, and there and then extemporised a kind of little dialogue. May I be forgiven those verses ! The public never noticed the little *ruse*, and they were not disappointed, and the result was completely successful.

In my performances of *Medea*, I was frequently obliged to meet an unforeseen emergency, and show presence of mind. Often when travelling in foreign countries having only to give one representation of *Medea*—and having one single child available in the company, the second, who had not to speak, had to be provided by the property-man. Generally I had to instruct him by gestures, as we did not understand one another. Once it happened that one of these poor little wretches, not being accustomed to the stage, grew frightened from the moment I appeared on the mountain carrying him in my arms. When he heard the applause with which I was received, and saw for the first time the foot-lights and the crowded pit, he began to cry and struggle, and endeavor to escape from my hold. I had to make a great effort to keep my head cool enough to commence my own part and prevent myself falling down the mountain, while at the same time I tried to make my prisoner understand by my caresses that he had nothing to fear from me, and that somewhat quieted him. Frequently his mother, or sister, or father was obliged to stand all the time at the wings making signs, and whispering comforting words in order to assure him he was in no danger.

But a worse thing than this once happened to me, at the end of the tragedy, at the most thrilling point, when, assailed by the Corinthians, I fled desperately across the stage, dragging my children with me by either hand, mingling my screams with those of the populace, and ending by throwing the two little ones on the steps of the altar of Saturn, where I feigned to kill them. While concealing them by my person— I remained immovable as a statue—one of the murdered youngsters began to howl, and in its fright suddenly got up and ran behind the scenes before I could do anything to prevent him. And just to think that the public was to imagine that I had murdered him! Although the audience was deeply impressed by the tragic action of this scene, yet it was impossible to avoid a hearty laugh at the sight of the dead child running away.

In April, 1856, I returned to Paris. As had been arranged the year before with M. Legouvé, steps were taken at once to put *Medea* on the stage as quickly as possible. In the analytical study of this tragedy—one of six which I have chosen from my *répertoire*, and which follows in the second part of this volume—the reader will find a minute account of the circumstances which led to my acceptance of the part, and of the events which preceded the appearance of the work, and the gratifying result of our labors on the night of the 8th April.

Medea ran for nineteen evenings, and it might have gone on for a greater number, if I had not been obliged to alternate it with those dramas in which I had appeared the year before.

From Paris we went to London. I gave my first performance in the elegant Lyceum Theatre on the 4th June, 1856, selecting *Medea* as the opening piece. The English public were so greatly prejudiced in my favor by the French, German, and Belgian newspapers, that they gave me the warmest welcome, and came in crowds to hear me, showing me the most flattering signs of sympathy and esteem.

Many of the most distinguished literary men in England were surprised that I had not added *Macbeth* —in my opinion the greatest work of Shakespeare— to my *répertoire*. I urged that a foreign, travelling company, could not undertake such a play, because of the want of scenery, and of the necessary number of actors. I was answered that in England, at that period, it was often found necessary to adapt such works, not only to the capacity and numbers of the actors, but also to the state and requirements of the audience, who were not able to criticise justly the times, the places, and the conditions under which Shakespeare's dramatic genius was developed.

I objected to this, as it seemed to me a sacrilege to adapt and mutilate the work of the greatest English poet. We Italians would not venture to touch a single line of our classics.

They assured me that it was done without scruple, in order to render it comprehensible to all intelligences. To say the truth, their argument was not illogical, and finally, as they proposed to assume the onus of the undertaking, I accepted, and on my return to London, in June, 1857, *Macbeth*, arranged and adapted for my company by Mr. Clark, was produced at Covent Garden. The capital Italian translation was by Giulio Carcano. Mr. Harris put it on the stage according to English traditions. The part of Lady Macbeth, which afterwards became one of my especial favorites, occupied me greatly, for I knew that serious comparisons would be drawn.

The remembrance of the marvellous representation of Lady Macbeth by Mrs. Siddons, and the traditional criticisms of the press, would, as it seemed to me, be certain to render the public very severe and hard to please. However, I devoted all my skill and knowledge to discovering and elucidating the exact meaning of the author, and it appeared to the English that I succeeded in identifying myself with this type of perfidy and crafty cunning, far beyond their expectations.

The drama was repeated several evenings, producing a deep impression on the audience, especially in the great sleep-walking scene. So fully, indeed, did I enter into the spirit of the part, that during the whole of the act my pupils remained immovable in their sockets, until the tears came into my eyes. And it is from this forced immobility that I date the commencement of my weakened eye-sight.

What it cost me to discover the proper intonation

—

of voice, the true expression of face, in this culminating scene, and, indeed, I may say, throughout my interpretation of this diabolical personage's character, I have told in one of the analytical studies already mentioned, and which will follow hereafter.

I went to Warsaw for the first time in November 1856. I may say that my acting in that city was most brilliantly successful ; but justice requires me to add that this result was facilitated by the remarkable appreciation shown me, on my first appearance, by the elegant and courteous ladies of the Polish society. I was made the object of endless and delicate attentions, and especially on the part of the Governor, Prince Gortschakoff, and the Princess his wife ; and this hearty welcome induced me to return thither in the following year.

In the beginning of 1859 I went for the first time to Naples in order to perform at the Fondo, the very elegant royal theatre, and on the evening of the 14th January, I commenced a short series of representations with *Medea*. How kindly and enthusiastic I found my audience it is more easy to imagine than describe. Little by little there grew up between us that wonderful magnetic current of sympathy which always nerved me to double my efforts to deserve their favor.

It was with much difficulty that I obtained the necessary permission from the Bourbon Censor to play the *Phædra* of Racine. I was certain that however much mutilated, there would be still quite enough beauty enshrined in the work to produce a very great impression and ensure its success. But

the result surpassed my expectation. In the short
space of fifteen performances, I was constrained to
repeat *Phædra* five times, an unusual event at that
date. The last of these was destined for my benefit,
and on the morning in question there was not a
place to be had in the theatre. For want of a sufficient number of boxes many ladies of high rank had
to be content with stalls. A cantata was specially
composed in my honor, and I might have been in a
garden, so great was the quantity of flowers showered
upon me. The reader may judge how such an ovation was likely to excite me, and what an impulse it
would give to the inspiration of the artiste. But
with all my pleasant remembrances of the occasion
is associated one anything but delightful.

During the magnificent scene in the fourth act,
when her fit of jealous fury causes Phædra to fall
into a state almost amounting to delirium, I so lost
myself in my part, that instead of starting back, crying, "Even in martyrs the soul lives!" I advanced
unconsciously towards the foot-lights and fell on
them. The audience rose with a loud cry; and
I should probably have been badly burnt had it not
been for the presence of mind of a young gentleman
who occupied a seat close to the stage. He, seeing
that the actress who played the part of the *confidante*,
Enone, remained stupidly immovable from terror,
gave me a sharp push backwards, thus saving me
from a terrible accident. But his efforts did not
entirely succeed in averting all the bad consequences
of my fall. The elbow of my right arm broke one
of the glasses covering the foot-lights, and when I

regained my feet I saw that I had sustained a serious
wound. Much worse might have happened to me
however. If the theatre had been lighted with gas
instead of oil—as it was before my arrival in Naples
—the gas having been suppressed in every public
building in consequence of an explosion which had
occurred in a man-of-war, and which was suspected
of being the result of some political plot—I should
probably have been burnt to death.

The stage was immediately invaded by a crowd
anxious to know how I was. Among the first was
the Count Siracusa, brother of the King Ferdinand,
bringing the Court doctor. When my arm was dressed they began to say that I owed that deplorable
accident to the presence in the theatre of a celebrated
jettatore. Count Siracusa, who also believed in the
evil-eyed, unfastened from his *breloques* a falcon's
claw set in gold, and gave it to me, saying: " I killed
this bird myself ; wear it in future against the evil-
eye." I have always kept this little keepsake.

I was taken to my hotel, and during two months
I carried my arm in a sling. This, however, did not
prevent me from fulfilling my engagements, and I
acted with my bandaged arm, taking care to moder-
ate the energy of my movements. After a short time
it healed entirely, but I still retain traces of the unfortunate accident in a large scar on my arm.

I went to Madrid the same year to give a series of
performances in the theatre of the Zarzuela, and
commenced on the 16th of September with Legouvé's
Medea. The theatre was crammed, and the reception given to me was very enthusiastic. We gave

our usual series of performances, and the success was greater and greater every night. Queen Isabella came to the theatre every night.

On the 21st I had to repeat *Medea*. I shall never forget that evening, marked by an event which left an indelible remembrance in my heart.

I went to the theatre at my usual hour. The actors' dressing-rooms opened out of a most beautiful sitting-room, and here I remained while my maid prepared my costume, talking, with my companions and some *habitués*, over the many magnificent and interesting historical things we had seen during the last few days, and discussing the traditional customs of that superb country, which greatly surprise those who make acquaintance with them for the first time.

"For instance," said I, "what was the meaning of that little bell which was rung along the street to-day by one of the members of a confraternity?"

I was answered that it was to collect alms for the soul of a man condemned to death, by name Nicholas Chapado, whose sentence was to be carried into effect next day. The unhappy creature was a soldier, who, in a fit of anger, had drawn his sword against his sergeant in revenge for a blow the latter had given him. Besides, I was told that his poor sister—ignorant of what had happened—being by chance in a shop hard by, seeing the brother of the company of *San Giovanni decollato*, who collected the alms, inquired who it was that was to be shot. When she heard her brother's name she fell to the ground in a swoon.

This history touched me to the heart.

"My God!" I exclaimed, "while we are here full

of gayety, and expecting applause and success, that miserable man is counting the moments he has yet to live!"

I tried in vain to forget this gloomy picture, while I was obliged to think of my costume.

Soon afterwards two people asked to speak with me. My husband told them that I was dressing, and, therefore, it was impossible to see me. When they found persistence was useless, they told my husband that their business was about poor Chapado, whose life they were trying to save. My husband came to me, saying:

"Do you know there is a man condemned to death to-morrow?"

"Yes," I answered.

"Well, these people think his life is in your hands."

I changed color, and in much agitation I asked him if he was in earnest.

"Quite," he said. "A deputation came to tell me so just now. It will return in a few minutes. The unfortunate soldier is an excellent youth; he can point to a career of eleven years of irreproachable conduct in his favor. He was the victim of a sudden fit of passion, for his sergeant, who hated him, struck him unjustly in the presence of his companions. Chapado only put his hand to the hilt of his sword, but that was enough for him to be condemned to death. The life of this man depends on the Queen. They say that she is very fond of you, and if you ask her to grant you his life, she will not refuse, although she has already declined to see a deputation of students."

"The Queen will think me a mad-woman if I make any such request!" I answered in the greatest dismay. "How should I be any more successful than those who have already supplicated in vain? No, I should never dare! never."

Just then the friends of the condemned man returned, and repeated all that I already knew. I was overcome, and could not say a single word, so great was my agitation at the idea that they were depending on my intercession. At last, however, I promised to try. But then, suddenly I found myself face to face with a difficulty. General Narvaez, Duke of Valencia, and President of the Council of Ministers, was generally hated for his excessive severity and harshness, and in consequence of this I was advised to make my application direct to the Queen, without any intermediary.

"No," I answered, "I am acquainted with the General, and have found him to be a frank, amiable, true, and distinguished man; I shall address myself directly to him in the first instance, as I should not take such a step without first informing him. I have always striven to keep the straight path, and have found that it answers."

"But you will throw away the life of this poor creature," they urged.

"Well, is he not already lost? The worst that can happen will be that I shall not be able to save him. Is not that the truth? Leave me to follow my own instinct." And I dismissed them; and they left me, shrugging their shoulders and shaking their heads, and perfectly confident of my ill-success.

Fortunately, the President of the Council was in the theatre. I sent to ask him to honor me with his company for a few minutes. Narvaez, who was always courteous, did not keep me waiting. He came, attended by his aid-de-camp, but I begged the latter to stop outside with my husband, while I invited the General into my dressing-room. I was alone with him. My voice, which betrayed the emotion under which I was suffering, my whole appearance, struck the Duke.

"General," I began, "you have often told me that so great is the admiration you honor me with, that you would scarcely refuse me anything. Pardon! pardon, then, for this poor soldier. I am a stranger in Madrid, but, from the interest taken in this young man by the inhabitants, I am sure he merits it. I was advised to go direct to the Queen with my petition without troubling you. I am aware that by your well-proved fidelity to her person, and by your wise counsels, which have averted so many dangers from the State, you have won Her Majesty's special esteem and regard ; and I am convinced that a few efficacious words from you would do more than anything to make her listen to my petition."

"My good lady," replied the General, "it is impossible. I am sorry, but it is necessary to give an example. Our revolutions always begin with the army ; a similar thing occurred a short time ago, you see the result of it. The entire municipality besieged the Queen just now to ask the same favor, and I advised her to be firm in not conceding it. The discipline is slackened, clemency in this case would be dangerous. We must give an example."

But I did not lose heart; I persisted in my request with all the enthusiasm which gives such eloquence to speech. The General began to yield; I recommenced my attacks. An internal conflict was visible on his face. My tears accomplished the victory, and, taking my hand: "Ah! Madame," he said, "how can I resist your entreaties! If the Queen consents, I bow to her decision. Now listen: Ask an audience of Her Majesty, which will be immediately granted. You will be received between the 'acts. Throw yourself at her knees, and plead the cause of this wretched man with the eloquence with which you have pleaded it with me. The Queen likes you. She will be perplexed—she will answer that the President of the Council would not agree to it. Then let me be called; I will hasten to obey the summons; and—you may hope."

These words so overjoyed me that I could not control myself sufficiently to reply. I could only wring his hand, and set myself to follow his advice.

The General had hardly left me before my friends crowded round me full of questions. "What has he said? Has he consented? Has he refused?"

"Gently, gently," I cried, "for pity's sake, leave me, leave me. I can tell you nothing; you must wait."

Immediately after the first act the Queen granted me the desired audience, and, accompanied by one of my managers, Signor Barbieri, a distinguished composer, I repaired to the Royal box. I was begged to wait a few minutes in the ante-chamber that led to it. Suddenly I heard a confused murmur of voices, of weeping, An officer of the Royal household, enemy of Narvaez, had made use of his position at Court to introduce Chapado's sister into the Royal box without previously informing the Queen, and it was her sobs and cries we heard imploring pardon. The door opened, the poor suppliant was carried out fainting. Narvaez, not understanding anything of the delay of his expected summons to the Royal box, just entered the waiting-room at the moment they brought me into Her Majesty's presence. I found her lying on a sofa hardly recovered from the emotion she had just experienced in her delicate condition. It was just a few weeks before the birth of Alphonso XII. The ministers were round her.

"How happy I am to see you, dear Madame! I was greatly in need of changing the sad current of my thoughts," she said to me holding out her hand graciously. I kissed her hand, and, without hesitating an instant, I threw myself at her feet, crying "Pardon, pardon, Madame, for Chapado! Let your Majesty be touched by my supplication, and pardon a faithful subject led away in a moment of forgetfulness by a punishment he considered an insult. He is a good soldier who will die for your Majesty. If my poor merits have availed to excite your Majesty's interest and favor, grant me this petition, which I make with uplifted hands."

"Calm yourself, Madame," said the Queen, without being able to dissemble her emotion. "I would

5

like to pardon him—but the President of the Council assures me that——"

Forgetting all etiquette, and without heeding that I was interrupting Her Majesty, I exclaimed:

"Only deign to give utterance once more to your clement intentions, and the Marshal, whose humane sentiments I am acquainted with, will not persist in his severity!"

Upon this Narvaez, who had followed me, bowed before his Sovereign without a word. The Queen, then pressing my hand, raised me to my feet, saying:

"Yes, yes, we will grant your petition."

Hearing the noise by which the audience had begun to express their displeasure at the long delay between the acts, I hastened to take my leave of Her Majesty, with a heart overflowing with contentment.

"Ah! what two different tragedies are being played to-night," she said to me; then, desiring a pen to be brought, she signed the necessary pardon, and an Adjutant ran at once to communicate the news to the poor penitent, who was already receiving the last ministrations of his Church.

The news having spread of my intercession with the Sovereign, a breathless crowd awaited me at the foot of the stairs, down which I flew rather than ran, crying, "He is pardoned! he is pardoned!" When I reappeared upon the stage I was greeted with a burst of acclamation and applause! In the enthusiasm of the moment the name of the Queen was confounded with my own. I intimated by my gestures that it was she alone who deserved their thanks;

while the Queen, graciously pointing to me, cried from her box:

"No! no! it is she, it is she!"

In a word, I owe to Isabella II. one of the most memorable evenings of my life; and the pen used to sign the pardon of a brave and honest man, which was given to me by Her Majesty, will be always treasured by my children as a token of the great joy their mother then experienced.

But, although the life of this soldier had been granted me, yet, in order not entirely to violate military law, it was necessary that he should undergo punishment. He was therefore condemned to imprisonment for life at Alcala. The sentence was severe, but it was a mere nothing to the loss of life. Notwithstanding, when the Prince of Asturias was born, I implored a commutation of the penalty and obtained it; his term of detention was shortened to six years.

It was during one of my later visits to Madrid that I desired to make the acquaintance of this unfortunate man; for the letters he had written to me, without having ever seen me, revealed a man of excellent heart, full of honor and the liveliest gratitude. I asked permission to visit him in his prison, which was a short distance from Madrid. This the Governor readily accorded to me.

When I arrived there, accompanied by my husband and one of my old friends, I was ushered into a room which served as a visitors' parlor. Presently Nicholas Chapado made his appearance, dressed in convict garb. He stood with his head bent down, grasping his cap convulsively in his hands. But so great was his emotion that at first he was not able to speak. He could only throw himself at my feet, and kiss my garments in a transport of joy.

Every one present was touched. I cannot repeat all the expressions of gratitude he at last used towards me, and which stirred me to my heart. I learnt afterwards that his irreproachable conduct had gained him the esteem of his superiors as well as of his companions in misfortune ; that, being promoted to superintend a gang of laborers, he won their affection and secured their obedience, and that the sergeant, who had been the cause of his misfortune, having fallen dangerously ill and being at the point of death, had sent for him to ask his pardon for the great injustice he had done him—a pardon which Chapado had not hesitated a moment to grant.

I promised to put in motion every means I could think of to secure his immediate and complete liberation. As soon as the news of my visit to this place of punishment spread, all its occupants were eager to see me, and when I descended the staircase, with the Governor on one side and Chapado on the other, they knelt while I passed, respectfully uncovering their heads. I cannot express the profound emotion which their presence caused me, or tell fully how this moving scene made my eyes fill with tears.

Having finally obtained Chapado's full pardon, every time that I revisited Madrid he would hasten to see me ; and when I furnished him with means to attend my performances, I could not wish for a more energetic *claqueur*. Between the acts, and even above the applause of the public, he could be heard, justifying his transports of delight by saying: "But don't you remember that she saved my life! that I was already in the chapel receiving the last sacraments of the Church! That it was she asked and obtained my pardon from Queen Isabella! That I love her more than a mother! That I would gladly give my life for her!" and he would end these fervent expressions of gratitude by again clapping his hands frantically, and crying, "Long live Ristori! long live Ristori!" at the top of his voice until the people round him were inclined to think he must be mad.

All the letters I received from him began with these words, "*Mi Madre guarida.*" They are of a remarkable style, as written by a common soldier, and all of almost Oriental imagery. Chapado at present keeps a fruit-shop in Madrid.

CHAPTER IV.

AFTER having visited Vienna, Pesth, and Italy, in April of the same year, I returned to Paris. Each time I reappeared there, it was my study to provide some new work for presentation to my intelligent French audience. During the preceding year, my friend Montanelli, a man full of talent, who passed his life modestly in exile because of the prominent part he had taken in the political affairs of our country, in order to secure her freedom, had proposed to write me a tragedy in three acts, on a most thrilling subject, taken from Plutarch, under the name of *Camma*. The plot was somewhat as follows: A priestess of Diana, famous for her beauty, had married the Tetrarch Sinato. Sinoro, prince of Galatea, caused Sinato to die by treachery, in order that he might espouse his widow, of whom he was much enamoured Camma having discovered him to be the assassin, feigned to surrender herself to his wishes, and went with him to the Temple to celebrate the marriage rites. These concluded by the bride and bridegroom drinking successively out of the same cup.

As priestess, it was Camma's duty to prepare the nuptial draught, and she contrived to mix poison with it.

(70)

The first to put it to his lips was the unsuspicious Sinoro, who died in terrible agony from spasms induced by the poison after the revelation by Camma of his premeditated guilt. Indifferent to life, Camma also drank, and expired rejoicing, according to her religion, in the prospect of a speedy reunion with her beloved Sinato in the Elysian fields.

A propos of her death, my friend sent me his work piece by piece, as it was finished, in order to have my opinion upon it. I found that the death scene was too prolonged ; that he made me talk too much. Full of this idea, I wanted to communicate it to Montenelli as speedily as possible, and I therefore sent him a telegram, which ran as follows :

" You forget that I am in a hurry to die, and that in the presence of the corpse of the victim with whom I have divided the poison I ought not to go on talking for ever."

Any one can imagine how such a telegram, addressed to a person of note in connection with the political events of the day, and necessarily under *espionage,* would amaze the telegraph clerk, who at once sent it to the Ministry ; and what a ridiculous figure he would make afterwards !

It was on the evening of the 23d April, 1857, that I made my first appearance in this tragedy, which obtained a great success.

In the year 1858 I again went to France, England, Austria, Germany, and Italy. In June, 1859, I signed a contract with the principal theatres of Holland, and began my performances at Amsterdam on the 21st.

As I was aware that the Dutch were reputed a

phlegmatic people, not easily roused, I did not expect a very warm welcome. What, then, was my
amazement to see the frigidity of my audience melt
like snow under a summer sun, and to be received by
them with an enthusiasm equal to that of any south-
ern nation. It is such unexpected and spontaneous
demonstrations which stimulate the actress, and give
an impetus to art. And my surprise had no limits
when I heard that it was intended to organize a fête
in my honor, which the newspapers, in speaking of
it beforehand, called "an Art Festival."

More than twenty thousand people of all classes
took part in the solemnity. There was a great number of operative, artistic, and learned associations
present, all preceded by their respective banners.
About 9 o'clock one evening this enormous crowd
began to defile under my windows, calling loudly for
me. They had thousands of torches and Bengal fires,
combining the Dutch and Italian colors. It was a
scene of real enchantment. But the crowding and
pushing were not without serious consequences ;
several persons were precipitated into the canals, but
happily, were rescued. In short, the spectacle can
be more easily imagined than described. In order
to give some idea of it, I will only say that I was told
the King make this remark about it.

" It is too little for a revolution, and too much for
a demonstration."

Leaving Amsterdam, I proceeded to make a tour
of this industrious country, visiting its principal
cities, and receiving everywhere the most cordial and
flattering welcome. At the Hague I was the object

of the kindest attentions, bestowed on me by the late
Queen Sophia, that cultivated patroness of the arts.
She continued her manifestations of interest in me
until her death, and gave me repeated proofs of it
every time I met with her. His Majesty the King
also honored me several times with his presence, and
the last time I chanced to see him, at Wiesbaden, he
proved the continuance of his esteem by presenting
me with the grand gold medal, instituted in Holland
to distinguish those who have deserved well of art.
It is not strange, therefore, that I eagerly accepted
an offer to revisit Holland. I returned there the following year, full of the remembrances which I have
thus succinctly narrated. I will not describe this
second journey, lest I should repeat myself, but I
cannot refrain from mentioning another monster
demonstration which was specially distinguished both
in the way it was conceived and carried out; and, in
order that its true spirit may be better understood, I
delight to mention that this period of my artistic life
(1860) coincided with the warlike feats of arms which
were then attracting the notice of the civilized world
towards Italy.

I was to arrive at Utrecht, and the scholarly youth
of that city, interested and fascinated by the marvellous prestige of Victor Emmanuel and Garibaldi,
desired to welcome me—an Italian *artiste*—with the
enthusiasm with which they saluted a new era for
our country. The entire population, together with
the youthful and intelligent students of that University, assembled to meet me at the station. An open
carriage awaited me, drawn by four horses. It was a

solemn progress, and to this day I can recall the satisfaction I experienced, for I fully understood that
this homage was not paid to me personally, but rather
to Italy.

The procession began to move. My carriage, in
which I sat with my family, was preceded by an
advance-guard on horseback. Part of this select
escort rode on either side and followed me ; and thus
I passed through the principal streets of the city on
my way to the hotel, amidst an immense crowd.

I appeared on the stage the same evening and
received a perfect ovation from my audience. When
the play was over, I was treated to one of those torch-
light serenades which are always so picturesque,
especially in northern countries.

The remembrance of this episode, which I should
have liked to describe more minutely, is perpetuated
by accurate engravings, and I shall always tenderly
cherish the first copy that was presented to me.

Early in October, 1859, I went to Portugal, where
I divided a course of twenty-four performances between Lisbon and Oporto. What an enchanting
country it is ! And what delightful recollections I
retain of my different visits there ! How can my
futile pen ever express the impression which I felt at
the sight of that magnificent panorama of Lisbon
seen from the sea !

What an appreciative Maecenas towards artists
was the lamented King Ferdinand ! To me especially
he was always courteous and kindly, and to this day
I preserve a drawing in water-colors he graciously
painted for my album. Every time I revisited Lisbon

I met with the same constant appreciation from the public, and the same consideration from the father-King. I was last in Portugal in 1878, and was delighted to receive the same welcome from the public, while the Royal family, of which Pia of Savoy is the principal ornament, gave me many manifestations of sympathy.

I must not omit to mention a very original performance, of which I retain a most pleasant remembrance, and which I gave in the February of the following year as I passed through Coimbra. As is well known, Coimbra is the seat of the principal Portuguese University, in which there is a most charming theatre destined for the amusement of the students; and only on rare occasions actors, who have obtained favor with the Lisbon public, on leaving there, are requested to appear upon the stage of this theatre. The Head of the University asked me to perform *Medea*. I assented with pleasure, as I was glad to perform before an audience, the masculine character of which had struck me the year before when I passed through the city. I had been at the same time greatly impressed by the picturesqueness of their costume.

When I was received by the whole of the students with their Rectors and Professors at their head, the picturesque costume of those young men reminded me of a *moyen age* picture. The students wear a sort of tail coat buttoned to the throat, short trousers, and a stand-up white collar; on the head a cap shaped like the one Dante wears in his portraits. A large cloak covers the whole person. This dress, entirely of black, acts as a kind of frame to the face and emphasizes all its coloring; and their beard, usually long and thick, gives additional prominence to their very dark eyes.*

As I have already said, I was to represent *Medea*, the *mise en scène* of which presented some difficulties which seemed to me hard to overcome. One of the fundamental statutes of the University forbids the appearance of any females as supernumeraries. How, then, was the scene with the Canephorae to be arranged? They were indispensable; but, behold! the students proposed an expedient worthy of their lively imaginations. They offered to array themselves as young maidens and enact the followers of Creusa. The proposal seemed to me all the more absurd because of their thick beards, but there was no help for it; and all I could do was to recommend them to hide their faces in the best possible way.

When I arrived at the theatre for the performance, I was solemnly received by the Professors and students. I found that these most polite young men had prepared me a dressing room, which for elegance and good taste could rival with the most elaborate and perfumed boudoir.

But I must pass on to the performance. The theatre was crowded; but I must confess my mind

---

* King Don Dinez founded at Lisbon, in 1288, a school for the study of general science. This study included faculties of art, of canonical and civil law, and of medicine. In 1290 Pope Nicholas IV. confirmed his foundation. In 1306 the King transferred the College to Coimbra, and constituted it a University, similar to those existing in other parts of Europe.

was preoccupied with the little arrangement for the Canephorae already mentioned. I was not at all sure that in its most touching scenes the tragedy might not be turned into a farce! Fortunately, this did not happen, though for one instant I feared my apprehensions might be well founded. In order to accustom myself to this most original set of supernumeraries, I had made them pass in review before me prior to commencing the performance. But, alas! during one of the most important situations of the first act, I chanced to cast my eye on a box close to the stage. And what did I see? Some of the Canephorae, who just before had been sent by Creusa to pray in the Temple of Diana, smoking, with the utmost indifference, long Havana cigars! How could I help laughing? How could I continue my part? Tried and experienced actress as I was, I could not withstand the effects of this ridiculous and unexpected sight. It was only by the greatest effort that I maintained my self-control, and I was forced to send and ask these new kind of Canephorae to be kind enough to withdraw from the front of the box.

Of my return to France from Portugal, through Belgium, I have the most agreeable reminiscences of a visit—unfortunately, too short—which I made to Hanover. The Royal Family gave me and my family innumerable proofs of the most affectionate benevolence. King George was not only interesting for the courageous patience with which he bore his blindness from the age of sixteen; he was, besides, a brilliant talker, well versed in art. The welcome

we received in the Royal home, where a beloved
mother ruled with a gentle hand, holds a high place
in my dearest recollections.

From Hanover I went to Paris. This was in
April, 1860. On the evening of the 21st, the annual
performance for the benefit of Racine's grand-
daughter, Mlle. Trochu, took place at the Comedie
Française. On this occasion they endeavored to
make the entertainment as varied as possible, and
thus it was that it came into the head of my good
friend Legouvé to try and persuade me, not only to
appear in the fourth act of *Phædra*, but to recite, in
French, a poem he had written for the occasion.
Although ready to take part in Italian in that chari-
table purpose, the reader may imagine I met his
second proposal with a decided and energetic negative ; for I was fully aware of the great difficulties I
should have to encounter both in the pronunciation
of a foreign language, the nervous excitement in
which I should find myself, and the critical character
of the important and severe audience which fre-
quented the Comedie Française. Besides all this, I
knew that in accordance with the traditional custom,
I should be surrounded by all the players attached
to the theatre during my French recitation.

But Legouvé was not to be refused so easily. He
persuaded me to recite, then and there, in a room to
ourselves, some verses which he had been repeating
to me in his excellent diction. To please him, I
consented, and Legouvé was so well satisfied with
my attempt that, opening the door of the room where
we were, he cried laughingly, at the top of his voice,

to some friends who were waiting my decision : "*La Patrie est sauvée! La Patrie est sauvée!*"

Encouraged by these demonstrations on the part of my friend, I set myself in good earnest to study his composition. *Audaces fortuna juvat!* I may say that my difficult task was successfully accomplished.

The republic received me like *une enfant gatée de la Maison de Molière;* but what gratified me still more was the warm approval of my most illustrious comrades for the time being.

The following was the programme for that evening :—

Athaliah.
The Fourth Act of *Phædra*, performed by Mdme. Ristori.
A tribute to Racine, by M. Amedée Roland.
Verses by M. Legouvé, recited by Mdme. Ristori.
Les Paideurs.

This successful experiment was the cause of an even more difficult and important effort.

Legouvé would not relinquish his desire of seeing me perform in French, and to persuade me he employed all his eloquence. He knew my deep gratitude to the French, to the Emperor, and to the brave army who had just made its triumphal entry into Paris from the victorious fields of Magenta and Solferino. Already more than once I had expressed my wish to thank the French public who had opened wide to me the road of all Europe.

"Here you have the opportunity," he said to me. "The efforts you are going to make will be the proof of your feeling. Nobody could interpret it differently."

He gained his cause. Once again I yielded to the force of eloquence. I considered, also, that I would satisfy the lively desire of the Parisian public to see me in such a difficult task as acting in their language. I consented to essay the drama, in four acts, which Legouvé had expressly composed for me, and in which I was to figure as an Italian, who, thanks to the considerate and delicate thoughtfulness of the author, might properly be expected to speak with a slightly foreign accent. When I was told the subject I was greatly pleased with it.

Beatrix, a young actress of considerable reputation, invited to pass from Court to Court, and from salon to salon, ends by meeting a young prince, who falls madly in love with her, and determines to marry her in spite of the difference in their position. She secretly returns the prince's affection, but, knowing that such union would be a cause of much sorrow to her lover's mother, of whose kindness she had been frequently the object, would not think of causing unhappiness in the family of her benefactress. Beatrix, not wishing to deceive, and not having the strength to resist, disappeared. I liked this part, as I felt interested in the sufferings and the heroism of this young actress, Beatrix. I was ready to set to work at once; and to facilitate the execution of our plan, Legouvé proposed to accompany me in a journey I was about to make along the Rhine.

It was one continuous rehearsal from morning till night. He availed himself of every spare moment to train me in my part, and to conquer the difficulties I had in the pronunciation, and displayed infinite art

in teaching me to soften down the rolling of the
Italian *r*, which pronounced close, as by us, is such
an element of expression and energy in our language, but which is so little accordant with the
smoothness of the French one. The final syllable
of the imperfect tense was also another subject of
our studies. These were quite finished by the time
our peregrinations were over, and we were thus enabled to make arrangements for the performance of
Beatrix at the Odéon in the following March. On
leaving Paris, I made another tour in Holland, went
up the Rhine, and visited Livonica and Courtrand.

In December of the same year (1860) I went to
St. Petersburg, where I returned in November 1861.
I was at Moscow in February 1861 and February
1862.

I retain the most pleasant recollections of this
period of my life. St Petersburg with its many
attractions will always remain impressed upon my
mind, and I shall never forget the welcome I received
from the public. Although the Court, being in
mourning for a member of the Imperial family, could
not attend the theatre, yet the Emperor Alexander II.
and the Empress desired to see me, and I was
therefore invited to spend an evening at the Winter
Palace. I recited the third act of *Mary Stuart*
before their Majesties. Nothing could exceed the
graciousness with which I was received. But how
enthusiastic the inhabitants of the north can be,
I was better able to judge from my welcome at
Moscow.

It is true that the youthful element predominates

6

in that ancient city, attracted there by the celebrity
of its University. Here, as in Holland, the students
distinguished themselves by their enthusiasm, but in
rather a different manner, and I greatly prize, and
carefully preserve as an object of the highest moral
value, the present which they made me of a gold
bracelet set with amethysts, symbolizing the globe,
on which reposed a glittering star—the star of Art.

University students, even in Russia, are not over-
burdened with riches! For this reason, therefore, I
cherish all the more the token of sympathy and affection they offered me.

On the morning of my departure the students, in
a body, awaited me at the station. Hardly had I
arrived when they clustered round me, and, as though
by enchantment, I found myself transported to my
compartment! My family followed me as well as
they could. Up to the moment of starting, my carriage was turned into a manufactory of autographs.
Hundreds of times I had to sign my name on bits of
paper, pocket-books, fragments of paper. The whistle of the engine gave the signal of departure, and
the train moved off amidst the most clamorous
demonstrations.

Such remembrances are most touching, and I wish
the same heritage of heart and affection to the actresses who shall come after me.

From Moscow I went to Paris, as I had to begin
the rehearsals of *Beatrix*. Little by little, as these
went on, the love for my part grew stronger in me.
I identified myself so thoroughly with the personage
I had seen created and developed under my very

eyes, that on the day of the first representation—March 25th, 1861—it seemed to me as if I were simply appearing in one of my customary parts, and the thought of the public did not trouble me at all. I felt quite sure that they would appreciate my most audacious attempt, accepting it as a tribute of Italian gratitude, and this thought was my salvation. Indeed, I felt so perfectly sure of myself, and so calm, that I remember I replied with a hearty laugh to the exhortations of my comrades who, just before I presented myself on the stage, entreated me to take courage, to have no fear! But when I actually went on, our old adage recurred involuntarily to my mind —"It is one thing to talk of death; and quite another thing to die."

However accustomed I was to the public of the principal cities of Europe, I felt some dismay at the sight of the crowd which filled the Odéon that evening. The unamimous applause with which I was greeted alarmed rather than encouraged me! Thinking how much was expected of me, I had to summon all the force of my strong will to my aid, to overcome that momentary hesitation. But I succeeded, and I repeated that part for forty nights. And while on this subject, I may mention that *Beatrix* met with the greatest success throughout the French provinces, as also in Holland and other countries. Some years later I gave it again in Paris for twenty consecutive evenings at the Vaudeville.

I travelled to Berlin, for the third time, in March of the same year (1862), performing for six evenings in the Theatre Royal. The Imperial family were prodigal of their affection, and the excellent Emperor William, then King of Prussia, crowned his favors by conferring on me the Order of Civic Merit.

From Berlin I was invited to give three perform- ances at the Grand Ducal Theatre in Weimar. On this occasion I was most kindly received by the Grand Duke and Grand Duchess, and I spent one evening at Court, when I was enabled to judge of the culture of this accomplished Prince, for he then repeated to me, from memory, many passages of Dante, which he had translated fluently; and on future occasions when I was brought into contact with him, I found that he understood and could speak our language most admirably.

Amid all my pleasant recollections of the kindness I received from the German Court, I especially re- member that to the King of Prussia I owe the honor of becoming acquainted with Meyerbeer.

It was near the King's birthday, and I was in Weimar for a brief series of representations, when the Grand Duke, who, as every one knows, is brother to the Queen Augusta of Prussia, requested me, in her name, to go to Berlin unknown to the King, and perform *I Gelosi Fortunati.* A beautiful and elegant little theatre was privately got ready in one of the apartments of the Imperial residence. The King was highly delighted with this affectionate surprise prepared by his Consort. The little play went off brilliantly, and after the performance supper was served at small tables scattered about the room. It was then that the King presented Meyerbeer to me, appointing him my cavalier for the rest of the even-

ing. What a recompense for the fatigue of my journey! and Meyerbeer, who was most agreeable, had
no difficulty in making his conversation interesting to
me. The next day he came to see me with his two
daughters, and we spent a pleasant hour, talking of
art and of Italy.

During the remainder of 1862, and up to December 1864, I revisited, several times, cities where I
had already given performances, making long stays
in my own dear country, especially in Sicily, whence,
in September 1864, I embarked for Alexandria, in
Egypt.

In the land of the Pharaohs I had an opportunity
of judging how art affected different nations. The
enthusiasm manifested for me by the society of Alexandria, the most cosmopolitan of the world, left
nothing to desire. On the evening of my benefit I
was overwhelmed with demonstrations of esteem and
kindness, especially from the Italian colony. In re-
sponse to repeated invitations, I next went to Cairo,
where I appeared at a temporary theatre, the old one
having been burnt down.

The 2d of December of 1864, saw me in Smyrna.
The voyage was long and most unfortunate. We had
taken passage in a steamer belonging to the Austrian
Lloyd's, called *The Empress*. As soon as we left
Alexandria we found the sea very tempestuous, and
when we neared the Colossus of Rhodes, the boiler
was found to be damaged. For forty-eight hours we
lay at the mercy of the wind and the waves. The
captain and the officers vied with one another in
bravery. Our signals of distress, though constantly

repeated, were in vain, and we suffered very much physically and mentally. We fancied that every wave that beat against the ship would be our destruction ; but, by a merciful Providence, and thanks to the immense efforts made by the officers, the damage to the machinery was repaired somehow, and we slowly returned to Alexandria.

Yet, exhausted as I was by all I had undergone, I felt obliged to re-embark in another vessel of the same line—the *Archduchess Charlotte*—a few days after.

I do not exaggerate when I say that I had a fierce struggle between my inclinations and my duty, before —in my condition of mental and physical suffering— I could decide on this step. But I may say that throughout my artistic life I have always succeeded, at whatever cost, in fulfilling my engagements.

I gave one performance of *Medea* at Smyrna, on my way to Constantinople, but at the latter city I was only able to give thirty, partly in consequence of the unfortunate voyage, and partly because of my great desire to arrive quickly at Athens. Yet, although my stay at Constantinople was short, it is full of pleasing remembrances to me.

I reached Athens on the 19th of January 1856. I could only give five performances. I had hardly arrived at the Piræus than I was already impatient to visit the Acropolis, and I satisfied this great longing of mine the day after my first public appearance, having for my cicerone the renowned archæologist and diplomatist, Raugabéy, now Minister at Berlin. My learned guide revived for me the world of Ancient

Greece with all its classic charms. What a boon for me to find in these sublime marbles all the noble attitudes which I had sought so ardently to reproduce before the public. I was in ecstasy before such wonders. Standing before the Caryatides I studied the Grecian drapery in order to reproduce at the first opportunity every detail of those wondrous folds. Mr. Raugabéy had almost to drag me away by force from that matchless bas-relief of the Victoria Actere, the graceful attitude of which I have still before my eyes.

The Temple of Theseus made a profound impression on me, as did also the theatre of Bacchus. What enchantment it was to see the dazzling rays of sunshine light up the summits of those imposing mountains, Hymethus, Penteticon, and Parnassus, which surround the Acropolis. What a panorama! What magnificent and surprising effects! How my heart beat at finding myself in the midst of those ruins which recall the history of so many centuries, and are such eloquent testimony to the truly beautiful in art which Greece gave to Rome ; or, I might say, to the entire world.

I tore myself away with difficulty from that sublime contemplation which had absorbed me, and increased my love of art. Alas ! how often art is sacrificed to the necessity of the moment ! and just then I had to experience this hard truth. Unfortunately, a previous agreement which I could not break, rendered me unable to comply with the courteous request of King George, who, seeing the enthusiasm manifested by his people (some of whom had made incredible sac-

rifices to attend my performances), tried to induce
me to take part in a grand representation which
should revive, in the nineteenth century, the costumes
and stage-effects of ancient Greek tragedy, as far as
was consistent with the exigencies of the modern
theatre.   It was to be a daylight performance in the
theatre of Bacchus, where all Greece would assemble.
That classic enclosure should be put into the best
possible condition for the entertainment by the Athe-
nian architects.

How can I describe my disappointment at having
to refuse this tempting proposal made me by His
Majesty?   For myself, I was only too delighted at
the idea of appearing upon the stage of that ancient
theatre in classic Greece; of reviving for a moment
the art of Sophocles and Æschylus; reposing, in
spirit, in the majesty of Olympus!   It would have
been a memorable event in my life.   But, unhappily,
the prose of that wretched contract overpowered the
poetical enchantment I would fain have shared.

Good-by, poetry; good-by, dear Athens; good-
by, my amiable guide.   I was bound to appear at a
fixed date in Paris, where I was to play at the Lyric
Theatre in French, in a drama by M. Legouvé, called
Les deux Reines.   What could we say to the cruel
play of destiny?   On my return voyage we touched
at Messina, and there I found a telegram from M.
Legouvé, informing me that, in consequence of some
political complications with the Holy See, Napo-
leon III. had prohibited *Les deux Reines.*

And to think that it was for this contract that I
had deprived myself of an unspeakable pleasure!

We divided between Naples, Leghorn, Florence, Milan and Turin, the time we were to have spent in Paris.

I returned to this metropolis towards the end of April 1865, in order to fulfil my engagement to play *Beatrix* at the Vaudeville! Just at that time Florence was solemnly celebrating the sixth centenary of Dante. Most of the intellectual world had been invited to honor the divine poet.

The Syndic was most urgent that I should go there to contribute, with Tommaso Salvini and Ernesto Rossi, in composing an artistic programme worthy of the occasion, and also to take part in the grand procession formed by representatives of Arts and Science, who, walking through the city to Piazza Santa Croce, were to be present at the unveiling of the statue of Dante. I was delighted to accept this flattering invitation; to associate myself with those two masters in art was for me a fortunate chance. Our meeting suggested the idea of making us play *Francesca da Rimini* together in the Cocomero (now Nicolini) Theatre, for a charity. Paolo was taken by Ernesto Rossi; Salvini played Lanciotto, of which part he made a surprising creation. I was Francesca. We vied with each other in passion and zeal, and new effects sprang forth as if by enchantment. Rossi showed well that he belonged to that school which has no masters, in the strict sense of the word, but which acts from the impulse of a superior genius. Educated in the precepts of Gustavo Modena equally with Salvini, Ernesto Rossi could never have become a celebrity without a special disposition and imposing talent.

The evening was an artistic fête, and to commemorate it a marble tablet was placed in the interior of the theatre. This was an event which I rejoice to have taken part in, and which I desire to record in order to pay a fresh tribute of affection and esteem to my two illustrious companions.

After having paid the honor due to the great poet and to my country, I hastened to return to Paris in order to resume the rehearsals for *Beatrix*, which was given on the 22d of May, my good Parisian public receiving me with the same expression of esteem as in the past years. From that epoch up to the end of July 1866, I travelled to Italy, Austria, Holland, France and Belgium.

My health was always remarkably good, although, unfortunately, I was never able to accustom myself to the sea. During my many wanderings I acquired a robustness of constitution that nothing could shake, and this, in its turn, developed in me an untiring energy which enabled me to guide and direct all our movements with the resolution and authority of a general at the head of his army. Every one obeyed me ; and this obedience I gained by the exercise of the strictest impartiality, for I was always ready to censure or correct those who failed to discharge their proper obligations, and to bestow praise without distinction upon those who merited it, while at the same time I treated all with kindness and courteousness.

As a rule, I found the members of my company willing to submit gracefully to my authority ; if any seemed inclined to assert themselves too loudly, the firmness of my demeanor speedily put them in their proper place.

Everything relating to the artistic management rested entirely in my hands. I gave all orders, made all arrangements, and occupied myself with all those great and small details which any one who knows the stage will fully understand, and which are so essential to the success of a performance. A special administration had charge of the business department. But I am proud to say that my husband was the soul of every enterprise. Since I am speaking of him my heart inspires me to state that he never ceased to exercise over me, during my whole career, a constantly benevolent influence. It was he who kept up my courage when I hesitated before the difficulties I met with ; he showed me the fame I should acquire, and pointed out to me the end I was to reach ; facilitating everything in the course before me. Without him I should never have dared to attempt carrying the banner of Italian Art round the world.

My hesitation at that moment was excusable, however, because my aged mother's infirm health was just then preoccupying me more than anything else, and I was tormented with the idea that I might lose her during my absence. And thus it was. She died several years afterwards while I was on the way to Rio de Janeiro. Ten years before I had also the grief of not being present to close my father's eyes in Florence, being at the time at Wiesbaden.

But to resume the thread of my narrative. I may say that I took the greatest pains to make myself noted as an example of punctuality. Throughout my long journeys, I met with some hardships. If any of my party grew faint-hearted, or feared to follow me, I tried to spur them on by my example. I was always the first to encounter any difficulties that might lie in the way. It happened to me once, in February 1872, as I was travelling between Moscow and Dunaburg, to have to cross, at night and on foot, a long bridge near Kowna, which had suffered such damage from the severity of the season that it had to be rebuilt. When we reached it, the workmen were still busy, lighted by flickering torches. The torrent beneath it, swollen by heavy rains and the quickly melting snow, was frightful to look at, and to add to its horror, we heard that that very morning, an unfortunate workman had fallen in and been drowned.

When my actors were told this, and saw how unsafe was the passage across the bridge, as it was encumbered with planks and beams of wood, they resolutely refused attempting to go any farther. Time pressed, for the train was waiting at the little station upon the opposite bank. If we remained there all night, we should have to do without any shelter. I was persuaded, from the representations made to me by the superintendent of the workmen, that there was no real danger if the passage was undertaken with caution. So, merrily and with some laughter at my craven-hearted companions, I walked across the long bridge, accompanied by my family, from whom, indeed, I was never divided. At this sight the entire company, huddled together like a flock of sheep, followed me slowly, stumbling and tripping as they came across the bridge, and I was able to reach Dunaburg at the hour fixed for our first performance.

In the beginning of September 1866, I visited, for the first time, the United States, where I remained until the 17th of May of the following year. Great was my impatience to reach that country and to be the first to carry my own language into the noble land of Washington, where, in the midst of a feverish devotion to industry and commerce, the arts and sciences still held a prominent place.

I commenced at the Lyric Theatre in New York, on the 20th of September, with *Medea*. I could not have wished for a warmer welcome than that which there greeted me.

From this epoch date friendships which neither time nor distance have cooled, and, writing these lines, I send an affectionate greeting to those who still remember me beyond the ocean.

Leaving New York, I was summoned to all the cities, large and small, of the States. But I shall never attempt here descriptions which have been written so often by master hands. In order not to repeat myself, I pass over the very warm receptions I received everywhere. The Americans were the first to introduce a most useful custom in the department of dramatic art which Europe was rather slow in following; I mean the weekly afternoon performances, which with us were only exceptions. It allowed women and young girls to be present at the play without interfering with their duties and studies, or exposing them to the fatigue of late hours.

In North America there are invariably two weekly afternoon performances; Saturday and Wednesday. The passing *stars* appear on those days in a house wholly filled by the fair sex. Their applause is naturally less noisy and more modest, but the bravos are always given with much intelligence and at the right moment. The young girls came in such crowds to my performances that I was often obliged to order the removal of the wings to make room for them even on the stage. I tried to measure my play in such a manner that my neighbors should not lose a single movement. My efforts were recompensed by the grateful expression on those young and pretty faces.

Giacometti's *Elizabeth* was a particular favorite with the Americans, from its fine scenic effects, and they came in crowds whenever I played it.

I visited an immense number of cities, but it would detain me too long to enumerate their names or describe them. The result was far beyond my expectations. I can say that I left hardly any city or town of the United States unvisited.

We left the United States, as I have said, in May, and returned thither on the 18th of October in the same year, beginning a new series of performances. My second journey across the Atlantic, in the steamer *Europa*, commenced in such stormy weather, that, when we had been a few days out, one of the deck stewards was swept overboard by a huge wave, and drowned. This unfortunate man had a wife and children at Marseilles, who were dependent on his earnings. It was a case that excited the sympathy of all the passengers, and a project was immediately set on foot to give an entertainment on behalf of the bereaved family. The Captain lent himself to it with all eagerness, and spared no pains to transform the dining-room into an elegant little theatre. The stage was marked off by a row of lights, which represented foot-lights.

I had the good fortune to find myself in company with the renowned singer, Madame La Grange, and, as I had my own troupe with me, we were able to provide an attractive programme. La Grange was to sing three of her favorite pieces; and I had to perform the scene between Mary Stuart and Elizabeth, in Scribe's tragedy: besides, a French gentleman offered to contribute with some singing.

By this time the weather had somewhat moderated, so that we hoped that the next evening, which was fixed for the entertainment, would be sufficiently fine for us not to suffer any inconvenience. But our hopes were not realized, and on the following morning the waves began to rise, and the wind increased in strength. The ship soon began to jump about and our faces lengthened considerably. I commenced to ask myself how I was going to act in this state of things. Towards evening, however, they mended a little, so that it was possible to begin at the hour fixed upon. I came upon the stage determined to triumph over the elements! In the best of spirits I began the beautiful invocation of Mary Stuart to the clouds; but the real clouds, alas! began to gather once more in the sky, and the sea to rise! At the entrance of Elizabeth, I became quite giddy—I stag-

gered—my throat grew dry and parched—I felt the
breaking out of the cold perspiration that heralds sea-
sickness. I hardly knew what I was doing! The
actor who was playing the part of Talbot, fearing that
I should never be able to hold out, ran for a smell-
ing-bottle, and made me smell it at every opportunity.
By means of this expedient I managed to reach
the end of the scene, being upheld by Anna whenever I seemed likely to fall! As soon as I was free,
I ran at once on deck, and threw myself into the arm-
chair. There I awaited Mdme. La Grange, my companion in misfortune, to hear how she had managed
to get through her part.

But from the place where I had taken shelter, I
could hear the audience shouting with laughter at that
poor French amateur, singing, with sepulchral voice,
" *Richard est mort, Richard est mort.*"

This fête of charity had a still more amusing episode next day. A passenger who had complained
energetically to the Captain for abandoning the care
of the ship while that entertainment was going on in
the salon, frightened at the always increasing waves,
put on his safety belt and passed the whole night
on deck. This most courageous gentleman shot furious glances at us, innocent causes of his imaginary
danger.

In my second visit to the United States I made an
excursion to Havana, in January 1868. This terrestrial paradise remains in my memory as an enchanting picture. But here, also, I am forestalled by so
many painters of this tropical nature, and of this life
so bewitching in its Oriental indolence, that I dare

not endeavor to describe them. Once more a hearty greeting to the Havannese, who filled our theatre every evening, and never ceased to applaud me.

On my benefit evening with *Camma*, and a little comedy, *Ciò che piace alla prima attrice*, where, at one point, disguised as Jeanne d'Arc, I recited the well-known adieux of Schiller, admirably translated by our lamented Maffei, the rush for places was enormous, all the boxes and numbered places having been secured many days previously. From 2 o'clock in the afternoon the Cazuela, which is the gallery reserved for ladies, was quite filled; and so afraid were they of not finding room, that they had their dinner served there.

On my return to the hotel an attempt was made to take the horses from my carriage, but this I strenuously opposed. I could not, however, prevent many young men from perching themselves on the axle of the wheels, and on the spokes, at the risk of falling under them, and climbing beside the coachman. I was literally buried under bouquets! I am often haunted by the magic spectacle of this tropical night when, beneath a sky sparkling with stars, I passed like a queen, in the midst of this enthusiastic crowd, between two rows of *volantes*,* from which the elegant occupants in ball-dresses kissed their hands to me, while the negro coachmen could scarcely hold their horses, frightened by the flaming torches. Of the thousand and one nights which I have passed *à la belle étoile*, in returning from the theatres, that was the most memorable.

---

* A kind of open carriage.

After I left the United States, in September 1868, I make another tour of nine months in Italy. We performed the very popular drama of Paolo Giacometti—*Marie Antoinette*—which had been so well received in the United States, but not before given in Italy. My liking for the subject, and my old friendship for the author, made me take a singular interest in its execution. I bestowed as much care on the style of the costumes as on the accessories. It was given at the Theatre Brunetti at Bologna.

My love of truth in art led me to visit the cell in the *conciergerie*, which was the last abode of the unhappy Queen, at the time when I was studying this part. I vividly recollect the sad impression it produced upon me, so much that I could with my imagination see the resigned martyr, and feel myself a partaker of her terrible sufferings.

I had wished to produce this tragedy in Italy before an intelligent public, capable of appreciating its grand situations. Circumstances having brought me to Bologna, for twelve performances, I settled to put *Marie Antoinette* on the stage on the evening of the 9th of November.

Many difficulties had to be overcome before I could obtain the consent of the authorities to its representation. When they were informed of the subject, they suspected, before they read it, that the tragedy would prove a most decided apotheosis of democracy. Then the republician party, persuaded that they would find in it a glorification of the French Republic, and suspicious of the attitude of the Government, made a great noise about its production;

but finally, thanks to the intervention of influential personages, who were convinced that I should never sanction anything to disturb public order, the interdict upon it was revoked.

All in good time came the longed-for evening, November the 3d. The number of guards was increased, and a piquet of cavalry added—precautions exaggerated, perhaps.

The public assembled in crowds ; and, as the action of the piece developed itself, the ultra-Liberals discovered that there was nothing in favor of the Revolution, and of their Radical opinions, and that, on the contrary, it utterly condemned that crime. It was, instead, the desperate case of this unfortunate royal family that impressed the greater part of the audience, and excited its sympathy even to tears. But this did not please the Radical fraction of it. At the close of the second act there were very decided expressions of disapproval, and these increased so greatly in the third act as entirely to drown the piece.

The Questor, who was in the stage box, grew pale with alarm, fearing the outburst of some disorder. Poor Giacometti wiped his forehead, making despairing signs from the wings ! On my part, impatient at the difficulties to be overcome, and indignant to see that a small minority tried to substitute their own evil passions for the tender emotions which up to that time had filled the greater number of the audience, I drew near the wing where the author was leaning ready to faint. " Come speak to the public ; you are a well-known Liberal. They will listen to you ! "

But Giacometti dared not. The situation grew more precarious. It was necessary for us to take some decisive step. I could contain myself no longer. Seized by one of my impulses of impatience I rose resolutely, advanced to the footlights, and signed that I wished to speak. In an instant general silence prevailed. Master of the situation, I addressed the audience as follows :—

"Gentlemen! In presenting to Italy this work of our illustrious compatriot, I believed I was acting wisely in selecting for its first critics the public of Bologna, noted everywhere for its intelligence and politeness. I would not wish anyone to applaud what they do not approve ; but in order to criticise rightly it is necessary at all events to listen without bias of party spirit. In this case much inconvenience has been caused to peaceble citizens, who came to the theatre for amusement and not for conflict."

My determined words gained me general applause, and impressed the authors of the disturbance. When the curtain fell, I was called before it several times, and I appeared holding poor Giacometti, trembling in his excitement, tightly by the hand.

The Questor, together with the other authorities, came to offer their thanks *and congratulate me on the courage I had shown, as though I had saved the country.* From this moment success was assured ; and so popular did the work become, that as I walked along the streets the women pointed me out to their companions with the exclamation—"Look! look! there is Marie Antoinette!"

But certain newspapers by no means abstained

from polemics. The tortures inflicted by the cobbler Simon on the unhappy Dauphin were falsified, or at least exaggerated! The sufferings, the humiliations, the martyrdom of the unfortunate royal family were stigmatised as poetical compositions! But at least good sense and historical accuracy triumphed over fanaticism, and *Marie Antoinette* was received everywhere with the greatest enthusiasm.

CHAPTER V.

SECOND VISIT TO AMERICA, AND OTHER ARTISTIC JOURNEYS.

I LEFT Italy in the beginning of June 1869, for Rio Janeiro, and on the 20th opened at the Flumineuse Theatre with *Medea*.

Although the strong desire to see me which existed among the Brazilians had drawn great crowds to the Theatre, among whom were their Majesties the Emperor and Empress, and the Imperial Princess, yet, to my amazement, when I presented myself on the mountain height with my two children, not a sound of applause greeted me! My reception was in fact icily cold. This extraordinary and unusual welcome almost stunned me for a moment, for the courteous manner in which the Brazilian public generally received *artistes* was well known from those who had experienced it.

But suddenly, at the first scenic effect, their coldness melted away! It was when *Medea*, in answer to her children's entreaties for bread, uttered the agonizing words—

" Gladly would I empty my veins to the last drop,
And say, Here, drink your nourishment from my blood."

This invocation uttered with trembling lips, and coming straight from the heart, excited a frantic

(102)

applause, and raised demonstrations which are the baptism of success. It rose to a paroxysm when Medea, turning to Creusa, tells her that were she to find her rival she would spring upon her like a leopard, tearing its prey limb from limb.

How overwhelmed I was with honors and distinctions by the Brazilians and their sovereign! He honored me with a friendship of which I am proud. Neither time nor distance have diminished my remembrance of it. Received at Court with my family, I cannot describe the kindness and graciousness I met in that Imperial family. I had many opportunities of admiring the culture and deep knowledge of the Emperor, who is versed in the literature of all languages, and is beloved by his subjects for the rectitude of his principles and his justice. Well may they be grateful to him, for his only aim in life is their well-being. The principal cause of his various journeys in Europe is the ardent desire that his country may enjoy the benefit of the latest progress made in science and art, in order to make his people great and prosperous.

I sailed for Buenos Ayres, carrying away the most agreeable recollections of my last evening at Rio, where, after the performance, I was accompanied to my pretty little villa in the suburbs by thousands of torches, and bands of music playing national airs; the streets through which I passed being strewn with flowers, while the Bengal lights gave us every now and then glimpses of the wonderful Bay of Rio de Janeiro.

On the 10th of September I performed at Buenos

Ayres. Fresh joys awaited me in that pleasant land,
where the numerous Italian colony, who there, as in
every distant region, honor the mother country, gave
me a truly royal welcome, almost as though they
were jealous of that offered me by the people of the
Argentine Republic.

I then went to Monte Video until the 26th October,
obtaining there the same results, and returned to
Italy by way of Rio Janeiro, where the echoes of my
first appearance there were not yet silent.

In September 1871, I revisited the Danubian Principalities, Bucharest, Galaby, Bracla, Jassy. From
this last place we had a most disastrous journey to
Russia. Means of transport were scarce and most
difficult to find. We had to traverse uncultivated
steppes utterly devoid of roads, except such as might
be called natural footpaths. We hired all sorts of
vehicles; they were only similar in one respect, they
were all open. They even wanted the necessary
means of sitting safely. We managed the best way
we could, and when we started on our journey we
had very much the appearance of a caravan of emigrants! The horses attached to the first carriage,
which was mine, had large bells fastened to their
harness, so that in the darkness of the night they
might serve as guide for the others. We were so
jolted about in the ruts of the uneven roads, that we
had to hold tightly to the sides lest we should be
shaken out of the carriages. The road, indeed,
looked like a frozen sea! It was the middle of October; the night was extremely cold, and though we
were wrapped to the chin in rugs and cloaks, of

which we carried a good supply, yet, as our vehicles were open, we suffered very severely from the temperature.

Early in the morning our drivers, without consulting us, halted right in the middle of a plain, and commenced to give the horses a feed of hay and oats. There was no dwelling-place in sight; so the luxury of a café or refreshment-room was not to be thought of. We resigned ourselves patiently to imitate the example of this patriarchal simplicity, and eat our breakfast in the open air! Seated on the ground, upon a rug, we set to work upon the provisions we had fortunately brought with us. The originality of the meal, the enormous appetites the cold of the night had given us, the fresh country air, and the merriment produced by the unusual spectacle, all combined to render that repast a most enjoyable one.

We reached Kischeneff on the 20th, and went to the best hotel in the place. What happiness after our nomadic expedition! Taking possession of our rooms in order to enjoy well-deserved repose, we became aware of the microscopic comforts upon which we had congratulated ourselves. Our beds were provided only with one single sheet. All the servants had gone to bed; we had to ring a regular alarm for these absolute necessaries. They informed us, without any circumlocution, that if we wanted more sheets we should have to pay for them.

Having got what we wanted, we were sleeping at last, when we were roused in the depths of the night by the cries of a woman resounding through the whole house, and they attracted us all to our doors; the bells were again set in motion, and the servants ran from all sides. They told us that all this hubbub was caused by a Colonel's wife, to whom her amiable husband was administering correction, of which she would have probably to preserve unpleasant remembrances!

The cries continued. Full of pity and indignation we sent the most vigorous of our party to the assistance of the unfortunate woman; his loud knocks at her door were followed by silence——when, behold! we see the victim make her appearance in the corridor in very light attire, angry, and calling out with stentorian voice: "What do you want? Mind your own affairs! My husband may beat me if he likes!" To which the least excited amongst us responded with a calmness which still makes me laugh: "Well, Madame, if this treatment is good for you, at least bear it without making such a noise! As for us, we want to sleep!" And so we returned to our beds.

From Kischeneff I went to Odessa, and thence to Kieff. Towards the end of 1872, after stopping at Berlin and Weimar, and making a tour through Belgium, I took up my winter quarters at Rome, in order to obtain the repose necessary after so many long journeys and the fatigues of the stage. And here I may say, that I only visited the Danubian Principalities, Turkey and Greece once, but I was in the other parts of the world twice, and even oftener, choosing always Paris or Rome as the places where I enjoyed the short rest I was able to obtain.

In 1873 I revisited London for the fourth time.

Having no new works to produce, and weary of playing always the same things, I felt the necessity of invigorating my mental powers by some strong emotion; in short, of undertaking some difficult task which had never yet been essayed by an Italian actress.

One day I fancied I had discovered what would satisfy this aspiration of my restless spirit. The admiration which I had always felt for the works of Shakespeare, and especially for his *Lady Macbeth,* made me conceive the idea of rendering in its original language the grand sleep-walking scene which is one of the most gigantic conceptions of this mighty poet.

I was impelled to essay this task by the strong desire I had to acknowledge, as well as I could, the affection and constant interest which the most intelligent public of the great metropolis of the United Kingdom had always shown me. But how was I to succeed in it? This was the question my wavering mind was always putting to itself.

I consulted one of my amiable acquaintances, Mrs. Ward, mother of the distinguished actress, Geneviève Ward. She not only encouraged me to put my idea into practice, but offered to help me in learning the scene.

I retained some small reminiscences of English studies made when I was a child, but there is no idiom so difficult to pronounce as the English, and the number of years which had passed since I had attempted it rendered me diffident, although at the same time I felt greatly attracted by such an arduous task. Thanks to my special natural facility for foreign languages, I was able, after fifteen days of indefatigable study, to undertake the ordeal; but as I had no wish to risk a failure, I proceeded with the utmost caution.

I decided to invite the theatrical critics of the most important journals of the city to my house, without telling them why I desired their company. They all very courteously accepted my invitation, and I then unfolded my project, and the idea with which it had inspired me. I begged them to hear me, and frankly and honestly give me their opinion upon my performance, assuring them that I should not be at all offended if it were unfavorable.

I then went through the scene I had been studying, with which they expressed themselves extremely satisfied. They only corrected me in two words, and they entreated me to announce my audacious attempt to the public.

But when the evening came for the representation, and the moment for that important scene approached, I felt my heart sink. But the kindly reception given me by the audience as soon as I appeared, greatly assisted me in regaining my composure. The fortunate result of my experiment was ample compensation for all my anxieties.

My desires, however, increased with my success. I aspired to yet higher flights. In a word, I aimed at no less than performing the entire part of *Lady Macbeth* in English; but the idea seemed rash, so that I dismissed for the time the tempting thought.

CHAPTER VI.

JOURNEY ROUND THE WORLD.

In May 1874, I began, with my husband, a journey round the world, having as companions our children and an old friend, General Galletti, who was a very pleasant fellow-traveller for us.

The order of our course was as follows—Bordeaux, Rio de Janeiro, Buenos Ayres, Montevideo, Valparaiso, Santiago, Lima, Vera Cruz, Mexico, Puebla, United States, San Francisco, the Sandwich Islands, New Zealand, Sydney, Melbourne, Adelaide, Ceylon, Aden, Suez, Alexandria in Egypt, Brindisi, Rome.

After making a beginning to our tour, as I have said, at Rio Janeiro, Buenos Ayres, and Montevideo, we embarked on board the splendid English steamer *Britannia* on the 15th of July, for Valparaiso. We passed through the famous Straits of Magellan, having Patagonia on one side, and on the other Terra del Fuego. I will not delay my narrative to indulge in any long description of the emotion I experienced as I contemplated for the first time the view that nature had spread before me. I will only say that the delicious weather we enjoyed, contrary to the prognostications made before our departure, permitted us all to remain on deck and strain our eyes in the effort to be the first to discover some point of view, or some object which had for us the charm of

novelty.   And we had not long to wait.   See! yonder
advances a *piroque*, making for our vessel.   It contains
a family of Patagonians, extremely tall in stature,
with straight countenances, and long thick hair, rough
and coarse as a horse's mane.   Their wide mouths,
huge cheek bones, and very white and prominent
long teeth, reminded me of my old acquaintances the
redskins, whom I had met many times during my
journeys through California.   I seem to see again
those very tall Patagonians, with nothing on but a
blanket of guanaco skin.

They made signs that they wanted tobacco and
something to eat ; and, in order to satisfy them, we
begged the captain to slacken speed, as it was usual
to do in this place and in such a case ; but for some
reason, which I do not now remember, he refused.
The natives, disappointed in their expectations, expressed their indignation by unmistakable signs of
anger, and I may say that the little I heard of their
language was not harmonious.   We were thirty-six
hours in traversing the Straits, and when we issued
from them at Cape Pilar we found the sea so rough
that it was with difficulty we could keep our feet.

I had lashed myself to the great ring which secured
the port-hole just above my berth, when the sea
struck the side of the vessel with such violence that
both I and my bed were thrown to the ground, and
there I remained suspended by the arm still lashed
to the ring.   I was too ill to extricate myself alone
from that inconvenient position.   The persons who
ran to help me stumbled also, thus offering a curious
spectacle.   In this way we began our acquaintance
with the Pacific Ocean.

At Valparaiso, on the 1st of August, I gave my first performance, opening with my favorite tragedy of *Medea*, the invariable success of which had caused me to select it on this occasion.

I remained two months in that city, Santiago, and Quillota. Not less than in other places was the favor with which I was distinguished by that public. The 18th of October I was at Lima, the beautiful capital of Peru. There, as usual, I began with *Medea*. I found an audience, intelligent, easily roused, and profuse in manifestations of courtesy towards me.

But we hardly escaped being witnesses of a civil war. I was far from foreseeing that amongst the few passengers taken on board the *Britannia* in passing Punta Arenas, just in the middle of the Straits of Magellan, there should be one who two months afterwards would disturb our quiet sojourn at Lima. This personage was rather short in stature, but of bold aspect, rather silent, and his rough manners did not prepossess us in his favor; also the gossip which circulated about him in our little floating colony was not such as to inspire us with the desire of improving our acquaintance with him. It was said that Señor —— had been head of a vast conspiracy tending to overturn the President of the Peruvian Republic. The plot was nothing less than to blow up the whole train which was carrying the President and the Ministers to the inauguration of a new line of railway. Rightly or wrongly, the individual in question was accused of being the instigator of this terrible crime, and he was exiled. This dangerous fellow-traveller landed at Coronel, the first Chilian port our steamer touched. We had arrived at Valparaiso when the news spread that, joined by a certain number of partisans, he had hired a mercantile clipper and hoisted sail for an unknown destination.

Our pleasant stay at Valparaiso and Santiago, had caused us to forget the name and deeds of Señor —— ; but, arriving at Lima, it came to our notice that he had disembarked on the Peruvian coast and was carrying on a guerilla warfare at the head of a little army against the troops of the Peruvian Government, which, accustomed to these vicissitudes, were not greatly affected thereby. Revolutions and counter-revolutions follow upon each other in this blessed country where the so ardently-desired post of President generally costs the life of the ambitious candidate who achieves it; such, at least, was usually the case up to 1874.

Besides the papers, which gave us every morning news of the war, we possessed a living gazette in the person of a native servant whom we had engaged to assist our own domestics. Although his business was only to market and go messages, he had pompously arrogated to himself the title of majordomo; and it was impossible to make him cross the street door. At every news unfavorable to the Presidential party, the majordomo affected a tragic tone and we were treated to his lamentations.

At first we could not understand why he should prefer to remain shut up within doors; but one day, our own servant forcing him to go out, he provided himself with a sword-stick, with which, he said, he would know how to defend himself, although he was not certainly a man ready to strike!

"How?" said the other. "You have to go to market, and not to fight."

"Why, don't you know," he answered, "the danger which threatens us at every corner of the street? The Government wants soldiers, takes them by force; and if they lay hands upon me, I am lost."

And such was the case, as we were able to certify shortly afterwards. A sergeant with two soldiers stood at every turning, taking conscript every man of the people he met; and, in case of resistance, he threw the lasso over him, in the same way as they use it to catch wild horses in the plains of Mexico.

Meantime Señor —— and his adherents advanced towards the capital. One fine morning the President started at the head of the whole Lima garrison to go and fight the enemy so dreaded by the great majority of the country, and only left the police to guard the capital. Of the whole population, we were the only persons astonished at what was happening, the inhabitants being long accustomed to similar events. One evening we had returned from a most interesting excursion along the grand railway line undertaken by Meigs, which leads from Oraya across the Andes to connect Peru with the river Amazon. In a few hours we had reached a height of 14,000 feet, crossing zones of the most varied vegetation, meeting with numerous flocks of llamas, sometimes free, sometimes used as beasts of burden. We were all assembled at table, relating to a Peruvian friend who was dining with us the impressions of the day, when

8

suddenly cries of "Sierra puerta, sierra puerta!"* were heard in the street. A terrified woman rushed into our *patio*† screaming: "Jesus! Maria! la revolucion!"

Our valiant Majordomo, more alarmed even than the woman, hastened to the street-door, which he closed precipitately and secured with bar and bolts. Curiosity impelled us to the windows, from whence we saw our neighbors, in hot haste, using the same precautions. The shots we heard at a little distance caused us prudently to draw in our heads.

"What is the meaning of all this?" we asked our guest, who, without showing the slightest discomposure, informed us:

"It is only a *Sierra Puerta.* Every time the President is forced to leave the city with the garrison to repress a revolutionary movement, it rarely happens that they who remain at home do not come to blows in the city itself. The police being too few in number to maintain order, are commanded to patrol the streets before returning to the barracks crying 'Sierra puerta!' Every inhabitant shuts the house-door and secures it as best he can, and patiently awaits the event. In the streets one might run the risk of a shot; but the houses are never invaded, and we may go on with our dinner."

This sublime indifference in no way modified our curiosity, and, despite his advice, we did not leave the windows. Nothing more was seen or heard, and

---

* Shut the door, shut the door.
† Court or yard.

the distant shots ceased. Soon after the doors were cautiously re-opened, the inhabitants re-appeared, and presently the police-guards again showed themselves in the streets, spreading reassuring tidings. It had been only a false alarm; the telegraph announced a great victory of the President over the rebels. "All's well that ends well," says Shakespeare. We opened the doors, laughing at the tragicomic interruption, and resumed our places at table.

In this capital the ladies are as beautiful as they are amiable. Many pages would not suffice to register all the affectionate remembrances which crowd upon my mind while I am writing.

On the 28th November we left Callao, the port of Lima, which is hardly a quarter of an hour distant, and we embarked on board the *Oroja,* surrounded by our new and charming friends, who had largely contributed to enliven our short visit to their country.

The voyage from Peru to Panama was most enchanting. The sea, always smooth, allowed even the worst sailors amongst us to stay on deck, reclining on our sea-chairs, following the flights of pelicans, and albatross, which traced long white and grey lines on the deep blue of the sky. We passed, almost touching them, the Islands of Lejos and the arid rocks of the Sylla de Prysta. But the scene quickly changes, and we see islands of fantastic vegetation, where all the rich fruits of the tropics grow wild.

The Isthmus of Panama is a terrestrial paradise; it is the ideal Eden of the poets!

Its flora is most varied and gigantic, and at once delights and bewilders the observer. The sky is azure, and much more diaphanous and vaporous than ours. There are sunrises and sunsets which are so many idyls of nature.

At Panama we left the *Oroja,* and in a few hours the railway took us from one ocean to another, across a marvellously beautiful country, which leaves an impression on the memory like a fairy tale. The high temperature, however, and the heavy, unwholesome atmosphere, caused us to experience a feeling of relief when we again left terra firma and set foot on the *Saxonia,* a German steamer, which carried us to the pretty town of St. Thomas, after a short stay at Curaçoa.

On the 16th December we took passage in an English company's steamer for Mexico. On the 25th, after touching at Havana, behold us again on board the *Ebro,* gliding placidly upon the shining mirror of the Mexican Gulf.

Each of us, going up on deck in the morning, feels a soft and, at the same time, melancholy emotion, and smile as we shake hands with our travelling companions. We are by this time no longer strangers to each other. Dislikes, if there were any, vanish —a common tie unites us ; every one sighs and longs for something. It is Christmas, and many a thousand leagues divide us from our homes and friends. The thoughts, which on such a day fly away like swallows beneath that sparkling sky, are mutually understood ; they bear an electric current from our hearts to those who are far away.

Our floating palace is in gala to-day, and since yesterday evening the dining-room no longer wears its everyday appearance; the pictures on the walls disappear beneath the wreaths of holly brought from England; broad ribbons running along the cornice bear white placards with " Happy Christmas " in capital letters. Garlands of flowers hang from the ceiling; the table from early morning has assumed gigantic dimensions, our captain having delicately thought of suppressing distinctions on this occasion, and inviting both second and first class passengers to march in file past the monumental plum pudding mixed in the kitchen on board.

At 7 we are all standing in our places, and the captain, having said a short prayer, salutes us all, as we sit down, with these words : " A happy Christmas to you all, ladies and gentlemen ! "

Dinner over, we go on deck again, where artificial fireworks are ready. Nothing can be imagined more fantastic than those streaming rockets and that golden shower on a beautiful tropical night in that silver-flashing sea, upon which our ship ploughed a luminous furrow. " Hurrah ! " burst forth the sailors in stentorian voices, adding the name of each country represented on board—formidable hurrahs flung into the air in the immense ocean solitudes, having found an echo in our hearts.

After the artificial fireworks a dance was improvised for the sailors and the steerage passengers, the captain opening the ball. The orchestra, composed of a hand-organ and a trombone—an original and certainly novel combination—was situated near. An enormous bunch of mistletoe was hung from a rope above the deck, and we sat all round enjoying the gayety of these good people, and sharing in their laughter every time that the dancers passed beneath the fatal plant, when, according to the old English custom, the gentleman has the right to steal a kiss from his partner.

By midnight silence and stillness once more reigned on board. As for us, we still remained awhile on deck in ecstatic contemplation of the beautiful sky where every star seemed to smile and shed its rays on us.

I could not make up my mind to return to my cabin. More than ever on this Christmas night I felt my heart full of deep gratitude towards God who had protected me and mine in our long voyage across the seas, and who was granting me this feeling of rest, tranquillity and hope for the work still lying before me. The ship's bell ringing 2 o'clock caused me to rise from my seat. A sailor passed near me : " A happy Christmas to you and your dear ones," I said, unable to resist the impulse of speaking to him the words with which our good quartermaster had received me on deck that morning.

We touched St. Thomas, Porto Rico, and Vera Cruz. Here I was received in a way which I cannot pass without mention. The municipality welcomed me officially, and provided me with lodgings and everything I required. In fact, I may say that I was the guest of the entire population, who presented me with flowers and poetry. I commenced my performances in the city of Mexico on the 31st December.

I will only observe that here also I was treated with the greatest consideration.

On this my second visit to Vera Cruz, I was still more greatly struck with the lugubrious aspect of the city. Not by accident did Cortes call it the " True Cross," in memory of so many comrades fallen victims to the Black Vomit and Yellow Fever, which prevail there almost continually. I confess that my apprehensions only ceased when we set foot on the French steamer *Ville de Brest*, which was to bear us to New York.

It was the 17th of February. From the preceding evening, however, to our dread of the climate was added the prospect of a most difficult start, since a strong north wind (frequent and alarming on those shores) was hourly increasing in violence. In fact, next morning the sight of the terribly angry sea amply justified our fears. The actors and part of our baggage were embarked early in the morning. But the sea grew rougher every minute, and when the time came to go on board, and we were on the pier, the boatmen, showing us the high and tempestuous waves which were dashing against the rocky shore, refused to row us to the *Ville de Brest*, which was dancing like a nutshell in the middle of the roadstead. Entreaties were of no avail, and it was only when we had gradually reached the offer of twenty dollars for each boat that they summoned up sufficient courage to venture upon that passage of three quarters of an hour. They were eternal, such was the trepidation to which we were a prey lest the boats should capsize at any moment.

With a sigh of relief we scrambled up the ladder
of the steamer as well as our drenched and consequently heavy garments permitted us. The captain
had been so polite as to delay his departure for more
than an hour, an unusual thing for a postal steamer.
A large part of our luggage could not be embarked,
the boatmen absolutely refusing to venture with a
heavy load through such a sea. We were forced to
resign ourselves to. leave it there until the next postal
steamer the following week, trusting in our good star
to find at New York what was indispensable ; for,
according to my engagements, I could not delay the
first performances. At last we were off, and while
the first rotations of the screw by degrees increased
the distance between us and the Mexican land, which
was disappearing in a grey and melancholy veil, one
hundred and fifty sisters of charity, expelled by the
Government, kneeling on deck, spite of the rolling
vessel, the impetuous wind, and the spray of the
waves, sang in a solemn hymn farewell to their
homes, friends, and country, where those holy women
were no longer to expend the treasures of their
charity. We were deeply moved at that pathetic
picture, representing so many humble sacrifices, so
much constant self-denial towards a most sublime
ideal ; and I saw not far from me a sailor wipe away
a tear with his rough and horny hand.

*   *   *   *   *

The passage from Havana to New York, where
the *Ville de Brest* left us, was as rough as the rest of
our voyage ; and we were very glad to land once
more. But, according to the proverb, "Troubles

never cease," I had no sooner landed than I began to feel the want of the luggage left behind. The New York theatres had not any large wardrobes, and many articles essential to our performances were missing from our trunks.

This state of things lasted for a month, and every time I went on the stage, arrayed in the makeshift attire I had been forced to assume in the place of my carefully-studied historical costumes, I felt almost unable to identify myself with my part. Thus, for example, the scantiness of my mantle constrained all my movements. The meagre accessories embarrassed me. At last, when these difficulties were at an end, I had my own belongings about me once more.

From the 27th of February until our departure for Sydney we remained in the United States, being everywhere received with kindness and most flattering evidences of sympathy. My artistic tour ended at San Francisco, where I embarked for Australia. Unfortunately, our last days in the United States were marked by a very sad incident.

My brother Cæsar, who was my constant companion, lost his wife after giving birth to her first child. It was impossible to abandon this poor little creature to the hands of an American nurse. The distance, the difficulty of communication, alike forbade it. What was to be done? An idea was suggested which we immediately seized. We must get a she-goat, which would provide the baby with nourishment until we reached Sydney. When the day of embarkation came, the small four-legged nurse was the object of all our care. But unfortunately, the sea was not equally well disposed towards her.

Our departure from San Francisco was fixed for the 21st June 1875. We had taken places on board the *City of Melbourne*, and had been told by the captain, Mr. Brown, that she would leave at twelve o'clock, while the agents on shore informed me later that it would not be until two in the afternoon. Everything was ready betimes. Trunks and cases, large and small, bags and baskets, were duly sent to the ship. As there was then only one departure a month from San Francisco to Australia we were very careful to be ready in time, in order not to risk being left behind. Therefore at noon, I and my daughter and the servants, went down to the quay, from which we were distant twenty minutes, while my husband and son were to call at the post office, and then join us on the pier. I found a crowd of people waiting to wish me "God speed"; but from the way they waved their handkerchiefs, as we approached, I saw at once that something had happened; and, in fact, they were beckoning to me to make haste, for the ship was already raising her anchor, as the hour fixed by the captain for her departure had passed.

Imagine what my feelings were. I called out to know if my husband and son had arrived, and when I heard they had not, I resolutely refused to embark without them. The captain, annoyed by my refusal, ordered the engines to be set going. My actors' united entreaties were powerless to move him; he was at that moment a regular ogre. My anxiety may be better imagined than described.

- Presently my husband and son arrived, breathless with their haste, for they had been informed of what had happened. But the captain, perhaps to punish us, had only made a pretended start, convinced, as he was, that my tardiness was due either to negligence or caprice. When we saw the steamer put back again we felt indescribably relieved. Assisted by my friends and acquaintances we flung our small belongings hastily on board, and threw ourselves into the first chairs offered us, overcome by the emotions we had experienced. But I was soon so much affected by the movement of the sea that I was obliged to retire to my cabin. Indeed, as soon as we left the harbor we were all *hors de combat.*

My brother, no longer able to look after the poor baby, came without hesitation to the state room I shared with my daughter. He deposited the little bundle in our arms, and hurried off to his berth. The juvenile traveller began to scream and fidget. My sufferings rendered me quite unable to look after it. An actress of the company, who had kindly taken charge of this poor little creature, hastened to our assistance. She put it in a cot in the ladies' cabin. But a few days afterwards our troubles increased ; the interesting goat, which had most satisfactorily performed her duties as nurse, in her turn became affected by the sea, and lost her milk. The reader will understand how critical the situation then grew ; everybody on board was interested in our case ; one ran to fetch some condensed milk, another brought some farinaceous food, which, he assured us, we should find an excellent substitute. To hear them talk, each seemed an experienced family man. We placed ourselves in the hand of Providence and let them try. Thank God! the baby throve under this strange nursing, and was fat, ruddy and handsome when we reached Sydney.

But to return to our journey. I gave the captain the cold shoulder for several days; but, seeing how skilfully he managed his ship, and noticing the particular interest he took in me and my family, I ended by condoning his rough manners, and we became capital friends.

The 29th we reached Honolulu in the Sandwich Islands, where we made a halt of twenty-four hours. The Italian Consul, good M. Schaefos, came to receive us on board and conducted us to a charming hotel with verandas buried in verdure—Dutch neatness, combined with tropical vegetation. We were enchanted, and ready to follow our guide through the ravishing country which surrounded the city. Scarcely in the hotel and our toilette made, we saw M. Schaefos come back with an invitation in English from King Kalakaua to breakfast at the palace. We were delighted at the prospect of seeing this insular king in the midst of a court we expected to find grotesque in primitive costume, all the women we had met in the town and country being merely clothed in a tunic of many-colored print, their heads crowned with flowers almost always yellow, and galloping astride on ponies, laughing continually among themselves. As to the men, the same costume and the same childish gayety. The Hawaians are so happy as to be convinced that we are not here below to bore ourselves. The court which reigns over these philosophers must be very amusing.

Always accompanied by our amiable consul, we made our entry into a beautiful garden where two aides-de-camp awaited us, handsome fair youths tightly girt in European uniforms faced with silver. They ushered us into the very simple vestibule of the house, all on the ground floor. The doors of the salon opened before us; two lackeys, in sky-blue livery and irreproachable silver lace, held both doors open, and we walked into a vast room, the walls of which were covered with the portraits of all the sovereigns of the civilized world. Our beloved King Victor Emmanuel smiled down upon us from his frame, seeming to bid us welcome. Our hopes of witnessing a savage court receded into dim distance, and when King Kalakaua advanced, graciously holding out his hand to me, I understood how definitely and completely our expectations were *cheated.*

The king, above middle height and whose face scarcely indicated the native color, wore an English coat and whiskers. His pleasing countenance and simple manner conveyed the impression of a perfect gentleman.

No more illusions. The king spoke the purest English, and one of his first questions was to ask whether we liked the valse "A deux ou à trois temps."

Lunch was served, and we took our places at a table resplendent with silver and Sévres china. To excuse the Queen's absence, His Majesty condescended to tell me "She is in the woods," and this was the only note which could recall us to the local tone. The repast was charming and the conversation interesting; the more so as, besides our consul, we had amongst the guests Judge Allen, our amiable travelling companion from San Francisco.

After lunch the king offered me his arm for a turn in the garden, where there was a pavilion in which a very tolerable band was playing. With quite European gallantry they went through our national Italian airs.

We should have remained a long time if the king had not been engaged to attend a concert given *en passant* by our fellow-passenger, Mdme. Murzka, to the court and the city. We had scarcely time to change our dress and make our appearance in the great hall, slightly ornamented, which serves for the public amusements of Honolulu.

We were hardly in our places when the king entered with the Queen—"returned from the woods "— on his arm. Love of truth obliges me to state that the august consort recalled more vividly than her husband Captain Cook's descriptions; and her ladies of honor did not disgrace the picture. The tone was decidedly accentuated. The Queen wore a low-necked gown and train of black silk, with the sky-blue scarf of some order. The king, dressed in a black suit, with polished boots, sat in his gilt arm-chair playing continually with his cane. Decidedly there are no more savages—at Honolulu.

At last, at midnight, after a comfortable supper at the hotel, we had gone again on board and retired to our cabins, when several knocks at my door caused me to open it and find myself in the presence of one of the blue aides-de-camp who had received us in the morning in the royal garden. He held in his hands a mysterious parcel wrapped in a vast red handkerchief, the ends of which he placed in my hands. It was a present from His Majesty, who had recollected the good opinion I had expressed about the fruit served at lunch. Between two *ceremoya* I found, as visiting-card, the portrait of Kalakaua II., with his autograph signature.

We left next day, and all the way to New Zealand had to contend against very bad weather. The small size of our vessel (only 800 tons) made this extremely trying, and for two days the sea was so rough as to make our captain rather anxious.

After a trying voyage of twenty-one days we reached Auckland, where we landed and spent a whole day. To walk without staggering, to sit at a table covered with a *white* cloth (a tint totally unknown on that ship-board), to have fresh and appetizing food, to dine peaceably without fidgeting oneself as to whether there was a cloud on the horizon or the wind was increasing, was such a satisfaction that it made us forget the discomfort and troubles endured.

The following morning we continued our voyage to Sydney, and entered that magnificent bay four days after.

On the evening of the 21st of July I made my first appearance at Sydney, which I left with great regret after a month of continual ovations. On the delicious hills of Port Jackson I have friends to whom I here renew the expression of my lively gratitude.

From Sydney I went to Melbourne, where I acted for thirty-four nights, with the same success as at Sydney, whither I returned on the 11th of October to take my farewell. Adelaide was to be our last halting place in this charming country. I closed my series of 212 performances on the 14th of December with the tragedy of *Mary Stuart.* During this artistic tour I traversed 35,283 miles of sea and 8,365 of land. (I kept the figures out of curiosity.) I spent 170 days upon the water, and seventeen days eight hours in railway trains. In a word, I left Rome on the 15th of April 1874, and returned there by way of India and Brindisi on the 14th of January 1876, after an absence of twenty months and nineteen days.

After all, I must confess that although I brought back the pleasantest memories with me, yet I was delighted with the prospect of repose—repose which I fondly imagined would be permanent, but which was, in fact, interrupted again and again! To taste the joy of returning to one's country, to revisit one's home—to find oneself again among relations and friends—to enjoy absolute freedom, a pleasure of which one had been long deprived, to be able to render aid to those less fortunate than oneself by appearing at performances or concerts—were, as it seemed to me, excellent reasons to confirm me in my determination to retire from the stage.

But that art fever, against which there is no striving, led me to give up once again that tranquillity so much longed for.

In short, on the 2d of October 1878, I started once more for a tour through Spain and Portugal.

I visited Denmark on the 4th of October of the same year, where I was so well satisfied with my reception that I returned again in the following November. From Copenhagen I travelled to Sweden, and opened on the 14th October with *Medea*, at that picturesque city of Stockholm, which has been aptly called "The Venice of the North."

Of what heights of enthusiasm did I not find the Swedes capable! With what a noble and lofty intellect King Oscar is endowed! Among the many foreign languages with which he is familiar I soon found that it pleased him best to converse with me in my own. I received many proofs of his sympathy, chief among them being the following. For my last performance I gave *Elizabeth*, Queen of England. His Majesty and the Court were present. When the play was over, the King, accompanied by his sons, came to my dressing-room, and, after having expressed his great satisfaction in the most courteous and flattering manner, he presented to me, with his own hand, a golden decoration, bearing on one side the device, *Literis et Artibus*, and on the reverse His Majesty's effigy, surmounted by a royal crown in diamonds.

An accident, which might have been fatal, happened during my brief sojourn in Sweden and Norway. The students of Upsala addressed me urgent entreaties to give them a performance in that great University. After repeated refusals I ended by yielding to the temptation of playing before that young and ardent public, and, at the risk of undertaking fatigues beyond my strength, I gave up the sole day

9

of rest left me between two performances; being engaged to play at Stockholm the 24th and 26th.

It was indispensable to travel at night and take a special train. The country through which we had to pass is intersected by broad and deep canals accessible to large vessels. Revolving bridges, the working of which is entrusted to a pointsman, alternately give passage to trains and ships. Hurrying away from Stockholm after the performance, stunned by the acclamations of the crowd who followed me to the station, I got into the train with my husband and my nephew, Giovanni Tessero. I had gone asleep immediately in my excellent sleeping-carriage, when towards one o'clock in the morning, I was awakened by a violent shock and repeated alarm signals. The train had stopped suddenly. We were told we had just escaped, as it were miraculously, from a great danger! The telegram which was to give warning of the passage of our train, containing only the cypher 12 1-2, was understood by the pointsman for half-past twelve noon; consequently we were not expected, and the abyss was yawning at only a few yards' distance in front of us. and in a few seconds we should have been precipitated into it, had not the engine-driver, whether from precaution or presentiment, slackened speed and stopped the train.

My nephew, Tessero, who had gathered these details, repeated them to us, shuddering at the peril so narrowly escaped. Meantime the pointsman was sleeping placidly, and not thinking of making the passage possible for us, so that we remained motionless for some time. But a comrade of his, upon

whom Morpheus had not so liberally strewn his pop-
pies, hearing the signals, closed the bridge and the
train could continue the journey.

The following day the innumerable telegrams of
congratulation I received were a new proof of the
affection entertained by that people for me. I heard
from our kind minister, Comte de la Tour, that the
morning after we left the report spread in Stockholm
that the train had fallen into the river.

But in contrast with this dismal recollection I
chronicle another very cheerful one.

Those delicious Swedish airs are still sounding in
my ears, which the youths of Upsala sang below the
balcony where the Governor courteously placed me
as we came from the supper he had given in my
honor. It was a real art festival. The following
morning at six, at the moment of leaving Upsala to
return to Stockholm, we found those wonderful student choristers in the waiting-room expecting me.

They received us singing a lively song, which was
followed by several others, growing gradually more
melancholy. When we got into our carriage those
fine young fellows ranged themselves on the platform
opposite us; and scarcely did the engine begin to
whistle than they intoned the national ditty called the
Neckers Polka, which Ambrose Thomas has so ably
interwoven with the many jewels comprised in the
death-scene of Ophelia in *Hamlet*. The snow was
falling in thick flakes—the train began to move slowly
—we could not leave the open windows until those
sad harmonies had gradually died away upon the
ear.

I returned to these beautiful countries in October and November 1880. Coming southwards the same year, for the first time during my long career I acted at Munich in Bavaria, giving four performances, which I have pleasure in remembering, because I had from the German actors more than elsewhere fraternal welcome.

At the end of 1880 I resolved to undertake no further engagements, but I speedily discovered, however, that such inaction suited ill with the energy of my temperament. For an actress may be compared to the soldier; the one desires the excitement and conflict of the stage, the other cannot resign himself to the monotony of peace!

And so, one day, the vague idea, which for seven years I had been cherishing in secret, came uppermost in my mind once more. Quietly and silently I resumed the occupation, so agreeable to me, of studying English.

I gave myself to it with ardor. In proportion as my lessons progressed to the satisfaction of my excellent mistress, Miss Clayton, so grew up within me the determination to succeed at every cost. Unfortunately the necessities of summer travelling, and of many other things, interrupted my beloved studies for six months of the year. Rendered impatient by these delays, I resolved to aim at nothing less than acquiring that facility and clearness of pronunciation which the stage requires, without troubling to perfect myself in the phrases used in conversation.

And, thanks to my tenacity of purpose, I succeeded. But what did not this minute and persevering study cost me. Was Demosthenes, with his pebbles in his mouth, on the sea-shore, more energetic than I in my study? In order to vanquish the greatest of my difficulties, that of pronunciation of the language, I invented a method which I think I may call somewhat ingenious. By the aid of ascending and descending lines, I was enabled to tell on which syllable of a word the voice should be raised, or lowered, or dropped. Thanks to other lines, which were either concave or convex, I learnt whether any syllable should be pronounced in a deep or sonorous tone. Assisted by certain French diphthongs, I succeeded in obtaining one of the special and most distinct English sounds, very foreign to a Latin throat; sometimes I added to the French diphthong another vowel sound, the value of which in our language corresponds to that of the French diphthongs *eu, aou,* and thus I gradually succeeded in obtaining the desired result, and acquiring that euphony so necessary to every language.

Such were the devices to which my pertinacious determination to succeed brought me!

Encouraged and animated by the opinion of competent judges, I was at last enabled to present myself upon the stage of Drury Lane on the 3d of July 1882, to play the entire part of Lady Macbeth.

I need not say what agitation and anxiety I went through that evening. The happy result alone could banish my trepidation. My friends came from all sides in my dressing-room to congratulate me on my success; they had the frankness to tell me what I knew very well, that I had not been able to get rid entirely of the Italian intonation, but they kindly added that the melody of our language gave a pretty originality to my reproduction.

After several repetitions of *Macbeth*, I undertook the part of *Elizabeth*, Queen of England.

At my first appearance, although the public were extremely courteous to me, I was by no means equally well satisfied with myself! I had been accustomed for many years to the same Italian actors, who understood exactly the interpretation I gave to every scene, and every point in my by-play. It was a very different thing to find myself surrounded by persons ignorant of my mode of acting, and having little in common with me. For a moment I felt my courage evaporate. But the obligation of duty undertaken reanimated and encouraged me. I endeavored neither to see nor hear, and succeeded in bringing the play to a conclusion more satisfactorily than I could have dared to hope for. In subsequent performances everything went better.

I made a tour through several of the English counties with these two dramas in September, October and November, with the best results.

During the winter of 1883, which I spent quietly in Rome, I had the pleasure of assisting at several performances undertaken in the cause of charity.

In the second half of the same year I revisited England, adding *Mary Stuart* and *Marie Antoinette* to my former *répertoire*. During my long stay there I had signed a contract for a long tour in North America, in order to reproduce before the Anglo-Saxon public across the ocean what I had just accomplished in the United Kingdom. I was *en passant* at Paris, waiting the hour of embarking on the *St. Germain*, which was to leave Havre the 18th October, when I was asked to take part in a performance to be given in the *Théâtre des Nations*, for the benefit of the cholera victims, by the *Comédie Française* and some distinguished singers who were also at the moment in Paris. My luggage was packed up or gone; I had no Italian actor with me capable of supporting me; but I accepted readily, because the purpose was for the relief at the same time of both French and Italian distress. My brother, Cæsar, who had come to Paris to see me off, agreed to support me along with a lady amateur, who was very willing to become an actress for a charity evening.

I was thus enabled in a few hours to put on the stage the sleep-walking scene of Lady Macbeth, which requires three characters. I added to my contribution the fifth canto of Dante's *Inferno*.

For many years I had not felt French hearts thrilling before me, and before leaving Europe I felt a real happiness in finding myself once again in communion with that good and dear public, who had given me my first joys out of Italy. A few hours afterwards I was on board the *St. Germain*, carrying with me, to cheer me during the long passage, the friendly articles of the whole French press, which thanked me for my last greeting to France.

For the fourth time I arrived in the United States under the happiest auspices, and began from Philadelphia a tour of seven months, which ended on the 4th day of May 1885. But before returning to my own country, I had the pleasure of acting *Macbeth* with Edwin Booth, the Talma of the United States. I was only able to give one performance in New York, on the evening of the 7th of May, at the Academy of Music, and one at Philadelphia ; but they were truly grand artistic festivals, and the public flocked to them in crowds. These satisfactory results incited the manager of the permanent company at the Thalia Theatre, New York, to beg me to act in Schiller's *Mary Stuart*, on the 12th, with his "troupe," I speaking English and they German.

At first it seemed to me too extraordinary an idea. I did not know a word of their language, yet at the same time I must confess this strange proposal had a certain fascination for me. I reflected that by paying the closest attention to the expression of my companions' faces, with a by-play in accordance with the situation when I was not speaking, I might be able to come creditably out of the ordeal. So, after some slight hesitation, I accepted the offer.

During the solitary rehearsal I was able to have with them, I was careful to have the words immediately preceding my parts repeated very distinctly, accustoming my ears gradually to their sound. By this means everything went on correctly. The performance was a success ; best of all, the greater part of the audience were persuaded that I was acquainted with the German language, and complimented me upon it.

The 23d of March 1885, we disembarked at Southampton from the German Lloyd's splendid steamer *Fulda*, happy after all to see our old Europe once more, and come to the end of the seven months' journey, during which space we had visited sixty-two cities of the New World.

We should never have been able to traverse such immense distances in so short a time if the industrial genius which presides in America over all the loco-motive enterprises had not come to our assistance. There is a company in the United States (which that of the *wagon lits* begins to imitate with us), which has for its object to let *car apartments* by the week or the month, which can be attached successively to trains for all destinations. (They are often used for pleasure excursions.) The necessity for lodging at inferior hotels at small towns is thus avoided ; one is not obliged to open trunks at every stopping place ; one can live as if at home, or as conveniently as if on board a yacht. This habit of locomotion is so much a part of American life that everything is organized at the stations for the provisioning every morning and at any occasional pause in the journey.

It was on leaving Philadelphia we took possession of our ambulating house. In the space of only 66 feet (English) we had anteroom, salon, two bed-rooms, with respective dressing-rooms, two rooms for servants, kitchen, pantry ; and, besides all this, there were a kind of iron cellars under the carriage, where the provisions were kept. Our sitting-room was particularly comfortable ; the hangings were furnished with *Mezzari* of Genoa. We had a piano, bookcase, *étagères* filled with all sorts of things, photographs, maps, and even hot-house plants, which accompanied us into the coldest regions.

We had hired our yacht on wheels for five months. We were often in motion for fifteen days in succession without being aware of the distance traversed; and when in the large cities we left it for the hotels, it was carefully kept in a shed in charge of two negroes appointed specially for that purpose by the Company.

Not without regret we left behind us in America that pretty habitation, thanks to which we had made, without fatigue, so long a journey.

Such are the principal events of my artistic life which my heart, guided by my memory, has dictated; and if in evoking my recollections I have been obliged to reawaken the praises bestowed upon me, it is because they are identified with each other, and above all because I experience a legitimate pride in recording them, attributing them in great measure to the homage paid so splendidly by the public, beyond the Alps and beyond the sea, to Italian art.

My readers will perceive that I have put on one side all pride of authorship, every pretension to style, and left on these memoirs the impression of that spontaneity which has all my life characterized my actions and my thoughts.

I do not pretend to posthumous fame with this book, which, from the depth of my retreat, I send forth to the judgment of the public; but as I cherish the hope that the vicissitudes of a life commenced so modestly, and the course I have accomplished, may serve for emulation and example to the young, who, having a serious vocation for the theatrical art, desire to face its difficulties and hardships.

One duty alone remains to me, that of reaching out a friendly hand to my faithful companions in arms ; to those who followed me across both worlds, and to those who have helped and contributed to our victories.

CHAPTER VII.

MARY STUART.

As the object of this work is a purely artistic one, and as, therefore, it does not come within its scope to discuss the various and most contradictory opinions which have been held by so many celebrated authors during the last three centuries about the guilt or innocence of the unfortunate Mary Stuart, I will only say that, for my own part, I was so convinced she had been the victim of undeserved cruelty and persecution, that I had no difficulty in forming my idea of her character. All the facts which a close study of her history brought to my knowledge confirmed me in the conviction I had always felt, that Mary Stuart was the victim of her own extraordinary beauty, her own personal fascination, and her fervent Roman Catholicism. That she was guilty of some indiscretions, which would probably have passed unnoticed in another woman, I do not attempt to deny; but they were certainly made the most of by those whose interest it was to ruin the unfortunate queen. Her enemies failed to take into account either her youth or the circumstances of the times in which she lived, and her juvenile frivolities have served as a foundation for many serious charges which have been brought against her. Her girlish imprudences have been painted in the darkest colors.

(140)

It is my firm belief that the gravest of these charges —such, for example, as her connivance at the murder of her husband—were embellished and distorted and magnified by her enemies to suit their own purposes and compass her destruction.

Every one knows how, in order that Mary might have no chance of defeating their machinations, she was kept a close prisoner for nineteen years, during which time she endeavored repeatedly, by means of letters, appeals and petitions, to obtain an opportunity of justifying herself before Elizabeth and the English Parliament, and disproving the accusations made against her. But all her efforts were useless; and, surely, in their failure may be found a proof that her persecutors feared to grant her request, lest she should succeed in convincing every one of her innocence.

And what chance had she of exposing the conspiracy against her, when her voice was silenced in a prison, when all assistance was denied her, when every effort she made only involved her more deeply in a maze of intrigue; when nineteen out of her forty-four years of life were passed in humiliating and miserable confinement.

The testimony of many historians proves that the conduct of this unhappy princess, from her infancy up to the death of Darnley, was without reproach. I fail to see, therefore, how such a woman as Mary Stuart, gentle, cultivated, fascinating and endowed with the most estimable qualities, could, in a moment, leave the paths of virtue for those of vice, could so completely forget herself as to commit crimes worthy only of the most depraved nature.   Yet this is what her inhuman persecutors would have us believe.

The real reason of all her sufferings was that, from infancy upwards, she had been guilty of three great and unpardonable sins.   She was the legitimate queen, she was a devoted Roman Catholic, and she was the most beautiful woman of her century.

These considerations, however, only sufficed to increase my sympathy with the unfortunate Queen, and I devoted all my abilities to a close study of her character, seeking to bring out in strong relief the nobility of her disposition, the dignity of the outraged sovereign, the sufferings of the oppressed victim, and the resignation of the martyr.

I was helped in this attempt by the care with which I had studied the historical period during which she lived, and by the investigations I had already made while preparing the part of Elizabeth.   And it is my profound conviction that no generous, impartial and sympathetic mind can fail to be touched by the sad story of poor Mary Stuart, who was an ornament to her sex, and who was driven to the scaffold by the mad jealousy of her rival, and by a long-continued course of cruel persecution.

*   *   *   *   *

Before entering upon any analysis of my acting in the character of Mary Stuart, I think it may interest the reader to give a short account of the circumstances which first led me to undertake this most important part.

Few persons would believe that the representation of the heroine in such a celebrated and world-renowned tragedy as this of Schiller's could have been confided to a girl of eighteen, who then, for the first time, assumed the part of *prima donna* (first lady), this Italian term not being confined to the principal singer in the opera, but also meaning first actress. But in Italy such is often the case. A manager (*capocomico*) engages an actress whom he considers suitable both in appearance and talent for the leading parts without considering her age.

When my engagement with the Royal Sardinian Company ended, I joined that of Romoaldo Mascherpa in the service of the Duchess of Parma, as first actress.

Now, although my four years' experience with the Royal Sardinian Company had made me quite at home upon the stage, yet the parts allotted to me had always been such as were suited to my years. When my father arranged for me to join Mascherpa he never dreamed that a travelling company would attempt tragedy, or that I should have any responsibilities beyond my years. Instead of this, however, the *capocomico* at once assigned me the most difficult and important parts, which would have generally been played by a much older and more experienced actress. My manager was an excellent old man, but his artistic abilities were of the most ordinary kind. He knew he was quite within his rights in giving me these parts if he chose to do so; and, as for me, I was simply expected to play them.

He began to entrust me with the most important, and some of these I had not even seen acted. My teacher, Carlotta Marchionni, of the Royal Sardinian

Company, having either given them up owing to advancing years, or never having played them; so that I had not even the advantage of her example to aid my inexperience. I first began to study the part of Mary Stuart in Trent. I was in despair. I felt certain I should fail; and neither my growing favor with the public, which I attributed entirely to my youth and personal appearance, nor the assurances of my friends and relatives, sufficed to encourage me. But as there could be no question of not fulfilling my obligations, I recommended myself to the protection of all the saints and angels, and applied myself resolutely not only to master Andrea Maffei's beautiful verses, but also to make myself well acquainted with the history of the unfortunate Queen and of her times. But for this I had scarcely any time, as I had also to superintend the preparation of my costume. I had, indeed, played some minor parts in tragedy while I was with the Royal Sardinian Company, but none approaching to this in importance. It was thought that I had a natural aptitude for such parts, but still required both experience and practice to make me perfect. I had no idea that I should begin with an undertaking of such magnitude.

I need not say that I never closed my eyes the night before my first performance. I was in a fever! I felt I should fail! The public would be unfavorable! The eyes which I knew would be fixed upon me seemed to my excited imagination knives piercing my heart. When I dozed for an instant my dreams were worse than my waking thoughts. Alas! a thousand voices seemed to be whispering in my ear:—

"You will never succeed ; the curtain will fall in the midst of a dead silence, and not a single friendly hand will applaud you!" My heart beat violently, a cold perspiration covered my forehead.

When my dear mother came at last to rouse me from these uneasy slumbers, the light of the sun dissipated at once the kind of incubus which had haunted me during the darkness.

The evening I had so much dreaded at last arrived! The public knew my trepidation, and the efforts I had made, and were leniently disposed towards me. From my first entrance upon the stage the audience perceived the care with which I had studied that character—a study which according to the Italian custom at that time, especially in the travelling companies, was done in a hurry. The appropriate costume, the historical head-gear, my slender figure, the oval shape and pallor of my face—the latter due, in great part, to the agitation from which I was suffering —my fair hair, and, in fact, my entire appearance, which recalled many of the traits of the unfortunate Mary, immediately gained me the sympathy of my audience, and a burst of spontaneous applause at once encouraged me and assured me of their indulgence.

I played as well as I could, and at the close of the third act, which is the culminating point of the play, I was called before the curtain several times, and greeted with the most flattering acclamations from all sides of the house. It seemed to me that I had conquered the world, and I had not a doubt that my *capocomico* would be equally proud of me, and would lose no time in congratulating me, and expressing his great satisfaction at the result of the experiment.

Judge then of my chagrin when, upon my asking him with girlish vanity: " I hope you are content now, are you not ? " the good old man shrugged his shoulders, raised his eyebrows, and with a provoking smile of pitying indulgence answered me : " Believe me, my dear little one, you have a marked turn for comedy, but, as for tragedy !—don't be offended with me for saying it—it is not for you, and I advise you to abandon it entirely."

It is true enough that I was fond of comedy ; but, in after years, I think I may venture to say that I was credited with some success in tragedy also.

These words from my *capocomico* completely paralyzed me.

Certainly, I did not then interpret the part as further study and ripened experience enabled me afterwards to do ; of course, being aware of what the public expected of me, I thenceforward set to work to analyze most carefully and minutely every situation in the play connected with Queen Mary ; and the great sympathy and pity with which her sad history filled me notwithstanding my youth, spurred me on in my investigation into every detail of her unhappy life.

I quickly grew to understand, also, what an important part the expression of my face, my carriage, and my demeanor must play in the representation of Mary Stuart. The public ought immediately to understand what they are called upon to judge. I felt that I must frame my countenance to resemble that of a woman in whom much suffering and many persecutions had not been able to extinguish the strength of mind that enabled her to bear the afflictions which beset her through life, yet who, withal, never forgot the dignity due to her rank, nor lost the faith which enabled her to bear so heroically the hand of God in the heavy afflictions of her later days.

It was, therefore, with an air of patience and resignation that I listened while my faithful Anna Kennedy told me how Paulet had rudely forced open my strong box, and rifled it of the papers, jewels, and even the crown of France, which Mary had carefully preserved as precious memorials of her past grandeur. And I answered her without a moment's discomposure, as though to prove that earthly vanities now counted for nothing with me—

> "Compose yourself, my Anna! and believe me,
> 'Tis not these baubles which can make a Queen:
> Basely indeed they may behave to us,
> But they cannot debase us. I have learnt
> To use myself to many a change in England;
> I can support this too."

Then, turning to Paulet, but still maintaining my calm and dignified demeanor, I addressed him in similar terms; while I met with angelic patience the scarcely concealed indignation of Anna at seeing me thus treated by my rough jailer.

I ventured, however, in accordance with my own deep conviction, though contrary to that of Schiller, to lay little emphasis on the lines in which the poet makes Mary accuse herself of complicity in the murder of Darnley, as it is evident that Schiller was led into this belief by the historians Hume and Buchanan, who were Mary's avowed enemies.

In the scene between the Queen and Mortimer, I showed how, amidst all my troubles, a gleam of hope did now and then spring up in my heart; and my eyes brightened at the possibility of my liberation. But as I glanced round my apartment, the sight of the grim walls which encircled me, and the remembrance of my miserable state, quenched the feeble. spark before it had well begun to burn. To Mortimer I laid bare my whole heart, for I saw in him a ministering angel sent by God for my deliverance. Very different, however, was my demeanor when I was visited by the perfidious Cecil, Lord Burleigh, the Minister and evil counsellor of Elizabeth.

When he appeared, followed by Paulet, to announce my sentence, I summoned all my royal dignity to my aid, in order to confound and humiliate my persecutors. Hearing myself accused by Burleigh in most insolent tones of being an accomplice in the conspiracy of Babington, and of rebellion against the laws of England, I assumed all the haughtiness of an offended Queen, of a calumniated woman, of an oppressed stranger, and replied—

> " Every one who stands arraigned of crime
> Shall plead before a jury of his equals.
> Who is my equal in this high commission?
> Kings only are my equals ! "

Burleigh went on to argue that I had already heard the accusations brought against me in a court of justice, that I lived under English skies, and breathed

English air; that I was protected by English laws, and ought therefore to respect the decrees of my judges. But I suddenly turned upon him with a frown, and replied in a mocking voice—

> " Sir, I breathe
> The air within an English prison wall.
> Is that to live in England : to enjoy
> Protection from its laws? I scarcely know,
> And never have I pledged my faith to keep them.
> I am no member of this realm ; I am
> An independent, and a foreign Queen."

Continuing in the same tone, I refuted, one by one, the false and subtle accusations which he made against me. But seeing at last how useless were all my efforts at exculpation, and convinced that it was in vain to adduce any proof of my innocence, when might was evidently to take the place of right, I ended in a voice which, despite all my efforts, betrayed some of the emotion I felt—

> " 'Tis well, my lord; let her then use her power ;
> Let her destroy me : let me bleed that she
> May live secure : but let her then confess
> That she hath exercised her power alone,
> And not contaminate the name of justice."

But here the feeling of bitterness which I could no longer restrain made itself manifest in the inflection I gave to the following words—

> " Let her not borrow, from the laws, the sword
> To rid her of her hated enemy ;
> Let her not clothe, in this religious garb,
> The bloody daring of licentious might.
> Let not these juggling tricks deceive the world."

Here, giving full and free vent to my indignation,

I turned with an expression of contempt upon those who were so eager to humiliate my royal powers, saying—

> "Though she may murder me she cannot judge.
> Let her no longer strive to join the fruits
> Of vice with virtue's fair and angel show.
> But what she is in truth, that let her dare
> To show herself in face of all the world."

And, with a glance of unutterable scorn at Burleigh, I hurriedly quitted the stage.

The author has introduced this scene most appropriately, in order to give an idea of the tension of mind of which Mary Stuart was the victim; and interpreting the execution from this point of view, I followed, with look and accent, the growth of the intricate web that was being spun around me.

The third act plainly shows how a most noble and elevated soul, full of religious enthusiasm and resignation, may yet be goaded beyond the limits of human endurance by the insolence and malice of persecutors.

Followed by my faithful Anna, I entered the pleasant park with a quick step, intoxicated by the freshness of the air, which not only chased the pallor from my cheek but gave my enfeebled body fresh vigor. Identifying myself with the situation, and endeavoring to draw on the spectator to share in the same emotion, I made evident the delight which momentarily possessed me, and which afforded such a painful contrast to the terrible sufferings to which Mary Stuart was subjected at that time; and to prove the reasonableness and truth of this interpretation, it will be enough to follow me carefully in the declamation of the next lines—

> " Freedom returns!   O let me enjoy it.
> Freedom invites me!   O let me employ it.
> Skimming with winged step light o'er the lea;
> Have I escaped from this mansion of mourning!
> Holds me no more the sad dungeon of care!
> Let me with joy and eagerness burning,
> Drink in the free, the celestial air!
> Thanks to these friendly trees, that hide from me
> My prison walls, and flatter my illusion!
> Happy I now may dream myself, and free;
> Why wake me from my dreams so sweet confusion?
> The extended vault of heaven around me lies,
> Free and unfettered range my wandering eyes
> O'er space's vast immeasurable sea!
> From where yon misty mountains rise on high,
> I can my empire's boundaries explore.
> And those light clouds which, steering southward, fly,
> Seek the mild clime of France's genial shore.
> Fast fleeting clouds; ye meteors that fly;
> Could I but sail with you through the sky!
> Tenderly greet the dear land of my youth!
> Here I am captive!   Oppressed by my foes,
> No other than you can carry my woes.
> Free thro' the ether your pathway is seen,
> Ye own not the power of this tyrant Queen."

But this joyous abandonment of soul speedily gave place to the most terrible emotions.   Hearing of the interview so unexpectedly accorded me by Elizabeth (although entirely invented by Schiller, forming the culminating point of this act), an instant I trembled from head to foot.   I would fain have fled away from the dreaded ordeal.   Nothing can better describe my state than the following lines, with which I answered the affectionate entreaties of Talbot, who tried every argument he could think of to induce me to meet my rival—

> " For years I've waited, and prepared myself ;
> For this I've studied, weigh'd and written down
> Each word within the tablet of my memory,
> That was to touch, and move her to compassion.
> Forgotten suddenly, effaced is all,
> And nothing lives within me at this moment,
> But the fierce burning feeling of my wrongs,
> My heart is turned to direst hate against her ;
> All gentle thoughts, all sweet forgiving words,
> Are gone, and round me stand with grisly mien
> The fiends of hell, and shake their snaky locks ! "

Then, touched by the persuasive words and affectionate advice of Talbot, that I should have an interview with Elizabeth ; with a more tranquil mind, but in tones of the deepest sadness, I said—

> " Oh ! this can never, never come to good ! "

The fear lest Burleigh, her bitter enemy, should accompany Elizabeth on her visit to Fotheringay added greatly to Mary's perturbation. When she heard from Talbot that Leicester alone would attend his sovereign, she could not refrain from a cry of joy, which was instantly checked by the faithful Anna, but passed unheeded by Talbot, intently watching for the arrival of Elizabeth. When I caught a glimpse of her I retired in terror to the back of the stage, seeking to hide myself among the trees and shrubs while intently watching the expression of her countenance.

After this, hearing the words which Elizabeth in her egregious vanity addressed to her suite, with the evident intention that they should reach my ears, and impress me—her unfortunate prisoner—with the adoration she was held in by her people, I murmured in a voice of the deepest sadness—

"Oh, God! from out these features speaks no heart!"

Meanwhile Anna and Talbot, with the most supplicating gestures, sought to encourage me to approach and prostrate myself before Elizabeth. At first I visibly resisted all their entreaties, but at last consented, though with an evident effort, and turned with faltering steps towards the Queen. I had now made up my mind to kneel before her, though I let it be seen how greatly the sense of my own dignity caused me to rebel against such a humiliation. But before my knees touched the ground, my whole nature seemed to revolt against such an act. I started back in an attitude which said more plainly than words, "I cannot do it," and turned to take refuge in the arms of my attendant, Anna. She, however, sank on her knees before me, and besought me by my holy religion, and by the overwhelming force of circumstances, not to persist in my refusal. At last, overcome by her entreaties, I raised her tenderly from the ground; and, intimating by my gesture the tremendous sacrifice I made in consenting to her request, with a deep sigh I exclaim—

"Well! be it so! To this I will submit."

Then with an intonation of voice suitable to the words, I spoke the following lines—

"Farewell high thoughts, and pride of noble mind!
I will forget my dignity, and all

My sufferings; I will fall before *her* feet
Who hath reduced me to this wretchedness.'

While I uttered the words I lifted my eyes to
heaven and pressed to my lips the crucifix I wore
attached to a rosary at my side, as though offering to
God the sacrifice I was about to make of my own
personal dignity.   Then, pausing for a moment, as if
in rapt meditation, to invoke God to grant me that
strength and courage of which I stood so much in
need, I addressed Elizabeth in a firm voice—

"The God of heav'n decides for you, my sister,
    Your happy brows are now with triumph crowned."

Here I stopped for an instant, expressing by my
marked hesitation how grave a matter it was for me
to add, by my abasement, to my haughty sister's
pride.   Then, as if by a sudden inspiration, I knelt
before her and cried out impetuously—

"I worship Him who to His height has raised you.

It is clear that in this most felicitous passage the
author wanted to show the public that it is not before
her, but before the Supreme Being, that Mary humil-
iates herself.   After a short pause, and in a supplicating tone of voice, I continued—

"But in your turn be merciful, my sister;
    Let me not lie before you thus disgraced; .
    Stretch forth your hand, your royal hand, to raise
    Your sister from her deep distress."

At an authoritative yet condescending sign from
Elizabeth I rose, sighing heavily.   Then, in a resigned, submissive tone I went on to reply to the
charges made against me.   I enumerated the various

acts of injustice from which I had suffered; and I called God to witness that in spite of myself I was constrained to accuse her of complicity in them. I pointed out that she had treated me neither fairly nor honorably; that, although I was her equal in rank, she had, in defiance of the rights of nations and of the laws of hospitality, taken no notice of the assistance asked from her, but had shut me up in a living tomb, deprived me of my friends and servants, and filled up the measure of her insults by dragging me before her arrogant tribunals. Here a gesture of resentment from Elizabeth recalled me to myself. I changed my tone entirely, for I realized how I had been involuntarily carried away by my feelings, and I added—

> "No more of this;
> Now stand we face to face; now, sister, speak:
> Name but my crime, I'll fully satisfy you,"

To which the inhuman Elizabeth made answer—

> "Accuse not fate! your own deceitful heart
> It was, the wild ambition of your house;
> As yet no enmities had passed between us,
> When your imperious uncle, the proud priest,
> Whose shameless hand grasps at all crowns, attacked me
> With unprovok'd hostility, and taught
> You, but too docile, to assume my arms,
> To vest yourself with my imperial title."

Dismayed at hearing the tone of contempt with which Elizabeth spoke of the Pontiff (Pius V.), and at finding herself charged with faults she had never committed, and conspiracies in which she had never engaged, Mary raised her eyes to heaven, exclaiming—

"I'm in the hand of God!"

and then addressed Elizabeth :—

"But you never will
Exert so cruelly the power it gives you."

To which Elizabeth replied in an arrogant tone—

"Who shall prevent me!"

I omitted no opportunity throughout this scene of showing the torture I was undergoing from Elizabeth's injurious treatment. Now I implored, by a gesture, the aid of Heaven; now I sought comfort from Talbot by a look which entreated him to become the judge of the iniquitious provocation I was enduring from my rival. I was on the point of putting my anger into words, when she said to me with all the venom of a serpent—

"Force is my only surety: no alliance
Can be concluded with a race of vipers."

At this I tottered as though I was about to fall. Both Anna and Talbot ran forward to support me. I thanked them affectionately with expressive gestures, and signed them to retire as the moment of my weakness was past. But, convinced by the harsh, haughty and insolent tone Elizabeth employed, that she never would acknowledge either my innocence or my legitimate rights, which I now saw I should be compelled to renounce forever, I turned my head slowly away from her, with a fixed, penetrating look, accompanied by a slightly ironical smile which seemed to say: "You are vilely abusing the power which superior strength has given you over your unarmed prisoner."

Then a sudden impulse of revolt against my evil destiny led me to question Heaven, with an expression of surpassing bitterness, whether I had really deserved such misfortunes? But the religious sentiment within me came to my aid. I besought pardon of the Supreme Being for my momentary rebellion against His will, and I inclined my head in meek submission, like a creature who recognizes the immutability of Providence, and accepts the martyrdom which is to be its lot.

And entering fully into the conception of the poet who has anatomized the character of this unhappy creature, I interpreted the rapid passage from resentment to pathos, as though the humble intonation of the words were the expression of a fleeting hope that she might be able to move her rival to pity. And, therefore, it was with a tone of the deepest affection I uttered the apostrophe, "Oh! sister!" in the hope that I should excite some sympathy in her heart. But as, according to the intention of the poet and the exigencies of history, the character of Elizabeth is not to be moved by Mary's affectionate entreaties, the Queen, with a contemptuous look, fixes her icy glance upon her victim, whereupon the latter breaks forth—

> " Rule your realm in peace :
> I give up every claim to these domains—
> Alas! the pinions of my soul are lam'd;
> Greatness entices me no more : your point
> Is gained; I am but Mary's shadow now—
> My noble spirit is at last broke down
> By long captivity: you've done your worst
> On me ; you have destroyed me in my bloom!

> Now end your work, my sister;—speak at length
> The word which to pronounce has brought you hither;
> For I will ne'er believe that you are come,
> To mock unfeelingly your hapless victim.
> Pronounce this word: say 'Mary, you are free:
> You have felt my power—learn now
> To honor too my generosity—'
>   Sister, not for all these islands' wealth,
> For all the realms encircled by the deep
> Could I before you stand inexorable
> In mien, as you now show yourself to me."

And I burst into a flood of tears. These just and temperate words, far from convincing Elizabeth, only aroused her ire and increased the aversion she had always felt for Mary. Without consideration for the rank and humiliation of her rival, she reviled her unrestrainedly with ferocious satisfaction. Reminding her of her lost prestige, she asks her—

> "Are all your schemes run
> Out? No more assassins on the road?
> Will none attempt for you again
> The sad adventurous achievement?"

She taunted her with her vanished beauty and fascination, and ended her insults by saying in a tone of contempt—

> "None is ambitious of the dang'rous honor
> Of being your fourth husband: you destroy
> Your wooers like your husbands."

At such a base outrage my face betrayed all the fury I felt. I all but hurled myself upon the speaker, crying: "Sister! sister!" but Talbot and Anna ran to me and held me back, while they did all in their power to calm my emotion. With a superhuman effort at self-control, I hurriedly, and with convulsive grasp, seized the crucifix hanging at my side and pressed it to my heart, exclaiming—

"Grant me forbearance, all ye pow'rs of heaven."

It was the predominance of the religious sentiment which came in as if unexpectedly to change the situation. To make the contrast still more vivid, Elizabeth contemplated me with sovereign disdain, deriding Leicester for having constantly declared that no one could look on Mary Stuart without being fascinated by her, and that no other woman on earth was her equal in beauty. Then, as if to exceed all her other insults, she said with an insolent smile—

"She who to all is common, may with ease
Become the common object of applause!"

At this all restraint became impossible. "This is too much!" I cried in my anger. Elizabeth heard me with a diabolical sneer, and interrupted me—

"You show us now indeed
Your real face! Till now 'twas but the mask!"

I attempted to answer her, but wrath choked my utterance; my face was distorted, my whole body trembled. At length, with difficulty, and in a half-suffocated, broken voice, I began to speak—

"My sins were human and my youth the cause;
Superior force betray'd me. Never have I
Denied, or to conceal it sought."

Then beginning to recover myself, and showing that I would give vent to the rancor so long pent up in my breast, eager to give insult for insult to her who had so grossly outraged me before everybody, I went on—

> "Of me the worst is known, and I can say
>   That I am better than the fame I bear."

Then, advancing towards the Queen, I cried in accents of fury—

> "But woe to you! when in the years to come,
>   The world shall rend from you the robe of honor,
>   With which your arch-hypocrisy hath veiled
>   The secret raging flames of lawless lust."

And my paroxysm of rage reached its height while, with flashing eyes, I hurled at her the lines—

> "Virtue was not your portion from your mother;
>   Well know we the foul cause that brought the head
>   Of Anna Boleyn to the fatal block!"

When the words had passed my lips I stood immovable for a moment, looking at Elizabeth with a glance that seemed almost to scorch her, and showing by my attitude what joy I felt in having thus in my turn humiliated my enemy. Elizabeth, mortally wounded at my insults, was to glare at me with eyes of savage hatred, Leicester and Paulet to run towards her endeavoring to pacify her, while Talbot and Anna hurried to me in mortal terror. The former, whose age and faithful devotion for so many years gave him the right to speak, began to remonstrate with me—

> "Is this the moderation, the submission of my Lady!"

To which, now quite beside myself, I answered—

> "Moderation! I've supported
>   What human nature can support. Farewell,
>   Lamb-hearted resignation, passive patience,
>   Fly to thy native heaven; burst at length
>   Thy bonds, come forward from thy dreary cave,
>   In all thy fury, long suppressed rancor!

> And thou, who to the anger'd basilisk
> Impart'st the murd'rous glance, oh! arm my tongue
> With poison'd darts!"

Meanwhile her courtiers gathered round Elizabeth, persuading her to depart; while I, after meditating in my own mind what still more terrible insult I could fling at her, suddenly faced round upon the English Queen and in utter recklessness exclaimed—

> "The English throne is sullied by a bastard,
> The noble Britons by a juggler fool'd.
> If right prevailed, you now would in the dust
> Before me lie, for I am your rightful King."

At this last excess I stood in a menacing attitude looking at her. Elizabeth freed herself from the grasp of Paulet and Leicester and endeavored to spring upon me; but, with all the authority of a haughty sovereign, I waived her back and signed to her imperiously to leave, which Elizabeth at last did, in a towering passion, her courtiers having to drag her away, as it were, almost by force. I watched her departing footsteps and felt that I had vanquished her. Seizing Anna's hand in a transport of joy at having thus obtained my revenge, and coming forward to the front of the stage, I, still in great excitement, exclaimed—

> "Within her heart she carries death. I know it.
> At last now I am once more happy, Anna,
> I have degraded her in Leicester's eyes!"

This idea seemed to intoxicate me, and with fierce satisfaction I added—

> "Oh! After years of sorrow and abasement
> I've felt one hour of triumph and revenge!"

11

And I left the stage in an agitated manner, followed by Anna.

From all the observations I have made, the reader will perceive that in the third Act, which forms an important part of the drama, I aimed above all else to set in full relief the great contrast between the widely different characters of the two cousins, who were rivals at the same time : one being unfortunate, while the other was omnipotent, and already fixed in the cruel intention of making Mary Stuart her victim.

In order the better to realize the justice of this interpretation it may be useful to recall what has already been observed, namely, that the meeting between the two queens was boldly introduced by the author, precisely that it might give him an opportunity of profiting by the certain effect of the contrast, and of bringing to light the stateliness and haughtiness of Mary Stuart, who knew and felt herself to be a queen.

As for me, I was careful not to forget to give sufficient prominence to the religious sentiment, which was an essential manifestation that could not separate itself from the troubled and agitated soul of woman.

As it is known that Mary does not appear in the fourth Act I pass on to the fifth.

But before beginning my analysis, I wish to give my reasons for disregarding Schiller's instructions about her dress in this Act. Many different accounts have come down to us of the attire in which she appeared on the day of her execution, most of which seem to me purely imaginary. Thus, for example, she has been sent to the scaffold by some authorities dressed entirely in red. Others have arrayed her in royal robes. Schiller represents her as wearing a rich white gown, a crown on her head, and a long black veil. Now, it seems to me this latter costume must be incorrect for two reasons. First, because it is scarcely likely that a woman who had been made prisoner in the flower of her age, when all the impressions of grief are most profound, and who had passed from a throne to a dungeon, a martyr to Faith could—after nineteen years of captivity and sorrow which had undermined her strength until she was obliged to ask support from Melville when she tried to mount the scaffold, because her knees, swollen by the damps of so many unhealthy prisons, refused to carry her—have retained so much vanity as to try and produce an effect upon the minds of those who saw her for the last time. Secondly, Mary could not have arrayed herself in this manner without the consent of Elizabeth. Is it likely that the latter would have allowed her rival the means of displaying those undoubted charms which had done more than anything else to excite her feelings against her, even supposing Mary had made such a request? And these convictions took root in me from the first days in which I began to study and guess at the difficult personality of Mary Stuart.

In fact, from the time of my first appearance in this character of the unfortunate queen, I had adopted the costume which seemed to me most strictly historical. By a very fortunate chance I found myself in London in 1857, the year in which the Archæological Institution had a grand exhibition of all the relics that could be obtained of the unhappy Mary Stuart. This exhibition was under the patronage of the Prince Consort. I was able to visit it. There were to be found many precious objects which had belonged to poor Mary up to the last hour of her life, and which had been preserved in old Scottish Catholic families devoted to the hapless queen. Among many other things I especially admired the white and blue enamel rosary which she wore (but which I, to produce a better scenic effect, had made entirely in gold), and the veil that covered her head when she ascended the scaffold which was a tissue of thread of gold and white silk, bordered all round with a narrow white lace, and having the royal arms in each of its four corners.

Among all the innumerable pictures which represented her in such different ways—one, whose authenticity is undoubted, because it was executed a few days after Mary's death, struck me most forcibly, and I can see it still with my mind's eye. It represented her execution at Fotheringay Castle, and is attributed to the painter Mytens. She is standing, dressed in a robe of black stamped velvet, surmounted by a short *surcoat* without sleeves, according to the fashion of the time. A white ruff encircles her neck. On her head she has a white *coif*, shaped like the cap which now bears her name, and a veil, also white like that which I have described above, covered her entirely from head to foot. A small ivory crucifix hangs round her neck, and two thin chains hold the two ends of the *surcoat* together across her breast.

In one word, this was the ideal costume I had already imagined for the part, except that I substituted a black *coif* and veil for the white ones, in the belief that by so doing I should give additional effect to the scene.

Mary, as represented in this wonderful picture, has in her hand a crucifix, at the bottom of which is a skull. The Queen, with outstretched arms, holds the sacred image propped upon the table, on the cover of which in the front part the artist has represented the tremendous scene of her execution. In this latter picture Mary is shown kneeling on the scaffold. Her upper garments have been removed, and allow her bodice of silk damask to become visible; and it was the color of this which probably gave rise to the fantastic accounts I had heard of her apparel. A thin streak of blood trickled from her neck, which had already received the executioner's first blow. His axe was uplifted in readiness for a second stroke. Several noble Lords and other personages are present at the execution; and in the background her attendants, the three faithful Maries, in deepest black. Three Latin inscriptions complete the picture. The first, in the right and upper corner, runs thus—

"Reginam serenissimam regum filiam uxorem et matrem, astantibus commissariis et ministris R. Eliz.—carnifex securi percutit atque uno et altero ictu truculenter sauciatae tertio caput abscindit."

Which may be translated—

"The executioner with one or two blows of his axe, smites the most noble Queen, the daughter, wife, and mother of kings— in the presence of the ministers and commissioners of Queen

Elizabeth; and, after cruelly wounding her, with a third stroke strikes off her head."

The second inscription, below the figure of the executioner, is as follows—

"Maria Scotiae Regina Angliae et Hiberniae vere princeps et haeres legitima Jacobi magnae Britanniae Regis mater, quam suorum haeresi vexatam, rebellione oppressam, refugii causa verbo Eliz. Reginae et cognatae inixam in Angliam, an° 1568 descendentem 19 annos captivam perfidia detinuit: milleque calumniis Senatus Angliae sententia haeresi instigante neci traditur ac 12 calend Mart. 1587 a servili carnifice obtruncatur, an° actat regniq. 45."

Or in English—

"Mary, Queen of Scotland, the true and legitimate heir to the throne of England and Ireland, mother of James, King of Great Britain, who, vexed by the heresy, and oppressed by the rebellion of her subjects, took refuge in England in the year 1568, confiding in the word of Queen Elizabeth, her cousin, was kept a prisoner by her perfidious relative for nineteen years, and, after undergoing much calumniation, was cruelly sentenced by the English Parliament, which was provoked by her heresy, and was put to death by the hand of the common executioner on the 18th February 1587, in the 45th year of her age and reign."

The third inscription was beneath the figure of Mary—

"Sic funestum ascendit tabulatum Regina quondam Galliarum et Scotiae florentissimae, invicto sed pio animo tirannidem exprobat et perfidiam, Fidem catholicam profitetur Romanae Ecclesiae semper fuisse et esse filiam plane palamq. testatur."

Or in English—

"Thus ascended the terrible scaffold, she who was Queen of France, and of flourishing Scotland; and with an invincible, yet pious soul, she reproved tyranny and perfidy, confessed the

Catholic faith, and openly professed that she was, as she had
ever been, a devoted daughter of the Roman Church."

Returning to my acting, I must observe first of all
that the change which takes place between the third
and fifth Act must always greatly strike the audience.
The dignity of my carriage was the only sign of
royalty remaining to me. Every trace of the sufferings which had tormented the Queen and embittered
her existence had disappeared. I expressed my
wishes and communicated my orders with the sweetness and serenity of a martyr ; so that when I presented myself to my attendants at the threshold of
my chamber, they were impressed with as much
admiration and reverence as though they had seen
an angel.

A long black veil covered me from head to foot.
In my hand I held a crucifix and a packet sealed
with black seals, which contained my last will and
testament. When I saw the sorrow of my servants,
whom I gently reproved, saying that they ought
rather to exult in the prospect of my speedy deliverance, a smile was on my face, and I added that I
regarded death as a friend. When I recognized my
faithful Melville among the crowd, I felt as though
he had been specially sent by Heaven to console my
last hours; for now, at all events, a true and unprej-
udiced account of the way in which I ended my life
would be given to the world. All the directions I
gave were characterized by sweetness and affection.
But feeling my courage failing, and being unwilling
to prolong this sad scene any longer, I at length said
in a resolute voice—

> " Come,
> Come all, and now receive my last farewell."

All knelt about me.   The sight, however, of those
mournful faces, of those arms outstretched towards
me, filled me with deep emotion, and, extending my
hands above their kneeling figures, I exclaimed—

> " I have been
> Much hated, yet have been much beloved."

Then I released myself from them, and took a
last sad and lingering farewell of each of these faithful hearts.

Henceforth I belonged not to the world.   Every
sentiment, every passion, was changed and transformed.   My only remaining regret was that I could
not enjoy the ministrations of a priest of my own
faith—

> "A priest of my religion is denied me,
> And I disdain to take the sacrament,
> The holy, heav'nly nourishment, from priests
> Of a false faith; I die in the belief
> Of my own Church, for that alone can save."

It was, therefore, with transports of ineffable joy
that I discovered, in Melville himself, an angel sent
by God to absolve me from my sins, and give me his
benediction.   With a cautious glance around to see
that no one was likely to disturb me, I took the crucifix, which hung from my girdle, and with great
compunction knelt before Melville, and began my
confession in an austere voice.   With words which
plainly showed my sincerity, I accused myself of having nourished a deep hatred against my enemies, of
having meditated revenge, and of having felt utterly

unable to pardon her who had so fearfully injured
me. But where I was wanting in spontaneity was
when Melville asked me if there were no other errors
which lay heavy on my heart; I replied—

> "A bloody crime of ancient date, indeed,
>   And long ago confessed; yet with new terrors
> It now attacks me; black and grisly, steps
> Across my path, and shuts the gates of heav'n:
> By my connivance fell the King, my husband;
> I gave my hand and heart to a seducer—
> By rigid penance I have made atonement;
> Yet in my soul the worm is gnawing still."

I always disbelieved many of the accusations
brought against Mary by her numerous and powerful
enemies, and I make this observation once more to
prove that there was nothing artificial about me.
Thus, it was utterly impossible for me to represent a
situation which I did not fully comprehend, and could
not clearly picture to my own mind. For this reason, I could never enter thoroughly into the spirit of
the confession which the author puts into the mouth
of the unfortunate Queen; for, in my own mind, I
was firmly persuaded of the falsity of the charges
brought against Mary Stuart.

Even on the scaffold Mary protested her innocence; was it likely she would lie when she was so
soon to appear before the Supreme Judge? And it
seems to me that the fact of her not being allowed
to justify herself publicly before Parliament, as was
her undoubted right, is an evident proof that those
authors are correct who have refused to see in the
aspersions cast upon her anything beyond calumny
and lies.

During that part of the confession where Melville, after having heard from Mary that she was free from all other sin, taxes her in austere tones with having been accessory to the conspiracy of Paris and Babington to murder Elizabeth, I maintained a serene front, and the calm and tranquil air proceeding from an easy conscience.   After a short pause, I said—

> "I am prepared to meet eternity;
> Within the narrow limits of an hour
> I shall appear before my Judge's throne;
> But, I repeat it, my confession 's ended."

Melville, still not wholly satisfied, besought me not to delude myself with vain words, if, indeed, I had in any way been implicated in such a grave fault; but again I protested my innocence, although I did not try to hide the fact that I had held communication with various Princes in the hope of "inducing them to aid in liberating me from the prison" to which I had been condemned by my persecutors.

> "Thou mount'st then, satisfied
> Of thy own innocence, the fatal scaffold?"

asked Melville.

> "God suffers me in mercy to atone
> By undeserved death, my youth's transgressions,"

I answered, alluding to the death of Darnley.

In spite of the tears that filled my eyes, the light of truth shone so plainly in them, and their expression was so full of faith in Celestial Justice as to give additional sublimity to the emotion of Melville, who absolved me with the most Christian words; and when his invocation to God was ended, placed his hand on my head and blessed me. I, still kneeling with my crucifix clasped in my hand, my face upraised, and a smile of perfect faith upon my lips, expressed by my attitude that I, even then, saw the heavens open before me, and realized the blessings so shortly to be mine.

After a few minutes passed in this kind of religious ecstasy, Anna appeared, greeted Melville most respectfully, and whispered a few words in his ear. He then raised me to my feet with a deep sigh; but my eyes still remained fixed on that luminous spot, through which my excited imagination led me to believe I had gained a glimpse of Heaven.

Melville addressed me sadly—

> "A painful conflict is in store for thee;
> Feel'st thou within thee strength enough to smother
> Each impulse of malignity and hate?"

To which I replied in a flexible, harmonious voice—

> "I fear not a relapse, I have to God
> Devoted both my hatred and my love."

On hearing the arrival of Burleigh and Leicester, the man once destined to be my husband, I did not alter the expression of my face in the least degree, and only returned to the thought of my misery when Cecil said—

> "I come, my Lady Stuart, to receive
> Your last commands and wishes."

And here, absorbed entirely in the thought of God, I thanked him with imperturbable calm; presenting some petitions for my friends and attendants, and for the repose of my body. Finally, I gave a message of farewell to Queen Elizabeth. But when Burleigh proceeded to ask the following question—

"You still refuse assistance from the Dean?"

I replied in a firm and decided tone—

"My Lord, I 've made my peace with my God;"

and I emphasized the words "my God," as if to show that my faith had been the constant guide of my life.

I then begged pardon of Paulet for having been the involuntary cause of his nephew Mortimer's death, but was interrupted by a cry of horror from my attendants. I turned hastily. The great door at the back of the stage had been opened, and at the sight of the executioner, the scaffold, and the guards with lighted torches, my gestures betrayed a natural weakness. I tottered back, my eyes closed involuntarily; Melville supported me, and seized the crucifix which was falling from my hand. But presently my senses returned; I murmured in a faint voice—

"Yes, my hour is come!
The sheriff comes to lead me to my fate!
And part we must. Farewell.
You, my worthy Sir, and my dear faithful Anna
Shall attend me in my last moment."

And, leaning on Melville and my servant, I advanced with uncertain steps towards the scaffold. Burleigh, eager to deny Mary this last consolation, interposed to prevent her friends accompanying her farther, on the ground that he had no orders authorizing him to permit this indulgence. To which Mary replied she was certain her royal sister would never permit her person to be profaned by the rough hands of the executioner; and she undertook that Anna's sobbing grief should not impede the executioner. Paulet joined his entreaties to those of the Queen, and Burleigh at last granted the favor.

From this time my face became transformed, and, looking upwards, I exclaimed, with the deepest religious fervor—

> "I now
> Have nothing in this world to wish for more.
> My God! My Comforter! My blest Redeemer!
> As once Thy arms were stretched upon the cross,
> Let them be now extended to receive me."

I spoke these lines slowly, clasping my hands together on my breast. Melville held up my crucifix before me while he guided my trembling steps. Suddenly I perceived Leicester standing rather in the background; and at sight of him I was seized with violent emotion. All my sad, terrible past rushed upon me once more. I tottered, and, unable to help myself, fell into the arms of the Earl, who stepped hurriedly forward to catch me. When I had regained my senses, I addressed him in feeble and trembling tones—

> "You keep your word, my Lord of Leicester; for
> You promised me your arm to lead me forth
> From prison, and you lend it to me now."

Seeing the great confusion of Leicester at these words, which were uttered in a tone at once of resignation and mild rebuke, I continued—

> "Farewell, my Lord, and, if you can, be happy!
> To woo two Queens has been your darling aim.
> You have disdain'd a tender, loving heart,
> Betray'd it, in the hope to win a proud one."

I had arranged that the Earl should show himself deeply moved at these accents. He was to turn to me with entreating gesture as if to exculpate himself, in order to give greater force to the following words which, with an almost prophetic expression, I pronounced—

" Kneel at the feet of Queen Elizabeth !
May your reward not prove your punishment.".

At this recall to earthly things, Melville, full of Christian fervor and in attitude of rebuke, pushes me to the front of the stage, holding the cross before my eyes ; the bell tolls, the drums beat ; we form a *tableau ;* I pressing the crucifix I wore to my lips. He says—

"Desire only to appear in the presence of Him who will shortly become your Judge, purified by your repeated victory over all earthly passions."

Profoundly moved, I raised myself, and again leaning on my confessor, still holding before my eyes the symbol of redemption. I turned slowly towards the back of the stage. At last I reached the steps leading to the scaffold ; here, Melville still at my side, still uplifting the cross, I turn once more, and by a gesture intimate to my weeping attendants I would pray Heaven for them. I stretched out my hands towards them in an attitude of benediction. Then, embracing the cross, I waved a last farewell to them all, and descended the interior staircase, followed by the executioner.

CHAPTER VIII.

MYRRHA.

ANY ONE who is familiar with the dramatic literature of our great authors, will easily understand that among all the tragedies produced by the immortal Alfieri, that of *Myrrha* is founded upon the most difficult and extraordinary subject of any which he has treated. And, in fact, to place upon the stage the spectacle of a daughter powerfully enamored of her own father, and assailed from time to time by impulses of fierce jealousy against her own mother, is undoubtedly a monstrous thing. But it will assuredly not be reckoned so unbecoming or incompatible with public morality, when it is remembered that this passion was inspired by an irresistible fate. Alfieri tells us that Cecris, Myrrha's mother, having boasted of the beauty of her daughter as superior to that of Venus herself, the offended goddess took her revenge by filling the heart of Myrrha with an incestuous passion. And thanks to his master hand, which has never had its equal, Alfieri has succeeded in making the representation of it not merely bearable, but even affecting.

In truth, the sight of the incessant and most painful conflict raging in a pure soul filled by such a terrible passion, a passion which causes remorse, shame, and scarcely-understood desires, and the enormity of which its victim herself can measure by the horror it causes her, must move the spectators to a feeling of compassion, and Alfieri has expressed this opinion at the close of his tragedy.

But if it was a difficult task for the author to treat such a subject so as to render it acceptable upon the stage, what must have been the burden of responsibility upon the actress who undertook to interpret it, and render it admissible, or even tolerable ?   Therefore, I may frankly say that this was the only character I studied during my artistic career, in the interpretation of which I was not at once successful, and it was the only one whose immense difficulty seemed to paralyze my intellectual powers.

For it appeared to me impossible adequately to depict the startling contrasts which succeeded one another without pause in the soul of this unhappy woman, who was vainly struggling against her destiny, and her living martyrdom.

How could it be shown that all that was guilty in her was not hers, but that hers rather was the virtue, the strength, with which she fought against the evil passion that filled her heart, fought against it even to taking her own life ?   How, step by step, could the overwhelming fury of that fatal sentiment be developed, and its incomprehended impulses and terrible results be set forth in their due proportions?

From the early age of fourteen, when, thanks to my natural and precocious development, I was able to undertake the principal part in *Francesca da Rimini*, up to the last day of my artistic studies, I was gifted with a great facility of imitation, which helped me to identify myself with my subject, and made me successful in every part. But in this of Myrrha I was dismayed by the many obstacles I encountered, and if any conceit had been likely to spring up within me, it would have been effectually annihilated, for during a considerable time it seemed to me the difficulties I encountered would surpass my ability to overcome them.

It was in 1848 that the unexpected change of Government made it possible to put upon the stage works hitherto prohibited by the Papal Censor, and my capocomico immediately conceived the idea of bringing out *Myrrha*, which was one of these prohibited plays.

It was just before the birth of the eldest of my four children, and it seemed to me most inappropriate for me, in my condition, to undertake the part of a young girl of twenty, the victim of such an unnatural passion. I, therefore, opposed the project as much as I could, but without success, for my Impresarii, Domeniconi, and Gaetano Coltellini, naturally counted on this play for filling the theatre. In my quality of dependant, I could not refuse my services, and, like my other companions in art, I was forced to consent.

In *four* days I learnt the part of Myrrha, which contains about 370 lines !

How was it possible for me thoroughly to study and enter into the meaning of even a quarter of such a task, or to identify myself with such a recondite character ? There was barely time to commit the words of my part to memory, as every one will know who is ac-

quainted with Alfieri's verses, and with his involved
form of expression.   The result was what might have
been expected, half a failure ; and I was so annoyed
that I declared nothing should induce me ever to appear again in this tragedy.   It was not until 1852
that wiser counsels induced me to change my mind.
Then our celebrated *prima donna,* and my very dear
friend, Carolina Internari, who displayed towards
me the affection of a mother, and who was devoted
to tragic art, speaking to me one day about Myrrha,
began to reprove me sharply for my cowardice in not
having again attempted the character.   When I persisted in my refusal, she offered me an inducement of
which I could never have dreamed.   Such was her
love for her art, and for the beautiful, that although
she had always taken the principal part in the play
and had been received in it with the greatest enthusiasm, yet if I would only consent once more to assume the part of Myrrha, she herself would play that
of the Nurse Euryclea, one of considerable importance certainly, but still one usually assigned to the
second lady of the company.   I was vanquished by
her generous proposal, my objections ceased, and I
resumed my study of Myrrha.   But what a study!
I meditated on every line, I analyzed each word, I
studied every look, until, at last, I began to fancy I
saw somewhat how this exceptional character should
be interpreted.   This study, in its complete and its
many details, was successful, and was received with
all the favor which was then bestowed on grand tragic
art, and the manifestation of which by the Italian
public differed widely from the convulsive aspiration

of the present day, and it found an appreciative
audience which showed inexpressible delight, often
amounting almost to delirium, in witnessing these
tragic representations.

Towards the close of 1852, after three months of
hard work, I presented myself upon the stage of the
Theatre Niccolini, at Florence—then the Cocomero
—to undergo my ordeal. The fact of having that
living incarnation of tragedy, Carolina Internari, to
support me in my effort, gave me such impulsive
energy, such fire and enthusiasm—my soul was so
keenly alive to the influence of that beautiful charmer
—that the very magnetism of her presence made the
blood to leap in my veins, my imagination carried
me, as if were, out of myself, and enabled me to
identify myself entirely with the miserable vicissitudes of Myrrha.

Thus it came to pass that I made this tragedy
entirely my own—mine exclusively—and it was this
which, when I played it at the Théâtre Ventadour, in
Paris, in 1855, procured me the favor of the public,
and of the French press, and afterwards that of the
other nations.

If the incestuous love of Myrrha was repugnant,
its repugnance was somewhat covered by the stress
which was laid upon her own innate chastity, and I
had so colored my interpretation of her character
with this nobler sentiment, as to bring out all its recondite and hidden beauties. My chief care was to
prove to the public, that although the subject appeared immoral, it was not really so in action. If, in the
old mythological fable, Myrrha is presented as whol-

ly odious and despicable, in Alfieri's tragedy the woman's passion is always dominated by the natural chastity of the young maiden, and indeed I heard several mothers remark, to my great satisfaction, "that they had not seen anything that could offend their daughters' modesty."

I will here recount a curious little anecdote in support of my assertion. A young lady who had just returned home from the theatre, greatly impressed by all she had seen, was talking over various points in the tragedy with her parents and friends, and she said : " But why was this Myrrha so strange, so dissatisfied ? sometimes she will be married, sometimes she wont : her parents are always of her mind. She herself fixes the day of her marriage, then she talks of putting it off, she tries to forget what just before she so ardently desired, and behold ! when the wedding is to take place, she, in an agony of anguish and fury, refuses her husband, reproaches her mother, and ends the tragedy by killing herself, after saying to her father, 'Ah ! thou would'st see that father recoil with horror if he knew it, Cinyras.' Whatever was the matter with her ? " Then the father of this young girl, whose penetration equalled his own, and who found himself rather at a loss for an answer, replied, with a wisdom worthy of him, " that the poor thing had probably been bitten by the tarantula." *

And indeed, a person whose intelligence is not very acute, may be excused for being somewhat be-

---

* The tarantula is a venomous spider found in some parts of Italy, whose bite is said to be fatal.— *Translator.*

wildered by the sudden and sharp contrasts of feeling in the tragedy.

In the first scene that Myrrha has with Pereus, her intended husband, I used every effort in my power to conceal the struggle that was raging within me, and to hide the real cause of my anguish, and of the aversion I felt towards every man but my father. But here and there, as it were, my weakness prevails over my resolution for an instant, and, as was evidently the author's intention, I let drop a word or two which gave some hint of the conflict through which I was passing.

Thus, for example, when Pereus says—

> "Now thou dost not disdain to be mine?
> No more to repent? no more to delay?"

Myrrha, who feels her courage is deserting her, answers :

"No. This is the day, and to-day I will be thy bride, but to-morrow let our sails be given to the winds, and let us leave for ever these shores at our back."

Pereus.—"What do I hear? What sudden contradiction is in thy words? It is pain to thee to leave thy native land, thy revered parents, and yet would'st thou depart thus for ever?"

Myrrha.—"I would abandon them for ever—and die of grief."

These passages are also a proof of the inflexible resolution of Myrrha, who, though certain she will die if separated from her father, yet prefers that separation to a prolonged residence near him.

I find it indispensable to touch as briefly as may be possible on certain ideas, certain passages difficult of expression, in order to enable the reader to form a better judgment of my interpretation of them.   Thus, in the third Act, when Myrrha is invited by her parents to confide in them, at the beginning, I advanced towards my mother with a firm step, as though my martyrdom were suspended for a moment, and coming opposite to her in an affectionate manner, I so contrived that the presence of my father was hid from my eyes.   Cecris, in advancing to meet me, said—

"Ah! beloved child! come to us—come!"

But as she spoke the words "Come to us," I became aware that my father was also before me, and, stopping as one struck by a sudden ague, gave my mother occasion for the second "Come," as though she would ask "Why do you hesitate?" her question being followed by my words, spoken in an aside—

"Heavens! What do I see? my father also!"

In answer to the affectionate exhortations of Cinyras, and the caresses of my mother, I allowed the public to guess the mental torture I was undergoing, by saying in another aside—

Are there torments in the world to equal mine?"

And when, pressed by my father, and persistently entreated by my mother, I saw no way of escape without betraying my guilty passion, I could control my feelings no longer, it seemed to me that my heart must break.

After a superhuman effort not to betray myself I murmured resolutely in an aside—

"Oh! Myrrha! this is thy last effort! O soul, take courage!"

And as the father, seeing the miserable condition of his child, and the suffering which oppressed her, said, in a tone of decision and authority—

"No! It would not be right. Thou dost not love Pereus, and it is unwillingly thou would'st give thyself to him,"

I exclaimed, with the cry of a soul which sees its last chance of escape from the fearful passion that is consuming it cut off—

"Ah! do not tear him from me—rather give me instant death!"

After a moment's pause, as though to regain my self-control, and excuse my vacillating state of mind, I continued—

"It is true, perhaps, that I do not love him as he loves me, and that I am not well assured of it myself. Believe me, he has my esteem, and that no man in the world could have my hand if he did not have it. I hope he will be dear to my heart as he ought to be. Chaste and faithful always I would live for him, and joy rekindle in my bosom. Some day, perhaps, life will return to me sweet and happy. If, at present, I do not love him as he merits, the fault is not in me—I, who abhor myself, have chosen him—I choose him again. I only wish and ask for him as a husband. This choice you have consented to with joy, let all be completed then, as I wish, and as you have wished. Since I triumph over my grief, so let it be with you; when I am happier I will go to the nuptials quickly, and you will be happier some day."

Identifying myself with the poet's ideal, I labored to reproduce the wonderful strength of will with which this unhappy girl repulsed her father's caresses, and adduced fallacious reasons as the unhappy cause of her mysterious sorrow, at one moment directing bitter imprecations against the cruel enemy who had wrought her such woe, while at another, feigning a calm she did not feel, a hope she was far from experiencing, all the time showing to the public, by occasional hints, her firm decision to die, if it were necessary, rather than live near the object of her shameful love. And who would not be moved to pity for the unfortunate maiden who had thus become the sport of such an adverse destiny, and whose soul was lacerated by such a guilty passion !

I was very careful not to meet my father's eyes, while at the same time I did not neglect any opportunity of showing the audience, by my expression, what jealous anger I felt at seeing my mother the object of his tenderness.

One of these occasions, of which I availed myself, was when Cinyras, after hearing the reasons his daughter adduces for the necessity of her separation from her parents, turns sadly to his wife, and says, as he embraces her—

"And thou, dear wife, standest there in silent grief. Consentest thou to her wish ?"

At this sight I made a hasty movement as though I would rush forward and hinder the embrace, then, seized with a sudden shivering, and bashfulness, I gathered my mantle about my person, and fled to the back of the stage. Afterwards I took leave of my parents in these words—

"I will withdraw to my room for a moment. I wish to go to the altar with dry eyes and with a smooth forehead to greet my spouse."

I exchanged an affectionate embrace with my mother,

but when my father drew near and attempted to clasp me to his heart, in order to avoid his caress, I bent before him in an attitude of simulated respect, allowing the terror with which I shrank from him to be plainly seen. Then, a prey to the most evident agitation, I rushed from the stage.

In the beginning of the fourth Act the author represents Myrrha so calm, serene and smiling as to make Nurse Euryclea say—

"It is a cruel joy thou showest now in leaving us."

And this joy appears as though it might be the natural consequence of the satisfaction experienced by Myrrha, in the belief that she has triumphed over all the obstacles which might prevent her departure, and has in this way freed herself from the fatal influence exercised over her. In a tranquil and sensible tone she says to Pereus—

"Yes, dear spouse, for that is the name I now wish to call thee, if ever I had an intense wish, it is to depart with thee at the dawn to-morrow. Oh! I desire it. I wish to be alone with thee. I wish no longer to see one of these objects, the witness of my tears, and their cause, perhaps. To cross new seas, to visit another kingdom, to breathe an air strange and pure, and to have thee for a protector at my side, a husband like thee, full of joy and love, such are my wishes, and all this will bring me back to what I once enjoyed. I trust I shall be less troublesome to thee. Thou must have some compassion for my state. My grief, if not spoken of by thee, will not long have root. Do thou not speak to me of the paternal kingdom, and of my deserted and disconsolate parents, nor of anything remind me that once was mine. Speak not their name. This alone will be the remedy to stay forever the fountain of my tears."

From this it may be gathered that when Myrrha is

not in the actual presence of her father, she is able
to conquer her internal strife, and to obtain the mastery over her passion. But, on the appearance of
Cinyras, in order to bring out more strikingly the
contrast between the following supreme situation and
the instantaneous effect which the sight of my father
produced on my heart, I was successful in showing
by incontestable evidence the icy coldness which ran
through my veins, my hair which stood on end—in
one word, the deep and invincible perturbation that
had seized me. The public, comprehending, identified itself at once (as the wave of involuntary emotion
let me plainly see) with the sentiments of this situation, which is one of the most moving in the tragedy.

The first returning symptoms of Myrrha's passion
are manifested when the priest intones the opening
verses of the nuptial hymn. Then her face assumes
the pallor of death, her limbs tremble. The only
one to perceive it is the nurse, who approaches her
in terror, and asks—

"Daughter, what is this? Thou tremblest! Heaven!"

To which Myrrha replies, still shaking and shivering—

"Silence, O silence!"

EURYCLEA—

"But yet——"

MYRRHA (resolutely and with authority)—

"No! it is not true. I tremble not"—

whilst burning tears run from her eyes. And this is
one of the most magnificent passages in this Act.

I remember what immense labor and fatigue it

cost me to arrive at the most exact interpretation of
the mental torment which her mother's persistent
demands as to the cause of her sorrow inflicted upon
Myrrha, and that this was aggravated by the struggle
caused by her irrevocable determination to consummate her marriage, even at the cost of her life.
These two true and powerful situations are admirably
expressed in the following words:

CECRIS.—" But why is this? Why changes thy face? Alas!
thou dost vacillate, and trembling, canst scarcely stand."

MYRRHA.—"Ah! for pity's sake, my mother, do not shake
my constancy by thy words. I know not of my face, but my
heart, my mind, remains firm and immovable."

Meanwhile, the priest continues repeating the third
strophe of the nuptial hymn—

"Let pure Faith and Concord, eternal and divine,
Make in the bosoms of these two their shrine,
And always in vain the fatal Alecto
With the horrible Furies
Released, moves her dismal nuptial torches
Before the strong pure heart
Of the honored bride who transcends all praise,
While the Furies rage in vain
And fatal discord from their path departs."

While the hymn goes on, Myrrha's breast heaves
with the violence of her effort to repress any outward
manifestation of the tempest that rages within her.
But at the words—

"While all the Furies rage in vain
And fatal discord from their path departs,"

it seems to me that she must have reached the
crowning point of her desperation.

The anger which possesses her can no longer be held back; the passion, which is consuming her like a poisonous serpent, bursts all bounds, and incites her to exclaim, half mad with rage—

"What say you? Already in my heart all the Furies have fearful possession. Behold with whips of vipers, and with dismal torches the mad Furies stand. See, these torches are what these nuptials merit."

Here I became entirely transfigured, as though seized with delirium, and, after a short pause, continued in a terrified manner—

".But what is this? The hymns ceased? Who holds me to his breast? Where am I? What said I? Am I already married? O wretchedness!"

As I spoke these words, I suddenly turned round, and found myself face to face with my father, who, with folded arms, gazed at me threateningly.

Struck by this sight, I felt the blood curdle in my veins, and, losing all my courage, with the cry—

"O misery!"

I let myself fall to the ground as though struck by lightning.

Little by little my mother and nurse succeeded in bringing me back to life again, though I was slow in entirely recovering my scattered senses. It was the magnetic effect of my father's voice that finally recalled me to myself, and, as I listened confusedly to his austere and menacing words, I replied in a weak and scarcely intelligible voice—

"It is true. Cinyras, be thou inexorable with me. I ask nothing else. I wish no more. He alone can terminate all the

sufferings of his unworthy, unhappy daughter. Into my breast
strike that vengeful sword hanging at thy girdle. Thou gavest
to me this miserable life. Take it from me. Behold, it is the
last boon for which I will supplicate. Ah, think! If thou
standest still, and with thine own right hand dost not kill me,
thou wilt compel me to die by mine own and no other."

How plainly Alfieri shows in this and other places
that Myrrha is powerless to conquer her love, and
that death alone can bring her rest and peace!

At the last words I fainted once more, so that I
did not perceive I was being supported by my father,
before he left me.

In the two following scenes Myrrha comes slowly
to herself, and, remaining alone with her mother,
there is a long interchange of sentiments of pity, of
anguish, and of remorse, and finally of jealous rage,
at seeing her hated rival continually at her side, and
of knowing that she alone possesses the affection of
Cinyras, and enjoys his tenderest caresses. Thus,
when Cecris says—

"Rather I would always from this hour watch over thy life";

Myrrha, beside herself with passion, interrupts her
cruelly—

"Thou watch my life? Must I at every moment, must I see
thee? Thou always to be before my eyes! Ah! first, I wish
that these my eyes were sepulchred in eternal darkness; with
my own hand I myself would wish to tear them from my brow."

And when Cecris adds—

"O heaven! What do I hear? Thou makest me to shudder! Thou hatest me, then?"

with savage desperation her daughter answers—

"Thou first, only, and everlasting mournful cause of my
every misery ——"

But, quickly the sight of my weeping mother recalled me to myself, and showed me what terrible
words must have issued from my lips, as by some
irresistible force. I was ashamed of having been led
into such excesses. My natural goodness of heart
triumphed, and blushing at the remembrance that I
had treated my mother so cruelly in my paroxysm of
jealous fury, and that I had so addressed her, I
besought her to kill me. Oppressed as I was by
the terrible conflict of emotions, I felt my strength
gradually forsaking me, and allowed myself to be
led gently towards my apartment by my mother,
exchanging caresses and kisses with her.

In the fifth Act the desolate Cinyras, aware of the
death of the unfortunate Pereus, determines to put
an end to the anxious life he leads, and, at every risk,
to have a clear explanation with Myrrha, and speak to
her with the decision and authority of a father. She
advances towards him.

The words which Alfieri has put into the mouth of
Cinyras, before Myrrha shows herself to the public,
clearly indicate what is her state of mind—

"Alas! Now she approaches with slow and reluctant steps!
It seems as if, in coming to me, she comes to die before my
face."

I presented myself, arrayed in a most simple Greek
dress of the finest white wool, with my hair plainly
arranged, an ashy paleness on my face, my eyes fixed,
my looks bent on the ground, my steps tottering and
uncertain.

My whole appearance at once made the spectators aware of the terrible conflict that raged within me, and prepared them for the inevitable catastrophe. At the sight of my father I remained as if petrified, and with head bent awaited my condemnation.

The remarks which Cinyras addresses to Myrrha with a view to discover the cause of her sufferings, show his conviction that it is really the flame of love which consumes her, but that it is a low passion, unworthy of her, else she would not have so carefully hidden it from all around her, or allowed it so to fasten upon her heart.

Without speaking a word, by negations, by interrupted and hardly expressed monosyllables, by gestures expressive of my grief, and by my unutterable anguish, I produced a by-play which formed, as it were, a dialogue with my father.

Thus, when Cinyras says—

" But who is worthy of thy heart if he could not have it—the incomparable, the constant and impassioned lover, Pereus?"

I so arranged that he, in addressing these words towards the side where he supposed Pereus might be, should turn himself quite in that direction, and I, by an involuntary impulse, intoxicated with love at the sound of that pitiful voice, with my arm outstretched towards my father, clearly implied that *he* alone was worthy of my affection. But when Cinyras suddenly faced me again, I lowered my gaze, and started back, terrified lest I should be surprised in that attitude. Then, seeing that I had been on the point of betraying myself, and feeling I had no longer the strength to parry his arguments, I whispered to myself, unheard by him, but in a deep, measured tone, full of bitterness—

"O death—death, that I so much invoke, wilt thou always be deaf to my grief?"

But every attempt at escape was in vain, my repeated denials were unavailing, every falsehood I uttered in my endeavor to avoid submitting to the absolute determination of Cinyras that I should reveal my secret to him, proved futile, until I interrupted him at last with the bitter cry of a stricken soul, and exclaimed—

"O heaven! I love—yes! since thou forcest me to tell it—I love desperately, and in vain."

Then, as if I hoped that this confession would prove sufficient, I entrenched myself behind my firm resolution to say no more, adding promptly—

"But who may be the object thou canst never, and no one else can know. He is ignorant of it himself, and I, too, deny it to myself."

My father made me a short answer, in which he protested that he would save his daughter at every cost, and seeing that I should not be able much longer to stave off my sad confession, I burst forth with energy, and almost beside myself—

"Save? What is thy thought? These self-same words hasten my death. Leave me, ah! leave me, for pity's sake, that I may for ever quickly drag myself from thee."

And I resolutely turned to fly. But my father's loving voice exclaiming—

"My daughter, only beloved one, what sayest thou! Ah! come to thy father's arms"—

chained me to the spot. Overpowered by the violence of my love, it seemed as though some invincible influence attracted me towards him. In my passionate rapture I threw myself into his arms, but, the moment he touched me, I started back full of horror, and repulsed him from me.

When, at last, no hope of escape remained, when there was no possibility that Myrrha could longer conceal the impious flame which was consuming her, in accordance with the intention of the author, who by a worthy inspiration of genius finds means to tell all in a single paraphrase, while saying nothing, I said, with a great effort, slowly and in a low voice, as though I feared for the very air to hear me—

"Oh! thou wouldest see that father recoil with horror if he knew it, Cinyras."

And after pronouncing that name as if my whole soul were in the word, I remained immovable for an instant, with my eyes fixed upon him, awaiting his answer.

But Myrrha's hour of torture is not yet over, for Cinyras, who has not understood the true meaning of the words he heard, threatens to remove his love from her altogether, and to abandon her to her own devices, if she will not reveal the terrible mystery that is consuming her. At this threat, Myrrha, not being able to endure the thought of abandonment by her father, loses every vestige of self-control, and, remembering the mother who will live forever happily at his side, gives full vent to her jealous fury, exclaiming—

13

"Oh! my happy mother! at least it will be granted to her to die at thy side."

The accent, the gesture, the look full of passionate love, enlighten Cinyras at once as to the true meaning of these sacrilegious words, and he retreats with horror from his daughter. Then Myrrha, overwhelmed by her infamy, and seeing no other way of escape from her dishonor, seizes with lightning speed the sword which hangs at her father's side, and plunges it into her heart, saying—

"My hand at least has been as quick as my tongue,"

and falls to the ground.

Supported in the arms of my nurse, when I heard Cinyras in the act of revealing the guilty secret to his consort, I endeavored to raise myself, and with piteous gestures implored him not to proceed, and to spare me the condemnation which must attend the knowledge of my fault. But my prayers were unavailing and I fell back once more on the bosom of my nurse. Left alone with her, and on the point of death, I spoke my last words in a feeble voice, and accents of reproof—

"When I asked thee for a steel, then thou shouldest have given it me, Euryclea. I then should have died innocent, now I die wicked";

and I fell back, dead, upon the ground.

I hope by this analytical study of my most difficult character to make the reader understand what immense efforts it required to enable me fully to enter into Alfieri's intentions, which evidently were to show how an impure passion conceived by an innocent soul, may be rendered capable of exciting a feeling of true pity on behalf of the miserable maiden who is the victim of the wrath of Venus.

In order to show how great were the repentance and remorse of Myrrha, Ovid makes her say—

"Oh, gods! If ye are accessible to the voice of penitence, I have deserved the most heavy punishment, and am ready to endure it. But that I may not offend the looks of the living remaining upon earth, nor those of the shadows which people the regions of death, exclude me, I pray, from both worlds, and by a metamorphosis divide me at once from the living and the dead."

The gods listened favorably to this request, and Myrrha's last petitions were granted. She was still speaking when the earth began to cover her feet and roots issued forth from her toe-nails to serve as a support to the trunk which commenced to form. Her bones turned into solid wood, keeping the marrow; her blood changed into sap, her arms into long branches, her fingers into smaller twigs, and her skin into rough bark. The visible evidences of her shame were hidden among the springing boughs, which had already reached her breasts and would soon encircle her neck. Myrrha, far from opposing the encroachments of the wood, welcomed it gladly and pressed down her face among the spreading foliage. Although with her body she had lost her former senses, yet she wept continually. Warm tears still flow from this tree, and these tears have great virtue.

The perfume which is distilled from it bears the name of Myrrha, and shall be celebrated throughout all future centuries.

> Est tales exorsa preces: "O, si qua patetis
> Numina confessis, merui, nec triste recuso
> Supplicium. Sed, ne violem vivosque superstes
> Mortuaque extinctos ambobus pellite regnis
> Mutatæque mihi vitamque necemque negate,
> Numen confessis aliquod patet. Ultima certe

Vota suos habuere deos.   Nam crura loquentis
Terra supervenit, ruptosque obliqua per ungues
Porrigitur radix, longi firmamina trunci,
Ossaque robur argunt, mediaque manente medulla,
Sanguis it in succos, in magnos brachia ramos,
In parvos digitos, duratur cortice pellis.
Itaque gravem crescens uterum perstrinxerat arbor
Pectoraque obruerat, collumque operire parabat
Non tulit illa moram venientique obvia ligno
Subsedit, mersitque suos in cortice vultus
Quæ, quanquam amisit veteres cum corpore sensus
Flet tamen et tepidu manant ex arbore guttae
Est honor et lacrymis; stillataque cortice Myrra
Nomen herile tenet, nullique tacebitur aevo."

CHAPTER IX.

MEDEA.

WITHOUT making any attempt to trace the legend of *Medea* from remote antiquity, I shall confine myself simply to time present, and merely say that the subject was dramatized about 1810 by the distinguished Italian, Giovanni Battista Niccolini. But although there were, here and there in the tragedy, some flashes of genius, although the style was modelled upon that of the ancient Greek plays, and passages were found which had been taken from Euripides and Seneca; yet it lacked those scenic effects which appeal so directly to the audience, and, as the dialogue was besides somewhat prolix, it was not represented so frequently as other plays by the same renowned author.

Another version of the tragedy was published shortly afterwards by the Duca della Valle, and as this was more concise and the scenic effects equally well preserved, although perhaps at the expense of the stately dignity of the Greek, the play became most popular, and there was not a first actress of any repute who did not essay it, nor a *capocomico* who did not endeavor to put it on the stage.

But I had always refused to accept the part, for nature had developed the maternal instinct in me to a very large degree, and I instinctively revolted from the idea of a woman who, by her own hand, and with deliberate design, could murder her children. Even on the stage I would not portray such a monster. And although my *capocomico* did his utmost to overcome my scruples, I was not to be persuaded out of my aversion.

When I arrived in France, as I have already said, in 1855, the disputes between the famous M. Legouvé and that genius of French tragedy, Rachel, were still recent. One day, after I had given a few representations at the Salle Ventadour, by which I was fortunate enough to gain the full sympathy of the Parisian public, my maid came to announce that two gentlemen desired to see me. I was still at dinner, for dramatic *artistes* are obliged to keep early hours, but I desired them to be admitted.

"I am M. Scribe," said one.

"And I M. Legouvé," added the other.

Who does not know these two names in Italy? Scribe's name is almost a household word there, and his plays of *Adrienne Lecouvreur*, *Luisa de Liguerolles*, &c., &c., formed an important and attractive part of my *répertoire*.

When, therefore, I found myself in the presence of so much talent, I felt much confused, although I was at the same time delighted to have made the acquaintance of two such representatives of French dramatic art. A gay and lively conversation speedily commenced, in the course of which I mentioned some of their works in which I had appeared, especially those of Scribe; and I was finally prevailed upon, by the courteous entreaties of both visitors, to recite certain lines from *Adrienne Lecouvreur*, which they were naturally polite enough to say gave them the fullest satisfaction. We got no farther during this visit; but a few days after M. Legouvé came again, when the following dialogue took place:—

M. Legouvé: "Why, Madame, do you not undertake my *Medea?*"

"For a very good reason, my dear Sir," I replied. "I have always been so fond of children in general that even while I was yet quite young, when I saw a pretty baby with its sweet little face, chubby cheeks, and fair curly hair, either carried by its nurse or led by the hand, I rushed to kiss it, without saying either 'With your leave,' or 'By your leave,' or caring a whit for the black looks bestowed on me by its attendant. You can imagine from this the intense affection I feel for my own children, and even upon the stage I could not bring myself fictitiously to kill those confided to me by the author! Now, in Italy, we have a *Medea* who is a favorite character with the *capocomici*, and actresses are only too glad to add her to their *répertoire;* but, as for me, however good the actress might be who played the part, I would never go to see her."

M. Legouvé: "Ah, well! my Medea murders her children in such a way that the audience is left to guess who does the deed, and do not actually see her do it."

"Pardon me, M. Legouvé, but you will never persuade me that the horror inspired by the mere idea of such a crime being committed by the heroine of the play would not prejudice the public against her."

M. Legouvé: "No, it does not, I assure you. Will you do me the favor and read my *Medea* for yourself, and you will then see with your own eyes the truth of my assertion."

"So be it, then, for I would not seem discourteous after your extreme politeness to me. But I hope you will not be offended if I warn you that it will never be possible for me to admit your work into my *répertoire*."

Without being in the slightest degree amazed at my frankness, M. Legouvé took his leave in these words:

"Yes, yes, only read it, and we will talk about it afterwards."

The next day, simply that I might not be accused of breaking my word, I devoted my half-hour of leisure, while my maid brushed my hair, to read the play. I did it, however, in the belief that I was wasting my time, for it seemed to me quite impossible that the author should have been able to avoid the final catastrophe. Thus I was by no means disposed to form a favorable judgment of the work.

It is, therefore, more easy to imagine than to describe my surprise when I discovered I was so much interested that I found myself indulging in such gestures and such exclamations that my astonished maid cried out: "Good heavens, Signora! what is the matter? I cannot dress your hair."

"Go on, go on," I answered, "it is nothing. Do not mind me."

When I had finished the first Act, which I found

far superior to any other play on the same subject
that I had seen, I exclaimed :

"Oh! it is beautiful! What magnificent situations! How could Rachel have refused to undertake
such a splendid part? I cannot understand it."

My interest increased after the second Act. I
waited the climax with the utmost anxiety. I longed
to see how my author would manage the murder of
the children, by their mother's own hands without
either making her actually do the deed, or arousing the
horror of the audience. Words failed me to express
the enthusiasm which the reading of the whole tragedy
inspired in me. Suffice it to say that M. Legouvé
found means to represent the murder to my sense as
both just and necessary.

The Corinthians had determined to seize the children and murder Medea, in revenge for the death of
the wretched Creusa, whom Medea had killed in a
moment of savage jealousy. What course remained
open to the persecuted mother? Should she yield,
and abandon her sons to Jason, certain that they
would be brought up in hatred of her. No, her
whole soul revolted against such an idea. To face
the infuriated mob, which had gathered against her,
would only be to court death for herself, without
saving her children ; and in this frightful dilemma,
she is seized by an overwhelming impulse herself to
destroy her offspring. Indeed, no other course is
open to her, possessed as she is by the Furies, and
therefore, quick as lightning, she plunges her dagger
into those innocent breasts. M. Legouvé had told

me the truth, and he had in this way succeeded in soft-ening the horror of this dreadful deed.

As she became aware of the roar of the advancing crowd, Medea looked about her for a way of escape, but on every side hearing the cries of men thirsting for her blood, and seeing that her children were on the point of being torn from her, she leaped with one bound on the altar of Saturn. The crowd poured in from every corner of the stage, completely surround-ing her, and their sudden exclamations of horror made the spectators aware of the terrible deed.

When I reached this point, my admiration of the masterly treatment quite overpowered me. I let the book drop from my hands, and henceforth exper-ienced the most ardent desire to attempt the part.

The next time I saw M. Legouvé I could hardly refrain from throwing myself on his neck with de-light.

"Yes, yes," I cried. "I shall be overjoyed to act your Medea, and we will arrange the last scene in such a way as to conceal the death of the children from the public. Without losing time, let us consider who shall translate your verses into Italian. Fortu-nately there were then among the Italian colony in Paris, many most eminent literary men, whom love of their country had driven into exile. Among these Montanelli seemed, upon consideration, the best fitted for the task, and he willingly accepted it. Our heroic compatriot, Daniel Manin, and many others, approved the choice; and it was decided that the play should be ready for the ensuing season.

When I returned to Paris in the spring of 1856,

eleven days were spent in arduous rehearsals, and in hastening the final preparations for the performance. People were already talking about it. I thought of nothing—dreamed of nothing—but Medea. The choice of my costume also greatly occupied my mind ; for all my researches had not enabled me to fix on anything I considered altogether suitable. At last the famous painter, Ary Schefster, whom I had the good fortune to know intimately, and whose esteem and friendship I was proud to possess—volunteered his aid. He designed my costume down to its most minute details, and really succeeded admirably, excepting being rather embarrassed by the large size of my mantle, which, though necessary at my first appearance on the stage, interfered somewhat with the various attitudes and gestures I had imagined. By simple and natural movement, he had arranged that I was to make the large and artistically disposed folds fall behind my shoulders ; to carry this out successfully was my care.

The 8th of April was fixed for the first representation, and I, who by a natural instinct would never have anything deferred when it had been once arranged, was determined that all should be ready for that evening—and ready it was. In those days a theatrical novelty excited the greatest and most eager curiosity. Both the French and Italian play-goers were in a state of excitement. The French were desirous to see and judge whether Mdlle. Rachel had really been wrong to refuse the part, after having not only approved, accepted and studied it, but also after having shown her artistic interest in it many

times, and having complimented the author on the
way he had conceived and carried out the part. The
Italians invested my experiment with an almost
national importance, and the excitement among them
was consequently immense. All those who sympa-
thized with our nation, or who were intimate with our
principal exiles, shared in their eagerness. Among
these I will only mention Alexandre Dumas, Jules
Janin, and my very dear friends M. and Madame
Planat de la Faye.*

Before the play began many persons came into my
dressing-room to offer me their best wishes for my
success. Among them was Ary Schefster, who
desired to see the effect of my costume, and decide
whether I had been able to arrange the folds of my large
mantle so as not to incommode me, while producing
the effect he desired. I showed him my ingenious
device for carrying out both purposes ; and when the
explanation was over, he hastened away to join his
family, so that he might not lose one word of the
play.

The Salle Ventadour was crammed with a large and
most fashionable audience. Madame de la Valliere,
daughter of the eminent M. Legouvé, was almost
overpowered by her emotions. The author, who

---

* These latter were on most intimate and affectionate terms
with Daniel Manin, whose sad exile and death they solaced and
comforted by their deep attachment. Madame Planat wrote
his life in two volumes, from the most authentic documents,
and in acknowledgment of her work, and of her great love for
Italy, the city of Venice conferred on her the honor of citizen-
ship.

knew that he had a high stake in the success of the evening, in consequence of the notoriety caused the year before by the Rachel incident, could not, with all his efforts, disguise his anxiety, which he betrayed by his minute attention to every stage detail, although he did it with the air of one who was watching over the interests of a friend.

As for me!—well! in spite of the interest every one showed in me, my hands were like ice, and I did nothing but rub them together with a constant and rapid movement, while I said to those who stood nearest me—"There seems to be a very great draught from the roof this evening; I am so cold, I am shivering all over."

The curtain rose—a most flattering murmur announced the attention and sympathy of the public. The magnificent lines of Orpheus (Signor Boccomini) were followed by prolonged applause. Oh! how these early manifestations of pleasure on the part of the audience, give heart and courage to the actors who have yet to present themselves.

At last the moment of my appearance arrived, and I stood already prepared on the platform of the shaking piece which represented the base of the mountain I was slowly and with difficulty to ascend. I carried my little Melanthe in my arms, while his tiny head rested on my shoulder, and the part of my ample mantle, which was afterwards to hang behind my back, and the arrangement of which had so preoccupied Ary Schefster, now covered half my head and almost the whole of my child's. I had placed the other boy, Lycaon, at my left side, making him put one hand within my girdle, as he leant against me in an attitude of utter exhaustion.

The songs of the Canephorae, who accompanied Creusa to the temple, preceded my entrance. When they caught sight of me the spectators burst into loud and prolonged applause, which only ceased when I began to speak. Arrived at the summit of the mountain, I stood for a moment in the attitude of a woman utterly exhausted. I was indebted for this "*pose,*" and for many others in my studies of tragedy, to the famous group of the Niobe, which occupies the Sala della Niobe in the famous Uffizi Gallery at Florence.

When I began to speak, my mournful and subdued tone of voice was such as to show that my prostration of body arose not merely from the toil and privations encountered during a long and arduous journey through valleys and over steeps, but also from the misery of witnessing the sufferings of my famishing children. Alas! what could I offer them but my blood! This state of mind Legouvé describes in the most moving and affecting manner.

Poor little Melanthe, who had sunk down quite worn out beside his brother on the steps of the statue of Diana, says in pitiful tones—

" Mother, I am weary."

MEDEA.—" Darling, you break my heart! no roof have we to shelter us. This bare rock must be your pillow to-day."

LYCAON.—" Mother, I am hungry."

At these heart-breaking words, I assumed an attitude of despair as though asking myself, " What can I do to help them ?" Then, almost beside myself, I exclaimed :

" Why cannot I open my veins to their last drop and bid them partake, and from my blood draw the nourishment they need ? "

This tone of prostration continued through the greater part of the Act.   But when I began to recount the sufferings I had endured through my lost love, then, like the drooping plants which are revived by the beneficent dew, I too regained my vigor ; and during the magnificent scene with Creusa, in which, step by step, I revealed the grief that was gnawing at my heart, dreading that while I was wandering about in my wretchedness, seeking some trace of my beloved who had left me, I should find him living happy in the arms of some rival—my whole appearance became transformed, my limbs worked convulsively, my eyes blazed, my mouth seemed to breathe forth poison ; and when Creusa asked me what I would do to Jason and his affianced bride if I came upon them, I answered with the aspect of a fury, looking at her with malevolent eyes, while I seized her hand and drew her to the front of the stage—

" What does the leopard in the forest depths, when pouncing on his prey with hideous roar ?   He bears it to his den, and tears the bloody carcass limb from limb."

As I uttered these last words I assumed the air of a wild beast gloating over his victim, while, with my hands, I made as though I were indeed dismembering my prey, my whole expression and attitude being calculated to excite the utmost dread and horror.

This posture, ferocious as it was, seemed to me strictly logical, and in accordance not merely with the disposition of Medea, but with that of every woman of strong character capable of extremes either in love or hate. And this conviction tended to make me a just judge, and served me as a pattern in the frequent transitions of the part. Thus, by profound study, I succeeded in developing this double passion as the author had imagined it, without departing from the truth.

But the scene changed with the unexpected appearance of Orpheus. At the assurance he gave me that Jason was still alive, my features lighted up with a passionate joy; but when I further discovered in Creusa the woman who was my rival, and heard her rashly defy my anger with the words—

"Hold! respect the hero who has plighted his faith to me";

I replied with a stern look—

"You love him?"

and Creusa said—

"Yes, I love him, and to-morrow the high priest will hail him as my husband."

Like a lioness who is determined her prey shall not escape her, I exclaimed in a mocking voice—

"You will marry him? We shall see."

I extended my right hand towards her with a resolute air, as though daring her to defy me, and stood thus until the curtain fell.

This first Act was received with the greatest enthusiasm, and I was called for several times by the excited audience. The Foyer (green-room), as it is named by the actors, was crowded with people. Admirers were profuse in their compliments, friends

wrung my hands with emotion too deep for words.
Others gathered round me in silence, unable to speak
their sentiments. M. Legouvé and I were indeed
the hero and heroine of the hour. All united in
expressing their astonishment at the wonderful way
in which each part had been studied and each detail
carried out after such a small number of rehearsals.
This would probably not have been so much a matter
of surprise in Italy, where theatrical conditions are
much less florid than among other nations, and where
it is essential to attract the public by the production
of constant novelties, and therefore but little time
can be given. In France on the contrary, the necessary preparations sometimes occupy six months.

The second Act abounds in fine situations and marvellous scenic effects, which offer the actress a large
scope for the display of her dramatic capacity. Chief
among the former is the scene between Medea and
Jason. When Jason reproaches himself with having
involuntarily condemned his children to a life of toil
and privation, and dreading to know that they should
be exposed to further shame and suffering, tells her
that he will do all in his power to rescue them from
such a fate, provided their mother sacrifice herself for
them, I eagerly ask—

"How?"

JASON.— By breaking our marriage tie !

I am for the moment stunned by such a proposal.
Then with a great effort at self-control, I add, with
scarcely repressed irony—

"Ha ! you will repudiate me !"

and already the tempest his words had awakened

14

within me made my eyes flash. I will not stop here to enumerate, even briefly, the thousand suggestions and questionings that passed between us in the few lines preceding those in which I answered his arguments with the sarcastic words beginning—"I have foreseen all," and gave place to the accents of hatred and revenge in keeping with Medea's indomitable temper, and which must breathe in every word of mine during the progress of the scene. And now I gave full vent to the fury that raged within me, which I had hitherto restrained in some degree. Weakness, passionate affection, were both forgotten in the just resentment of an outraged, humiliated soul, injured in its tenderest and strongest feelings, and all my fury burst forth as I answered him—

"Yes! Lacerate my heart with thy base treachery, discard me and elect another in my place. I can understand it, such crimes are of thy race. But to speak of thy children, to feign anxiety for their welfare while thy heart is busy with adulterous plans, to mingle their innocence with thy guilty thoughts, and shield thy infamy beneath the name of *father!* This exceeds all bearing—this thrills me with horror."

After my absolute refusal to consent to the rupture of our marriage tie, and ascertaining from his cruel and insulting words that he defied my anger, and that all affection for me had died within him, in spite of myself I remained strangely agitated. My deepest grief, however, was when, weary of my reproaches, and caring little for my refusal, Jason informed me that the very next day I should be banished the country, and Creusa would become his wife, while the winds that drove me from his shores would waft

me the strains of their wedding hymn. These men-
aces seemed to petrify me. My love changed to the
deepest hatred. Like a torrent of burning lava I
poured forth the words—

"Blood! Blood! Oh, for something wherewith to wring, to
lacerate his heart! something atrocious—fearful—hideous—
some punishment unknown to human nature, but equal, if it be
possible, to my hatred."

And like a wounded wild animal, I paced round and
round the stage, as though seeking for some new and
terrible mode of vengeance. Even the voices of my
children, who ran towards me, calling me by the en-
dearing name of mother, could not calm my fury;
for when they appealed to me with the words, "Hear
thy sons!" I replied vehemently—

"The children of Jason are no sons of mine!"
LYCAON: "Dost thou love us no longer?"
"No [I answered in bitter accents], accursed race! hence!—
all, all I hate, but ye far more than all! Because ye spring
from *him;* because to him I owe ye, him whom ye both
resemble."

Then, beholding the forlorn air of the poor little
innocent ones, I cried—

"Oh, Jason, wilt thou pursue me with thy semblance and thy
sons!"

And the affection which reigned all-powerful within
me awoke once more; deeply touched, I continued—

"Thy children! no, no,—mine!"

I stretched out my arms towards them in a transport of maternal affection, and they at once rushed
into my embrace. I threw myself upon a seat, took

the youngest on my knee, and pressed the other with rapture to my heart; thus forming a group which produced the greatest effect upon the audience. My true mother's love overflowed in my next words—

"I whose love for you has known no bounds, I who in this wide world have naught but you; I hate you? I send you from me? Wretch that I am! What are you to Jason, you unfortunate children of Medea! I should have broken my own heart, but not touched his! Does he know anything of you? His heart is filled with one idea, one name, one love,— Creusa!"

As I uttered this name all my fierce jealousy once more awoke within me. The children, terrified at the change, shrank from my embrace. Left alone, the sole idea of vengeance possessed me. I would destroy my rival. I would stab her, for—

"The heart then serves as guide to the blow, my arm would grudge to leave its work to poison."

I pulled a dagger from beneath my peplum, and at sight of it exclaimed with savage exultation: "Oh, joy!" Then in a deep voice and cautious tone I continued—

"At night, gliding stealthily along the sombre walls, I will enter, spectre-like, the room where she sleeps, and when I see her prostrate on her downy couch, and at my mercy, I will brandish on high my avenging weapon and plunge it in her bosom to seek out her soul. When she opens her eyes she will see *me!* At her death-cry the palace will awaken. Lover, friends, and parents will rush in horror-stricken, and behold Medea standing, avenged, over Creusa's lifeless corpse!"

While I uttered these last words I drew myself up in such a manner as to appear of gigantic size, holding my dagger tightly clasped aloft, so that men might well have been thunderstruck at my aspect.

At the unexpected appearance of Creusa, the idea of instantly carrying out my revenge came like a lightning flash into my mind, and filled me with a savage joy, but I rapidly hid myself behind a column in order to choose a propitious moment to fall upon her. As I followed Creusa with the intention of surprising her, we suddenly came upon one another face to face. The unhappy girl was looking for me, with the generous intention of warning me that an excited crowd was besieging the palace and thirsting for my blood—

"'Tis thee these angry crowds pursue. Let them but cross the threshold, and thou art lost! I come——"
MEDEA : " For what?"
CREUSA : "To save thee!"

This answer disarmed Medea's wrath, who, with a quick return of the instincts of her royal race, repeated in astonishment—

"Thou to save me!—save me!"

When I had spoken, I suddenly became conscious that I was still grasping my dagger, and, ashamed of myself, I hastened to hide it in silence.

Then followed a short scene with Creusa, in which I prayed and besought her, in accents full of anguish, to leave me the man who was all the world to me ; but at her repeated refusal my hatred returned in tenfold force. I rose up, ready to spring upon her, when Creonte, alarmed by her daughter's cry, came, in terrified haste, to her rescue, followed by a crowd of people. In the last scene, while my children cling closely to my side lest they should be dragged from

me by the infuriated mob who carried stones in their
hands ready to cast at me, Orpheus suddenly appeared, and addressed the raging multitude in an authoritative voice—

"Let him who loves not his own sons, be the first to tear
these children from their mother!"

At sight of him the people, awestruck, stood aside,
letting the stones fall from their hands. Creonte,
Jason, and Creusa felt in their turn the irresistible
fascination of the divine poet. Reassured by the
words of Orpheus who promised me a safe escape, I
wrapped both my sons in my mantle, and, certain
that all would now be well, retreated slowly, murmur-
ing to myself—

" At last I have found my revenge."

I need not insist upon the effect all these situations
produced on the public.

The stage was arranged in a truly artistic manner
for my appearance in the third Act. On the side to
the left of the spectator, a large curtain, draped in
the Greek style, indicated the entrance to a room,
which was reached by a short flight of steps. When
the drop scene rose Jason was discovered listening
impatiently to the admonitions of Orpheus.

Creusa comes on the scene unexpectedly, leading
his children in either hand, and delighted by their
caresses. It is quite a domestic group, and gives
opportunity for the expression of many tender sentiments towards the children on the part of Creusa,
who desires to adopt them both as her own. Jason,

full of these glad prospects, withdraws, followed by his dear ones and by the gloomy Orpheus. At this instant I show myself on the threshold of my chamber. I descend the first step with one foot, and, raising in my right hand the heavy curtain, I remain in the shadow of it, a cold observer of this new proof of Jason's treachery.

In the short monologue that follows, I confirm myself all the more in my thoughts of vengeance, and only wait the fall of night to fly with my children while the palace is full of the jocund guests who are celebrating the auspicious wedding of Creusa! These last words I pronounce in the sarcastic tone of one who has prepared quite a different close to the festivities. Here Orpheus returns, bringing an order from Creonte. He tells me that among the answers he had received from the oracle was one warning that the presence of Medea at the marriage would be fatal to the bride; and he ordered me to depart instantly, but without my children. Such a decree pierces Medea's heart, for her maternal love is stronger than her hate, and she entreats Orpheus to intercede for her with the king that he will restore her sons to her. In the following scene everything conduces to show the strain of humanity existing in this woman who is subjected to such severe trials, and this study served to prove how difficult it is to give a correct representation of such a strange personality, and to bring out in their true analogies the constantly opposing and contrasting passions by which she is incessantly torn.

Finding all my prayers and entreaties vain, I hum-

bled myself so far, at last, as to beseech the inflexible
Jason to allow me to depart with my sons; but hearing that he would only consent for one to accompany
me, I turned with the most moving expression of
countenance towards Creusa, the king, and Jason,
and besought them again, with reiterated prayers, to
grant my request. But the decision was irrevocable.
Then, seeing myself abandoned even by my children,
who were clinging to Creusa in dread lest they should
have to go with me—deaf to every word of comfort
that was addressed to me, I implored to be left alone,
a prey to my grief. Presently I discovered that my
children were gone, and with a breaking heart I
cried—

"My sons! my sons!"

and fell, as though deprived of my senses, on the
steps of the altar erected to Saturn. After a short
pause, I commenced the following powerful monologue :—

"Alone! Alone in the world! Father, husband, children!
all are gone! Thou weepest, Medea, thou! . . ."

But a feeling of shame succeeded that of despair.
I blushed as I saw my hands glistening with the
tears that had fallen from my brimming eyes, and I
exclaimed—

"And Jason? He triumphs! Yes! thanks to me his every
wish is fulfilled. Our union was a burden to him. I have dis-
solved it. He asked for my sons, and I have surrendered them
to him! My own hand has given him to his beloved one!"

Then, step by step, I went over the wrongs I had
endured, until, stung by the remembrance that I had
myself—

" Unconsciously aided and assisted Jason in the accomplishment of his happiness,"

my fury broke forth once more, and while I said the
words—

"My own hand has given," &c.,

I leaped to my feet, and shook my head resolutely as
though to free myself from the load of shame which
seemed as if it would crush me.   But the picture my
imagination drew of the transports of Jason and his
bride, was too much for me ; I shouted—

" Oh, ye infernal gods !   Help me ! help me !   Blood ! tears !
groans !   The avenging steel !   All these I crave !"

At this point I decided to exterminate them all—

" As yet I scarce know what I do.   But I am resolved some
hideous crime, throughout this terrified land shall shroud me
with a veil of horror, stained with blood !—that of Jason,
Creusa, her father, my own children——"

But the recollection of those dear ones suffices somewhat to calm my fury, and I began to be horror-
stricken at the idea of killing them with my own
hand.   However, as I reflected that such a blow
would overwhelm Jason with eternal sorrow, I crushed
back the cry of my better nature ; giving to the following verses all the force of the madness I no longer
feared—

" Let me die, provided only that Jason's grief be sempiternal,
—that my fell deed create for him innumerable tortures, and
that the infernal deities of my own land do claim him for their
natural prey !   Oh, thou pale god of gloomy Tauris !"

And here turning towards the statue of Saturn, I
burst out impetuously—

"Thou, Saturn, above all others, whose worship doth delight in infant slaughter,—hear me! Thy terrible altars love the blood of children sacrificed by their mothers' hands! This dread offering thou shalt have from me! But, in return, I claim thee as an accomplice! Fix then an undying vulture into Jason's breast, which shall gnaw his heart eternally. Increase his love for Creusa; for then her loss will cause him tenfold grief. Grant him even goodness and a parent's heart, that, wandering and outcast, he may live a prey to sorrow, and die as desperate as I shall die!"

At this moment my children reappear, led by Creusa's nurse; I stayed my wild words when I saw them, terrified at my scarcely uttered oath. I commanded them to avoid me lest I should be forced to sacrifice them to the implacable deity. But, hearing that Jason awaits them at the altar, as though to make them witnesses of his perfidy, every feeling of pity vanished, and I was again a prey to my mad fury, and ordered them to approach me. I arranged that after the words—

"Thou hast rightly said! Time presses,—the hour is at hand! Let them draw near. No! no thought of pity shall move me! father and son struck by the selfsame blow must both——"

Melanthe and Lycaon should throw themselves before me, grasping my knees with their tender hands, and raising their eyes to me in pitiful supplication; I am moved by their touch; I let fall the arm lifted to strike them; my voice softened, my hands as they dropped encountered theirs, and that contact produced such a sentiment of affection in my soul, that I forgot my thoughts of vengeance, and, deeply moved, I exclaimed in a voice overflowing with tenderness :—

"Their hands! their little hands, I feel their touch! I hesitate; my heart fails me—in spite of myself my lips incline to theirs. Ah! the struggle is too hard!"

Stooping to kiss them, but recollecting the oath I had just before sworn to Saturn, I turned to his altar, as though imploring the deity to grant me one brief moment of joy before I dealt the fatal blow. Contemplating my sons, the maternal sentiment awoke once more in all its strength within me! After brief struggle I burst into tears, and cried out like one intoxicated :—

"No, the effort is too great. Hence ye black designs! I have found my children!"

Thus saying, I fell on my knees between them, covering them with kisses, and pressing them with transport to my heart. At this moment Orpheus hastened towards me, urging me to seek safety in flight with my sons. I welcomed his proposal eagerly, when suddenly a distant and confused murmur of voices stayed our steps. A maid servant, dishevelled and in tears, ran in to announce that Creusa was dying, murdered by a poisoned veil. Distractedly I cried out—

"Yes! mine! the one I gave her!"

When Orpheus in a fury exclaimed—

"Wretch, let thy sons be torn from thee!"
"Never!"

I replied ; and, seizing little Melanthe, I held him

under my arm, while with the other I dragged
Lycaon. I tried to escape, hurrying precipitately to
the right side of the stage, but the noise of the infuriated mob drove me back in terrified haste to the
other. In vain I sought safety in every direction.
The cries of " Death ! death ! " which resounded
throughout the palace, forced me to try some other
way. At that moment the mob broke in on every
side, like an overwhelming torrent, seeking to tear
my children from me in accordance with the king's
command, who urged them on with the cry—

"Seize them ! to death with her ! "

I exclaimed desperately—

"Never ! you shall not have them ! "

and I made one bound to the altar of Saturn, dragging my children after me. The furious crowd
surrounded me, closing me in on every side ; when
suddenly a cry of horror burst from every throat,
which told that the awful sacrifice had been consum-
mated. The people fell back from such a sight, and
let the audience see Medea with her murdered sons
lying behind her at Saturn's feet ; her eyes sternly
set, her face stony, her whole attitude befitting that
of a statue of remorse.

After a brief interval of general horror, the voice
of Jason was heard crying—

"Leave me, by my hand must she perish ! "
ORPHEUS: "Approach not ! "
JASON: "The children ! "
"Slain ! "

answered the afflicted Creonte. Jason now hurried
in, asking desperately—

"Murdered? Who, who has murdered them?"
"Thou!"

exclaimed Medea, drawing herself up in an imposing and ferocious attitude, and extending her arm towards Jason, like an image of an inexorable destiny!

And here the curtain fell.

I applied myself to the study of this subject with irresistible transport of volition. So that I may say that I played and considered MEDEA as the study in which I delighted most, and which induced me to have recourse to all the resources of Art.

To use a common phrase, I considered this tragedy my *Cheval de Bataille.* I studied deeply the contrast between two passions which, if they are not common, are not even extraordinary, Jealousy and Hatred; and from the one and the other necessarily deriving itself, Revenge. It was a study exemplarily philosophical, finding its origin and explanation in the tenderness of the human soul. I have endeavored to express it in the best manner I was able. Returning to the past, and feeling myself live again in the impressions of those hours, it seems to me I have understood it as I ought and as I could.

CHAPTER X.

PHAEDRA.

It is worthy of notice that Racine, in composing his magnificient tragedy of *Phaedra*, was indebted, for some of the most truthful and beautiful parts of it, to dramas already produced by those great masters of tragic composition, Seneca and Euripides. Both their tragedies, however, were called *Hippolytus* (after the hero instead of the heroine of the piece).

This is what Racine says in the preface to his *Phaedra*:—

" Quoique j'aie suivie une route un peu differente de celle de cet auteur [speaking of Euripides] pour la conduite de l'action, je n'ai pas laissé d'enrichir ma pièce de tout ce qui m'a paru éclatant dans la sienne." *

And in fact, he, among others, found the scene between Phaedra and her nurse Œnone, so full of truth and pathetic sentiment, that he imitated it very closely when he introduced Phaedra in the first Act.

Euripides, however, represents her as resolute to die, because she cannot vanquish, with chastity,

" that guilty and impure love."

---

* " Although I have followed rather a different plan for the development of the action to that chosen by this author, yet I have not hesitated to enrich my piece by adding all that seemed to me most excellent in his."

(222)

The means imagined by Racine completely to alter the character of the action at the close of the first Act are masterly, and quite original. He makes her attendant Panope announce to the Queen the reported death of Theseus at the very moment when the former, overwhelmed with remorse for her illegitimate passion, and certain that she can never satisfy the impure flame which renders her odious to herself, has decided to allow herself to die of weakness.

Like a flash of lightning, the joyful news penetrates to her heart, for in this event she sees a way of escape out of the difficulty which rendered her nefarious love hopeless.

" The cards are broken which make our love a shame and a disgrace." *

The voice of conscience is silenced. The sweet hope that Hippolytus, when the death of her husband becomes known, will come to her, flashes across her mind like a ray of sunshine amidst a furious tempest, and like a young girl who for the first time hears loving lips whisper sweet words into her ear, Phaedra listens to the insinuations and persuasions of her nurse, swayed the while by a thousand varying emotions ; and with a smile flickering upon her pallid lips, she decides to save her life, surrendering herself entirely into the hands of Œnone, and pretending that it is only for the " love of her son," that she renounces her firm intention to die.

Racine, by introducing this incident into his trag-

---

* " Vient de rompre les neux
Qui faisaient tout le crime et l'horreur de nos feux."—*Racine.*

edy, has proved himself to have fully comprehended all the truth and beauty of the way in which Seneca, in the third scene of the second Act, makes Phaedra discover to Hippolytus the passion she cherishes for him.

He represents first her perplexity of mind as she resolves to tell her secret, then the gradual steps by which she is led to her sudden confession, and finally the horror of Hippolytus as he listens to her, and his scornful disdain. Racine differs from Seneca, however, by placing the carefully spun web of lies which Œnone prepares to save her beloved and unfortunate mistress in the third Act; and he substitutes a noble repulse of her attendants' evil proposal, for the wicked and tacit consent which Seneca makes Phaedra give to the culpable plan, against the carrying out of which the older dramatist does not make the Queen raise a single objection. At the same time it is true that Phaedra, even in Racine, consents to Œnone's proposal to accuse the innocent Hippolytus of attempting an outrage upon her, but this is justified by the terrible position in which the author places her.

Theseus, though believed to be dead, returns, and may discover at any moment her fault and her shame. Certain as she is that the man she loves will not keep silent about her guilty passion, Phaedra, although very shortly before she had shown the greatest horror at the idea of Hippolytus suffering for her fault, saying—

"I! dare I oppress and blacken innocence!"
"Moi, que j'ose opprimer et noircir l'innocence!"—*Racine.*

now, when she sees him approach with his father, is overwhelmed with fear. Her senses almost desert her, and hardly comprehending the words of Œnone, she gives a hasty assent to them, as being the only way in which she can save herself from the fury of her consort, and avert her own dishonor.

> PHAEDRA: "Ah! I see Hippolytus, I see my fate written in his insolent eyes! Do what thou wilt, I abandon myself to thee. In my perplexity I can do nothing for myself."*

Seneca, Euripides and Racine make Phaedra die in three different ways, and for three different reasons. According to the first, when she learns the tragic end of Hippolytus,—an end caused by the false and wicked accusation she brought against him in revenge for his refusal to listen to her—and sees the mangled remains of the miserable youth whom his father has sacrificed for her sake, she is seized with sudden remorse, and bursts into a paroxysm of fury. She throws herself in despair on to the body of Hippolytus, tearing her hair in her grief, acquaints Theseus with all the enormity of her fault, and with her perfidy; and as, in her judgment, death alone is a fit punishment for her misdeeds, she kills herself, with her own hand, stabbing herself with the dagger she holds, and presenting it to her consort.

Euripides in his *Hippolytus* makes Phaedra the victim of celestial vengeance, and, as such, worthy, in a sense, of pity. This is augmented when Phaedra, seeing the furious rage of Hippolytus, at the

---

*PHÆDRA: "Ah! je vois Hippolyte,
    Dans ses yeux insolents je vois ma perte écrite.
    Fais ce que tu voudras, je m'abandonne à toi;
    Dans le trouble où je suis, je ne puis rien pour
      moi. *Racine.*

indecent passion felt for him by his stepmother,* and revealed to him by the slave Œnone, overwhelmed by shame, enraged at the knowledge that Hippolytus knew of her love for him, and desirous to save herself from ignominy, decides to die, and accomplishes her fatal purpose by strangling herself with a rope. This climax would diminish the enormity of her guilt, and render Phaedra an object of compassion, were it not for the words Euripides makes Diana use to Theseus, after the terrible death of Hippolytus, and from these it is evident that Phaedra, before taking her own life, had conceived the wicked design of preparing a written document in which she accuses Hippolytus of having driven her to desperation, and caused her to do this dreadful deed in order to avoid being dishonored by him. This base and ignoble calumny causes her to become at once an object of scorn and loathing, and changes the pity that would otherwise have been felt for her into disgust and horror.

These are the lines which Euripides makes Diana address to Theseus—

> . . . τί τάλας τοῖσδε συνήδει,†
> παῖδ' οὐχ ὁσίως σὸν ἀποκτείνας,
> ψευδέσι μύθοις ἀλόχου πεισθεὶς
> ἀφανῆ; φανερὰ δ' εἷλεν σ' ἄτα

*   *   *   *   *

---

* According to mythology, Hippolytus was a son of Theseus, husband of Phaedra, by the Amazon Hippolyte.—*Translator.*

† See the *Hippolytus* of Euripides, lines 1286–1289 and 1310–1312. An approximate English translation runs as fol-

ἡ δ᾽ εἰς ἔλεγχον μὴ πέσῃ φοβουμένη,
ψευδεῖς γραφὰς ἔγραψε καὶ διώλεσε
δόλοισι σὸν παῖδ᾽, ἀλλ᾽ ὅμως ἔπεισέ σε.

Racine depicts the end of this Queen in more
noble fashion. Oppressed by the shame of having
revealed her improper passion to Hippolytus, crushed
by his scorn, and the horror with which he received
her avowal, quailing beneath the scrutinizing glance
of Theseus, feeling herself guilty, and driven wild
with jealousy at discovering in Aricia her more fortunate rival, dreading the wrath of her father Minos
when she should descend into Avernus, assailed by
remorse for having, when almost beside herself, consented to the perfidious insinuation of Œnone by
accusing Hippolytus of her fault—Phaedra swallows
one of the most potent poisons. And thus, already
bathed with the dews of death, she drags herself
before Theseus, summons all her little remaining
strength to her aid, and proclaims the innocence of
Hippolytus, her own fatal passion which she had im-
puted to him, and the perfidious consent she had
given to Œnone's proposal to accuse Hippolytus in
her stead. She asserts that she would have preferred
to end her life by the dagger, but that at any cost
she must first confess her crime, and her remorse,

---

lows:—"Because by an iniquitous death thou hast killed thy
son, O wretched man, art thou therefore pleased? A false and
vaguely worded paper written by thy consort hath led thee to
consent to this evil deed . . . but thy wife, terrified she would
be convinced of his fault, wrote lying words, and by her trickery
persuaded thee, and led thy son to his death."

and therefore she has selected a slow poison. She dies a lingering and agonizing death, unaware of the miserable end of Hippolytus.

That Phaedra was unaware of it is proved by the following lines; Panope, in Scene v., Act 5, comes breathless, to Theseus, saying—

PANOPE: "I am ignorant what project the Queen meditates,
My lord, but I fear everything from the transport which agitates her.
A mortal despair is paint on her countenance:
Her complexion has already the pallor of death.
Already driven with ignominy from her presence,
Œnone has cast herself into the deep sea—
Men know not what has driven her to this desperate act—
And the waters, closing over her, have hidden her for ever from our eyes."

THESEUS: "What do I hear?"

PANOPE: "Her death has not calmed the Queen;
Trouble seems to be growing in her uncertain soul.
Sometimes, to flatter her secret sorrow,
She takes her children, and bathes them in her tears;
Then, suddenly, renouncing all maternal love,
Her hand, with horror, pushes them away from her.
With uncertain steps she drags herself irresolutely, here and there.
Her wandering eyes recognize us no longer;
Three times she has commenced to write, and changed her mind.
Three times she has destroyed her hardly begun letter.
Deign to see her, my Lord, deign to succor her." *

---

* PANOPE: "J'ignore le projet que la reine médite,
Seigneur; mais je crains tout du transport qui l'agite

At the close of this scene Theramenes presents herself, and narrates, amidst her tears, the tragic end of Hippolytus, which happened near Mycenae, where his lacerated body was left. Nothing was known of this terrible accident in the royal palace, therefore it is evident Phaedra did not kill herself in despair at Hippolytus' death, but for the reason already stated.

Perhaps some people may consider as superfluous this minute comparison of the tragedies of Seneca, Euripides, and Racine, this analysis of the various ways in which they severally treat the personality of Phaedra—this detailed narration of incidents in Phaedra's life, as though its vicissitudes had been hitherto unknown. But in the hope that my studies may contain some interest for readers who have seen me on the stage, as well as for those who have not

---

Un mortel désespoir sur son visage est peint;
La pâleur de la mort est déjà sur son teint.
Déjà de sa présence avec honte chassée
Dans la profonde mer Œnone s'est lancée
On ne sait point d'où part ce dessein furieux;
Et les flots pour jamais l'ont ravie à nos yeux."

THESEUS: ' Qu'entends-je?"

PANOPE: "Son trepas n'a point calmé la reine;
Le trouble semble croître en son âme incertaine.
Quelque fois, pour flatter ses secrètes douleurs,
Elle prend ses enfants et les baigne de pleures;
Et soudain, renonçant à l'amour maternelle,
Sa main avec horreur les repousse loin d'elle;
Elle porte en hasard ses pas irrésolus;
Son œil tout égaré ne nous reconnait plus.
Elle a trois fois écrit, et, changeant de pensée,
Trois fois elle a rompu sa lettre commencée.
Daignez la voir, seigneur; daignez la secourir."

had the opportunity, I have thought it might be useful to give these important details, for the benefit of those who might not entirely remember them, in order that I might awaken within them a desire to know how I had elaborated my interpretation of the part—a matter of which the reader who has the patience to peruse the following pages, will be able to judge.

After the account I have given of the immense difficulty I encountered in my study of the personality of Myrrha, by Vittoria Alfieri, it would be natural to suppose that I should find that of Phaedra all the easier. And this is partly true, because the contrasts in the latter are less strange and difficult, but, at the same time, it must not be forgotten that the interpretations of these two characters have not a great deal in common, although they were both victims of the revenge of Venus.

It is to be noted, however, that Venus did not hate Phaedra, but Hippolytus, and, in causing Phaedra to conceive a powerful and incestuous passion, she selected her as the only means that was available to avenge herself on Hippolytus, because

"he had called her the worst of the goddesses, because he was backward to the laws of love, and because all his worship was given to Diana, daughter of Jove, whom alone he adored, proclaiming her ' the greatest of the gods.' "

These words Euripides puts into the mouth of Venus in the first scene of his tragedy. Myrrha, likewise, was the instrument of Venus' vengeance on her mother, Cecris, who had imprudently

"ventured to boast that she had a daughter, whose extraordinary beauty, grace, modesty, and wisdom attracted more people in Greece and the East than had ever in former times been drawn to the sacred worship of Venus."

The effect of such malediction launched against two such different natures would of course be entirely distinct. The one, a modest, chaste maiden, driven by a strange, mysterious influence to conceive an execrable passion, overwhelmed with horror at her own guilt, sought death in order to save herself from dishonor. The other, perfectly aware of the lengths to which her reprehensible feeling would carry her, gave way to it without the slightest effort at self-control, and put an end to her existence simply because she dreaded the revelation of a love which was not returned.

Myrrha died because her weak and youthful nature did not possess strength enough to enable her to dominate her ardent passion, of the discovery of which by its object she lived in daily dread, and she killed herself when, by an overpowering influence, the confession of her secret was wrung from her lips.

But Phaedra, fascinated and bewitched by the beauty of Hippolytus, recognized no obstacles to the accomplishment of her desires; with her own lips, and by her own free will, in passionate accents, and with burning looks, she revealed to the object of her love the flame that consumed her; and it was the knowledge that another woman was preferred to her that hastened her end, not any remorse for having wrongfully accused Hippolytus of her fault, and for leaving him to become the victim of his father's rage.

Having thus explained on what lines I conducted my psychological study of these two distinct personalities, who were under the power of an equally abnormal passion, and had therefore so many points in common, I will now proceed to explain more especially how I interpreted, studied, and represented the personality of Phaedra.

Racine precedes the entrance of Phaedra in the first Act by some lines spoken by the nurse Œnone, which picture the Queen in an almost dying state, and only anxious once more to behold the light of day. I think it necessary to quote them, in order that the reader may form a better idea of how I should be likely to appear on the stage.

> ŒNONE: "Alas! my lord! what trouble can be equal unto mine?
> The Queen doth fast approach her fatal end;
> 'Tis vain that night or day I leave her not,
> She dies in my arms of a malady she hides from me.
> Some evil influence disturbs her mind;
> Her grief distracts and tears her in her bed.
> She longs to see the day, and her profound sorrow
> Orders me to keep every one away from her." *

And in fact Phaedra enters, pale and prostrate, hardly able to stand, and supported by her maidens, while she scarcely retains strength enough to articulate.

It was my careful study to find the exact tone of

> *ŒNONE: "Helas! seigneur! quel trouble au mien peut être
> égal?
> La Reine touche presque à son terme fatal.
> En vain á l'observer jour et nuit je m'attache
> Elle meurt dans mes bras d'un mal qu'elle me
> cache;
> Un désordre éternel règne dans son esprit;
> Son chagrin inquiet l'arrache de son lit;
> Elle veut voir le jour, et sa douleur profonde
> M'ordonne toutefois d'ecarter tout le monde."

voice in which a person in Phaedra's condition would be likely to speak, a tone which would convey that her state of exhaustion was due to moral, not physical causes, and which could therefore be at once changed to a more joyous key should any unexpected or pleasant event occur.

Thus I repeated all passages expressive of weariness and discomfort, in recitative fashion, using a kind of doleful monotone. But when the strain of profound melancholy was interrupted by any extraneous suggestion that roused my feelings, my voice grew stronger, and more impulsive, as it were in spite of myself, for a moment, then sank suddenly down again within my chest, for lack of bodily vigor to maintain its pitch.

For example, Œnone reproaches Phaedra on account of her self-abandonment to a grief which is destroying her, for concealing it from every one, and such conduct, bringing misfortune upon her children, constrained, as they will be, to submit to a foreign yoke, that of the son of an Amazon, and she expresses herself thus :—

ŒNONE : "You offend the gods, the authors of your life;
　　　　You betray the husband to whom you plighted your troth.
　　　　And you betray, too, your miserable children,
　　　　Whom you precipitate into a miserable bondage.
　　　　Think that the same day that takes from them their mother,
　　　　Will give hope to the son of the stranger,
　　　　To that fierce enemy of you and yours,
　　　　That child which an Amazon has carried in her bosom,
　　　　That Hippolyte.

PHÆDRA: Oh, Heavens!
ŒNONE: This reproach touches you!
PHÆDRA: Wretched woman! what name has escaped your
      lips!" *

This dialogue is an exact imitation of Euripides.
During the utterance of these lines I remained, at
first, as though I were insensible, and I paid little
heed to the reproaches of Œnone until she began to
speak of the children. But when she said to me:

    "You will give hope to the son of the stranger,"

my body shuddered, and during the two succeeding
lines—

    "To that fierce enemy of you and yours;
      That child which an Amazon has carried in her bosom."

my prostration ceased, my brow darkened, my whole
person trembled, I gasped for breath. But when I
heard the words,

      "That Hippolyte!"

the repetition of the fatal name drew a sudden cry of
pain from my agonized heart;

    "Miserable woman! what name has escaped your lips!"

---

* ŒNONE: "Vous offensez les dieux, auteurs de votre vie;
        Vous trahissez l'époux à qui la foi vous lié;
        Vous trahissez, enfin, vos enfants malheureux,
        Que vous precipitez sous un joug rigoureux.
        Songez qu'un même jour leur ravira leur mère,
        Et rendra espérance au fils de l'étrangère,
        A ce fier ennemi de vous, de votre sang,
        Ce fils qu'une Amazone a porté dans son flanc,
        Cet Hippolyte.
  PHÆDRA: Ah Dieux!
  ŒNONE: Ce reproache vous touche!
  PHÆDRA: Malheureuse! quel nom est sorti de ta bouche!"

I cried in my agony, and I fell back upon my chair. At last, in answer to the renewed entreaties of Œnone that I would reveal the cause of my anguish, I resolved to speak, but my voice came with difficulty, and it only gained strength again when I began to deplore, in a plaintive tone, the fate of the mother and sister who were also victims to the hatred of the implacable goddess, and to the question asked in the greatest anxiety by Œnone—

"Do you love?"*

I replied in a hopeless tone, like a wild beast who has received its death-wound,

"I am suffering all the pangs of love!"†

My impetuosity reached its culminating point when, after Œnone had exclaimed,

"Hippolyte! great Heaven!" ‡

I answered with quick resentment—

"It is you who have named him!" §

and, making a long pause, I remained standing in a scornful attitude. But when the paroxysm was over my recovered energies once more abandoned me, and I fell back again on my chair.

After a glance round to assure myself that no one was listening, I began to narrate the origin of my fatal love, and the pretexts that had been invented to

---

* "Aimez-vous?"
† "De l'amour j'ai toutes les fureurs."
‡ "Hippolyte! grand dieux!"
§ "C'est toi qui l'a nommé!"

separate Hippolytus from me, and I commenced speaking in a faint, hoarse voice, in order to show the state of prostration to which the preceding mental struggle had reduced me. But as I continued my narrative, by degrees I grew more animated, and when I began to express the ineffable delight which the remembrance of the dear countenance of Hippolytus brought to my heart, my own face was irradiated.

> "In vain upon the altars my hand burnt the incense ;
> When my mouth uttered the name of the goddess,
> I adored Hippolytus. I beheld him everywhere,
> Even at the foot of the altar where I offered sacrifice,
> I offered all to the divinity I dare not name." *

The appearance of my attendant, Panope, recalled me to myself. I resumed my wonted dignity, gathered together my wandering fancies, but at the announcement she made to me of the death of Theseus, my whole appearance underwent a sudden change, expressive of a mixture of amazement, surprise, and ill-concealed joy at finding how unexpectedly the obstacle which interposed to prevent the completion of my desires, had been removed. I controlled myself with an effort, hiding my thought even from the faithful Œnone. Then, when Panope had gone away, I listened to the flattering words of the nurse with the complacency of one who staggers beneath the weight

---

* "En vain sur les autels ma main brûlait l'incens ;
Quand ma bouche implorait le nom de la déesse,
J'adorais Hippolyte, et la voyant sans cesse,
Même au pied des autels que je faisais fumer,
J'offrais tout à ce dieu que je n'osais nommer."

of some unexpected happiness, which he dare not allow himself to believe in, lest it should vanish like a beautiful dream. While Œnone continued her discourse, endeavoring to persuade me that now I might see Hippolytus without fear, and that my passion had nothing singular about it since the obstacle had been removed that made it culpable, I turned my person in such a way that she could not perceive my face, which I had prudence enough still further to hide from view with the rich and ample veil that enveloped me from head to foot. Thus I was able, by means of a by-play in accordance with the feelings that agitated me, to express to the public how the words of the faithful nurse acted like a healing balm on my lacerated heart, and brought me back once more to life and love. Then, dissimulating the real reason of my change, I allowed it to be guessed that consideration and affection for my son was the sole motive that decided me to cling to life, and causing Œnone to precede me, I leant my right hand on her shoulder, and quitted the stage with slow steps, as though my limbs had not yet re-acquired their pristine vigor.

The renowned La Harpe holds that Phaedra did really determine to live for the *sake of her son*, but such is not my opinion, and the words used by her in her confession of her love for Hippolytus confirm my idea, and I will further prove it by arguments which must, it seems to me, be admitted just.

During the second Act, in the admirable scene* of

---

* This scene is a copy of that in the second Act of Seneca's tragedy of Hippolytus, adapted by Racine with inimitable art, and the greatest effect.

the interview between Phaedra and Hippolytus, I make my appearance with uncertain steps, urged and encouraged by the nurse, Œnone, to recommend my child to his care, but I consider that this was simply a pretext to discover the feelings of Hippolytus. Had it been otherwise, Phaedra fearing, as she feared, the irresistible ascendency the man she loved possessed over her, and feeling the fascination he exercised upon her senses, would have avoided every occasion of meeting, lest she should betray and lower herself. I was so convinced of this, that at the beginning of the scene my words came slowly and with difficulty from my lips, as I said—

> "I come to unite my tears to your sorrow,
> I come to you, as to a son, to explain my trouble."*

The Italian translator of Racine's play has rendered these lines as follows :—

> "De' miei propri affanni,
> Vorrei parlarti . . e . . di mio figlio."

and the punctuation indicates, what the disjointed character of the words proves, that, Francesco dall' Ongaro was of my opinion ; and his conclusion is confirmed by the manner in which both the author and the Italian translator return to the subject in the succeeding passage, which in English runs thus :—

> " If you should hate me, I should not complain of it,
> My lord ; you have seen me strive to hurt you ;
> But you could not read to the bottom of my heart ;

---

* "A vos douleurs je viens joindre mes larmes ;
Je vous viens pour un fils, expliquer mes larmes."

I have sought to offer myself to your enmity,
I would not suffer you to approach the shores which I inhabit;
In public and in private I have declared against you,
And desired that seas should roll between us.
I have even decreed by an express law
That no one should dare to pronounce your name before me.
If, however, by the offence is measured the pain,
If hate alone can attract your hate,
Then, never was woman more worthy of pity,
And less worthy, my lord, of your enmity."

We give the Italian translation referred to above, and the French original, in a note.*

---

*PHÆDRA: "Nè che tu m' odii gia t' accusa! Avversa
  Sempre a te mi vedesti, e in cor, signore,
  Leggermi in cor tu non potevi. Io stessa
  Esca all' odio porgea, che non soffersi
  Viver con te sulla medesima terra.
  Nemica tua, non che segreta, aperta,
  Volli che il mar ci separasse: imposi
  Che niuno osasse innanzi a me nomarti;
  Grave torto, lo so; ma se la pena
  Dee l' offesa uguagliar, se l' odio solo
  Grida vendetta, non vi fa giammai
  Donna più degna della tua pietade
  E men degna, signor, dell' odio tuo!"

In the French the passage runs as follows:—

"Quand vous me hairiez, je ne m'en plaindrais pas,
  Seigneur; vous m'avez vue attachée a vous nuire.
  Dans le fond de mon cœur vous ne pouviez pas lire;
  A vôtre inimitié j'ai pris soin de n'offrir;
  Aux bords que j'habitais je n'ai pu vous souffrir;
  En public, en secret contre vous declarée,
  J'ai voulu par des mers en être separée;
  J'ai même défendu par une expresse loi
  Qu'on osât prononcer vôtre nom devant moi.

These last lines are not at all such as would be
likely to be spoken by a woman anxious to conceal
her real sentiments; they are rather the utterance of
one who wraps up in a circumlocution of words and
phrases, with a double meaning, an idea whose true
significance she desires to make understood. Convinced for all these reasons of the justice of my
interpretation, I decided to speak the passage in a
manner which should convey unmistakably the *double
entendre* I felt it contained ; and I accompanied these
words with lightning glances, which, taken in con-
junction with the tone of my voice, showed the effort
I was putting on myself to restrain the passion which
was devouring me, and which I could hardly refrain
from manifesting openly. Later on, I showed the
audience by my gestures how deeply wounded I was
that Hippolytus had not understood me, and when
the latter, believing in Phaedra's repentance for the
hatred which she had borne to him, sought to excuse
her conduct by saying that every other mother would
have behaved in like manner to a step-son, whose
love for her own children made her jealous, I, feeling
that the passionate restraint I had laid upon myself
was beginning to affect him, attempted once more to
make him understand me, by saying in a slightly
impatient tone—

Si pourtant à l'offense on mesure la peine,
Si la haine put seule attirer la haine,
Jamais femme ne fut plus digne de pitié
Et moins digne, seigneur, de vôtre inimitié."

Racine.

"Ah! my lord, I dare to protest that Heaven has exempted me from this common law.
It is a very different care which troubles and preys upon me."*

But, as gradually the scene progressed, I was no longer able to control the passion that possessed me. The revelation of it burst from me suddenly, as a stream that has been dammed up overflows its banks. Voice, gestures, and accent, all united to express the idea that I was in the condition of one inebriated with love, of one who cares for neither modesty, sobriety, or dignity, provided only she can enjoy the forbidden and guilty delight she so ardently desires.

And Hippolytus scorned. Suddenly my eyes were opened, and with a shudder that convulsed my whole person, I recognized in his conduct the influence of the terrible Eumenides. With the speed of lightning I seized the sword he had dropped, after drawing it in his first irresistible impulse to slay me, and turned it against my own breast. At this moment, Œnone, who had been listening unseen, rushed forward, threw herself upon me, seized my arm, though she did not succeed in wrenching the weapon from my grasp, and by main force dragged me from the stage. This most perilous scene with Hippolytus has great difficulty for an actress, because if she overpasses by a hairbreadth the line laid down by scenic propriety, the

---

*"Ah! seigneur! que le ciel, j'ose ici l'attester,
De cette loi commune a voulu m'exempter!
Qu'un soin bien different me trouble et me devore."

Racine.

16

audience would find the situation repulsive, and the effect would be greatly injured.

The first scene of the third Act, between Phaedra and Œnone, consists only of an alternation and succession of reproaches, remorse, hopes, fears, rage, illusions, and contrary plans.

How Hippolytus has grown odious in her eyes because of the humiliation he has inflicted on her! How she excuses him, and blames herself for having judged with too great severity the inexperienced youth, ignorant of the laws of love! In this perplexity she devises a means to retain his heart, which speedily absorbs all her thought, and she makes her faithful Œnone her messenger. But when she hears from her devoted and terrified nurse that Theseus is still alive, that he will shortly stand before her, I assumed, with a rapid transition, the attitude of one who is almost petrified by the sudden and amazing news she has received. In a voice so indistinct that it is little more than a murmur, I say—

"My husband is living, O Œnone! that is enough.
I have made the unworthy confession of a love that outrages him.
He lives, and I wish to know no more."*

and I repeat the words "that is enough," in a tone implying "all is over for me."

From this moment the idea of seeing myself confronted by my outraged consort, of not daring to

---

* "Mon époux est vivant.   O Œnone, c'est assez.
J'ai fait l'indigne aveu d un amour qui l'outrage.
Il vit, je ne veux pas en savoir d'avantage."

meet his look for very shame, began to fill me with a terror that overmastered me. I grew delirious, everything about me seemed "to gain voice and words," in order to apprise Theseus of my fault.

By this manifestation of total physical weakness and mental aberration, I sought to account in some measure for the ready consent which Phaedra gives to Œnone's infernal proposal, and I succeeded in showing how oppressed I was with an immeasurable dread of the appearance of Theseus and Hippolytus. Those better impulses which had caused me instinctively to reject Œnone's infamous proposal when it was first made, had now deserted me. In the utter impossibility of avoiding a meeting with my husband, I addressed to him the few lines which tell of my profound grief, my bitter remorse, as well as the shame I felt at appearing before my outraged consort, and the man who was the fatal cause of my trouble.

Full of confusion, and feeling that I had not strength to utter another word, I fled precipitately.

Most masterly is the fourth Act of this tragedy, in which the transcendent genius of Racine is fully revealed. He has most certainly not been influenced either by Euripides or Seneca, in the arrangement of this part of the classic work. It is rather modelled on Shakespeare, and shows all the devious workings of a human soul, and the causes and effects which have produced its disorganization.

When Phaedra, repentant, and tormented by remorse, comes trembling to Theseus to implore clemency for his son, and perhaps also to reveal the falsity of the accusation made against him, it might be plainly seen from my face, and from the way I spoke, what an effort and struggle it had been to me to decide on this step.

I uttered my first words after I came upon the stage in a supplicating tone, with my eyes fixed upon the ground, because I had not the courage to meet the anger of my husband when he heard the truth.

On learning from Theseus that Hippolytus "dared to insult the character of Phaedra by accusing her of lying," I bent down my head towards the ground, as though humiliated, and confused, and desirous to conceal my shame in the depths of the earth.

But when I further heard that " Aricia only was the woman Hippolytus openly confessed he loved, who only possessed his heart and his troth," the power of art worked such a complete transformation in my appearance that the spectator was overpowered by it.

I heard no more what Theseus said, I remained insensible to everything he preferred against his son, I understood only the tremendous revelation he had made to me.

Left alone, I gave vent, little by little, to the fury I had restrained until that moment. My whole being was penetrated by the dreadful truth, which in an instant had struck death to my heart. Then, slowly, in a tone of the most bitter scorn, and a voice growing in power as I proceeded, I uttered the stupendous lines in which are revealed, one by one, all the torments of a wonderful spirit :—

    " Hippolytus can feel, and yet feels nothing for me !
    Aricia has his heart, Aricia has his faith !

Ah! Heavens! when the inexorable ingrate
Armed himself against my wishes, with such a proud
    eye, and haughty countenance,
I thought his heart was for ever steeled against love,
Was equally adamant to all my sex.
And yet, another has conquered his audacity,
In his cruel eyes another has found favor." *

To the scorn which was akin to simulation, succeeded an explosion of wrath, as I exclaimed—

    " I am the sole object he cannot bear." †

And, no longer able to restrain my impestuous rage,
I paced to and fro upon the stage; then, seeing
Œnone, I ran precipitately towards her, to inform
her of what I had learnt. With savage fury I recalled one by one the terrors, the burning desires,
the torments I had suffered, in order to show that they
were all as nothing in comparison with the tremendous
grief which at that moment racked my heart. My
mind, unsettled from the burning dart of jealousy
that was rankling in my bosom, could only see the
image of my preferred rival, smiling, and in sweet
converse with Hippolytus! This imaginary joy

---

   * " Hippolyte est sensible, et ne sent rien pour moi !
     Aricie a son cœur, Aricie a sa foix !
     Ah ! Dieux ! lorsqu'à mes vœux l'ingrat inexorable
     S'armait d'un œil si fier, d'un front si redoutable,
     Je pensais qu'à l'amour son cœur fermé
     Fût contre tout mon sexe égalment armé.
     Une autre, cependant, a fleché son audace,
     Devant ses yeux cruels une autre a trouvé grace."

   † " Je suis le seul objet qu'il ne saurait souffrir."

seemed to kill me, the idea of the felicity of these two souls was insupportable.

The thought of vengeance flashed across my mind. I had already given Œnone instructions to murder Aricia, when I stayed her hand, because I wished that my own should do the bloody deed. I listened now only to the dictates of jealousy, that venomous asp which was rending my bosom. It seemed to me well to induce my husband to punish my rival, by stirring up his hatred against the family to which she belonged; then for a moment reverting to myself, I was constrained to meditate on my own faults, the enormity of which had driven me entirely beside myself.

Mad as I was, it seemed to me that I breathed only incest—lies. I desired to dip my avenging hand in innocent blood.

I saw, I discerned nothing more; in my delirium I felt myself transported to the presence of my father, Minos, the great judge of lost souls in hell. Already it seemed to me that the fatal urn, in which are enclosed the decrees containing the punishment inflicted on the departed, fell from his hands, while he strove to devise a sharper punishment for me. I fancied I saw him fling himself upon me to kill me, and with a bitter scream I made as though he was already grasping me by the hair. I writhed about in my efforts to escape his fatal grasp. I pressed my hands against my head to try and avoid that furious anger, and with a cry of anguish I exclaimed—

"Pardon! a cruel god has betrayed thy family:
Recognize his vengeance in the passions of thy daughter.

> Alas! my sorrowful heart has gathered no fruit
> From the frightful crime whose shame follows me;
> Pursued by evil to my latest moment,
> I lay down my life in torment," *

and I fell fainting to the ground.

In order to increase the scenic effect, I had arranged that after a *long pause* Œnone should fall on her knees beside me, and with kindly and persuasive words raise my inanimate form, until it rested partially upon her knees, while I slowly, and gradually, recovered my scattered senses, and broke out into reproaches against her. Hearing her assert, in her anxiety to condone my fault, that the gods themselves had committed it, I gradually regained sufficient strength to withdraw from her, and let her see with what scorn and anger I received her suggestion; but when I crossed to the other side of the stage the nurse followed me, and falling at my feet, and clasping my knees, entreated pardon. Then I turned upon her in all my rage, and hurled at her Racine's celebrated invective, so justly famous in French literature.

> "Away, execrable monster!
> Leave me, the sport of my miserable fate.
> May a just Heaven render thee worthy payment!
> And may thy punishment for ever terrify

> * "Pardonne! un dieu cruel a perdu ta famille:
> Reconnais se vengeance aux fureurs de ta fille.
> Hélas! du crime affreux dont la honte me suit
> Jamais mon triste cœur n'a recueilli le fruit;
> Jusqu'au dernier soupir de malheurs poursuivie,
> Je rends dans les tourments une penible vie."

> All those who, like thee, nourish by cowardly dexterity
> The failings of weak princes,
> Urging them to go the way to which their heart inclines,
> And smoothing for them the road to crime.
> Detestable flatterers!   Most unhappy present
> That celestial anger can make to kings!" *

and in a paroxysm of fury I disappeared from view.

The fifth Act presents no great difficulty in its interpretation.

Phaedra only shows herself for a moment at the end of the tragedy.   She is dying, supported by her attendants, the victim of the poison she had swallowed to still for ever the fearful pangs of remorse for the faults committed through fatal blindness.

In a spent voice, I unfold to my husband my incestuous passion and the false accusation brought against Hippolytus, but as the effects of the deadly draught grow more potent, the words come less and less distinctly from my lips.   As my agony increased I was placed in my easy-chair, and I breathed my last with my body half-falling from the grasp of one attendant, while all the other people were kneeling around me, in sign of their deep grief and reverent respect.

---

* " Monstre execrable,
Va ; laisse-moi, le soin de mon sort deplorable,
Puisse le juste ciel dignement te payer !
Et puisse ton supplice à jamais effrayer
Tous ceux qui, comme toi, par des lâches addresses
Des princes malheureux nourrissant les faiblesses,
Les poussant au penchant où leur cœur est inclin,
Et leur osent du crime aplanir le chemin.
Detestables flatteurs ! présent le plus funeste
Que puisse faire aux rois la colère céleste ! "

CHAPTER XI.

LADY MACBETH.

THE study of this character presented the greatest difficulties to me.   For I saw in Lady Macbeth, not merely a woman actuated by low passions and vulgar instincts, but rather a gigantic conception of perfidy, dissimulation, and hypocrisy, combined by the master hand of Shakespeare into a form of such magnitude that it might well dismay any actress of great dramatic power.

Long and close examination led me to conclude that Lady Macbeth was animated less by affection for her husband than by excessive ambition to share the throne which seemed within his reach.   She was well aware of his mental inferiority to herself, of his innate weakness of character and indolence of disposition, that was not to be stimulated into action, even by the thirst for power which was consuming him, and she therefore made use of him as a means for attaining her own ends, and took advantage of the unbounded influence her strong masculine nature and extraordinary personal fascination enabled her to exercise over him, to instill into his mind the first idea of crime in the most natural way, and with the most persuasive arguments.

Not that Macbeth himself was without proclivities towards evil.   Shakespeare plainly shows the germs

(249)

of ambition, and the chimerical fancies that existed in his brain, and were carefully hidden from every one, solely because they seemed impossible of realization. And his real nature cannot be better described than in the first soliloquy put into the mouth of Lady Macbeth, who, with her profound perspicacity, had comprehended every shade of his character. This will be brought out more fully when I come to analyze the message. It would have seemed easier to credit Lady Mecbeth with some feelings of personal tenderness for her husband, had it not been that she was to share the power and dignity with him; but this being so, I maintain that it was not merely ambition and love for her consort which led her to instigate him to evil, but also her desire to mount the throne. It is Lady Macbeth all through who lures on her hesitating husband to commit the deed from which his more cowardly nature shrinks. It is she who tauntingly reminds him of his oath, who reproaches him with pusillanimity; and when he still hesitates, it is she who declares she would drag her infant from her breast, and dash its brains out, sooner than break her plighted word. It is difficult to credit a woman of this kind with any of the feelings of ordinary humanity.

But my own idea on the subject did not prevent the continuing of my studies with the greatest diligence. I made myself thoroughly acquainted with the play and with the interpretations given of it by the most eminent *artistes*. I read all the literature I could obtain on the subject, and my pleasure may be imagined, when I found, in *The Nineteenth Century*

Magazine for February, 1878, the magnificent paper on Mrs. Siddons, and her acting in the character of Lady Macbeth, by Mr. G. J. Bell, Professor of Jurisprudence in the University of Edinburgh. Amongst many other interesting passages I should like to quote the following :—

> Her (Lady Macbeth's) turbulent and inhuman strength of spirit does all. She turns Macbeth to her purpose, makes him her mere instrument, guides, directs, and inspires the whole plot. Like his evil genius she hurries him on in the mad career of ambition and cruelty from which his nature would have shrunk.

Having thus shown, as I flatter myself, both by arguments and undeniable evidence, that my interpretation of the personality of Lady Macbeth is probably very similar to that which Shakespeare conceived, and portrayed both in his own words and by the nature of the facts, I will pass on to analyze several other important points in this difficult part.

Much criticism has been expended upon the way in which the letter, sent by Macbeth from the camp to his wife, should be read. Shakespeare represents Lady Macbeth as coming upon the stage with it in her hands, but many persons consider that natural anxiety to know its contents would have made her tear it open at once, without waiting until she could read it to the audience.

Instead of which, it seems to me far from likely that Shakespeare, who was as great a philosopher as he was a poet, and who possessed a marvellous insight into human nature, should have availed himself of the frivolous expedient of making Lady Macbeth read her letter aloud upon the stage, simply to inform the spectators of its contents, and show the intense mental struggle she must have gone through prior to appearing before them. Only an inexperi- enced writer of small inventive power and a novice in his craft would have resorted to such a puerile device.

It would have been far beneath the great genius who passed from the sublime to the beautiful with the rapidity of lightning.

The intention of the author certainly seems to have been to represent Lady Macbeth as receiving the note at the moment she appears upon the scene, and such a representation must be most simple and natural. Presenting herself, anxious and agitated, she makes the public understand that, by means of the writing she holds in her hands, she would prob- ably be able to reveal to them events which would change her whole future existence and raise her to the summit of greatness, provided that circumstances should conduce to the fulfilment of the designs work- ing in her mind.

I decided to read the letter straight through, and as if, in coming on the stage, I had already made myself acquainted with its first words, only pausing after those sentences which told how recent events had actually seemed to fulfil the prophecies long ago made to her. Thus, when I found that the three fatal sisters had vanished into thin air, after predict- ing Macbeth's great future, and greeting him with " Hail ! King that shall be ! " my expression was one of mingled awe, and superstitious amazement. Then when I finished the letter I made a long pause, as though to allow time for my mind to analyze each phrase wherein the supernatural powers pointed out the destiny I had had prefigured to me as likely to be accomplished.

But, afterwards, I remained for a moment sad and doubtful, considering and fearing the weak nature of my consort. However, reflecting on the most salient points of the message, I said :—

"Glamis thou art, and Cawdor thou shalt be,"

and to the last three words, "thou shalt be," I gave a supernatural emphasis and expression.

I was much gratified later on, by finding from the excellent article by Professor Bell, to which I have already referred, that Mrs. Siddons was also accustomed to declaim this passage in " a lofty, prophetic tone, as though the whole future had been revealed to her soul," and that she accentuated the words "thou shalt be " just as I did.

This is another convincing proof that Mrs. Siddons understood equally well the importance of analyzing the contents of the letter, of pondering every phrase of it, and of transmitting its mystic signification to the public, even amidst her deep fever of ambition, and naturally her expression of it would have been very different if she had been aware of what the paper contained before coming upon the stage.

I considered that I should be acting logically, and in accordance with the spirit of the words, if, while I spoke the following lines describing the character of Macbeth, I imagined him already standing by my side, and I therefore fixed my stern and piercing gaze upon his supposed figure, as though I would wrench from him the most hidden secrets of his soul, and imprint my own words upon his mind in letters of fire.

> " Yet do I fear thy nature;
> It is too full o' the milk of human kindness,
> To catch the nearest way.   Thou would'st be great;
> Art not without ambition, but without
> The illness should attend it.   What thou would'st highly,
> That would'st thou holily; would'st not play false,
> And yet would'st wrongly win; thou'dst have great Glamis,
> That which cries, thus thou must do, if thou have it;
> And that which rather thou dost fear to do,
> Thou wishest should be undone."

Then, to show that my pre-occupation had ceased, and that I ardently desired the return of my husband to begin and weave the web of evil arts and spells, as I spoke the lines—

> " Hie thee hither
> That I may pour my spirit in thine ear;
> And chastise with the valor of my tongue
> All that impedes thee from the golden round,
> Which faith and metaphysical aid doth seem
> To have thee crowned withal."

I returned to the left side of the stage where the entrance might be supposed to be (and where Macbeth might be expected to enter), while to express the cessation of my reflections, I began to form in my own mind the plan which the reading of the letter naturally suggested to me.

The terrible soliloquy in this scene, which follows the departure of the attendant, who has announced his master's speedy arrival, reveals all the perfidy and cruelty of this woman, who was neither more nor less than a monster in human shape, and shows with what supernatural powers she arms herself in order to succeed in leading her husband to become the instrument of her ambition. In one word, she is henceforth 'Macbeth's evil genius. With him it is still a question of " I Will," or " I will not." This woman, this serpent, masters him, holds him fast in her coils, and no human power will come to rescue him from them. In consequence I uttered the first words of this monologue in a hollow voice, with bloodthirsty eyes, and with the accent of a spirit speaking from out of some abyss, and, as I continued, my voice grew louder and more resonant, until it changed into an exaggerated cry of joy at the sight of my husband.

Throughout the following scene with Macbeth I preserved a cold, dignified, and calm demeanor, and I ignored the trivial scruples with which he received my guilty suggestions, as totally unworthy of consideration, confident that his weak and irresolute nature must eventually succumb to my stronger one. I conceived the plan of making use of by-play at the exit of the two personages to impress the overwhelming influence I exercised over him, silencing any further remonstrances on his part, by drawing his left arm round my waist. In this attitude I took his right hand in mine, and placing the first finger on my lips swore him thus to silence. Then I gradually and gently pushed him behind the scenes, towards which his back was now turned. All this was accomplished with as much delicacy and so many magnetic looks, that Macbeth had to own their fascination, and yield to my will.

The hypocrisy and feigned humility of Lady Macbeth when she went out afterwards to meet King Duncan, were excessive, and it was with most perfidious, yet well chosen words, that she invited the good old monarch to enter the Castle. In the subsequent scene with her husband, there are two things which it is necessary to delineate correctly and bring out in the most striking colors. First, the contrast between her wicked arts, when she energetically rebukes Macbeth for his cowardly fickleness in not wishing to see himself in that place he recently so much desired, because of a puerile awakening of conscience, and second, the infernal skill with which she tries to persuade him that the crime is easy, simple, and natural, and impossible to be discovered. Various are the terrible passages in this masterly scene ; that, when she reproaches him for having left the supper table so hastily that his absence might well excite comments, and he replies by imploring her to forget the evil scheme, and not make him guilty of the basest ingratitude, she answers :—

> " Was the hope drunk
> Wherein you dressed yourself ?   Hath it slept since ?
> And wakes it now to look so green and pale
> At what it did so freely ?   From this time,
> Such I account my love.   Art thou afraid
> To be the same in thine own act and valor,
> As thou art in desire ?   Would'st thou have that
> Which thou esteem'st the ornament of life,
> And live a coward in thine own esteem;
> Letting *I dare not*, wait upon *I would*,
> Like the poor cat i' the adage ? " *

---

* The proverb registered by Haywood in 1865, runs as follows :—" The cat would have fish, but dare not wet her feet."

MACBETH : Prythee, peace,
   I dare do all that may became a man,
   Who dare do more is none."

Lady Macbeth (terrified lest her ambitions have been raised only to be disappointed), cries in fiendish tones :—

" What beast was it then,
That made you break this enterprise to me?
When you durst do it, then you were a man;
And to be more than what you were, you would
Be so much more the man. Nor time, nor place
Did then adhere, and yet you would make both :
They have made themselves, and that their fitness now
Does unmake you. I have given suck; and know
How tender 'tis to love the babe that milks me :
I would, while it was smiling in my face,
Have plucked my nipple from his boneless gums,
And dashed the brains out, had I so sworn, as you
Have done to this ! "

Here the perplexity which is Macbeth's characteristic induces him to ask his consort impatiently—

" If we should fail ? "

to which she replies in a scornful tone—

" We fail !
But screw your courage to the sticking place,
And we'll not fail. Here Duncan is asleep,
(Whereto the rather shall his hard day's journey
Soundly invite him) his two chamberlains
Will I with wine and wassail so convince,
That memory, the warder of the brain,
Shall be a fume, and the receipt of reason
A limbeck only : When in swinish sleep
Their drenched natures lie, as in a death,
What cannot you and I perform upon

17

The unguarded Duncan? What not put upon
His spongy officers; who shall bear the guilt of our great
    quell."

The second Act may be dismissed in a few words, as the situations in it are quite clear, and arise naturally out of the progress of the action, and they offer no difficulty in interpretation, although embracing the dreadful vigils, and fearful agony of mind endured by Lady Macbeth. It is easy to understand the anxiety she felt to know the result of her well-laid schemes for the murder of Duncan, her joy at its completion, and the agitation into which the frenzy and remorse of her miserable husband would be sure to throw her. The repeated and incessant knocking at the gate of the Castle, which began at this precise moment, would be another source of alarm, because Macbeth's state of utter prostration might draw suspicion upon him, and lead to the discovery of the plans conceived in her mind with so much satanic skill.

The situations in the third Act are of great importance, and I therefore give a most minute and careful analysis of them, in order to make apparent that I had tried to seize the precise meaning intended by the author. In this Act, which shows, more than any other, the wonderful genius of Shakespeare, Lady Macbeth can give much additional force, if not by words, at any rate by her skilful by-play, and can increase or diminish its many dramatic beauties. For example, according to my interpretation, the entrance of the assassin who comes to announce the murder of Banquo, and the attempt on the life of his son

Fleance to Macbeth, and which causes him to experience two such great but varying emotions, would not escape the vigilant eyes of Lady Macbeth. Therefore, at the sight of the assassin, who presents himself on the threshold, she alone perceives him speaking in subdued tones to her husband, notes the repressed movements, and keeps him constantly in view. For she fears some imprudence on the part of Macbeth, remembering that he had told her shortly before, that a great thing would soon happen, which would amaze her.

I considered that in this scene Lady Macbeth would be terribly afraid lest the guests should observe this strange colloquy, in such a place, and at such a moment, and might conceive grave suspicions which would defeat all their projects. Hence I found it necessary and opportune to engage in a kind of double by-play, that is to say, with an air of the greatest courtesy to take part in the conversation of the guests, and the toasts they drank to me, remaining, however, always upon their seats, while at intervals I cast furtive and timorous glances towards the group made by my husband and the murderer.

At last, in order to make Macbeth aware of the danger he ran of betraying himself by some imprudence, I said in a clear voice, and with much ostentation of gayety :—

" My lord,
You do not give the cheer, the feast is cold
That is not often touched, while 'tis a making,
'Tis given with welcome ; to feed were best at home
From thence the sauce to meat is ceremony.
Meeting were bare without it."

With the same by-play, but in a yet more distinct tone of voice, in which an accent of reproof mingled with my half serious, half facetious words, I gave another warning—

> " My worthy lord,
> Our noble friends do lack you,"—

in such a way, however, that I made Macbeth alone understand, by the power of my significant glances, what this second appeal really meant.

This was apparently justified by my insinuations that he was wanting in courtesy to his guests, and was neglecting them. Afterwards, I experienced the greatest agitation and dismay at the discovery of Macbeth's incomprehensible and frightful visions, seeing him on the point of revealing all the secret of our crimes. Evidently, in this situation, every expression used by Lady Macbeth, and every effort made by her to hide the hallucinations of her husband, and bring him back to himself by the most bitter although subdued reproofs, required the closest study, for it is essential to remember that an appearance of gayety must be preserved upon the countenance whenever it is turned towards the guests, in order to excuse the strange demeanor of the husband on the ground of an ancient malady.

At last, when the increasing frenzy of Macbeth rendered vain every effort to restrain him, his wife was obliged to dismiss her guests in an agony of fear, in order to remain alone with him, and put an end to a situation which had become both impossible and dangerous.

From the moment of their departure I dated the commencement of the mental prostration of their unhappy hostess, which ended at last in total derangement. In order to justify this, I found it necessary to imagine some by-play which should convey an idea of her depression and discouragement, possessed as I was by the sad conviction that it was in vain to fight against destiny, which had become adverse with lightning-like rapidity. I let it be seen how remorse had begun to torment me.

At the close of the Act, at the moment of disappearing, I showed that I experienced a feeling of pity for Macbeth, rendered by my means the most miserable of men, and in saying to him,

" You lack the season of all natures—sleep."

I took his left hand in my right, leaned against his shoulder, and then, with my head now bent towards the ground in an attitude of sorrowful meditation, now raised to heaven with an expression of dismay, now turning towards my husband with a look full of vivid remorse that agitated my soul, I drew him gently towards our room, in the same way that one would lead an exhausted maniac. Then, when we reached the limits of the scene, I made Macbeth, who was terrified by a fold of his mantle getting between his feet, have another fearful paroxysm. With a sudden rush he passed to the other side. Frightened, yet forcing myself to master my own terror, I could not help, in spite of my efforts, letting the public see I was shaken, but with a gentle violence, I succeeded in pushing Macbeth behind the scenes, endeavoring to calm him by affectionate means.

This by-play, which was in strict accordance with the spirit of the scene, always produced an immense effect upon my audience.

Lady Macbeth has only one short scene in the fifth Act, but it is one of Shakespeare's most magnificent conceptions, and tries the powers of an actress to the uttermost. This woman, this colossus of physical and moral force, who, by a word, had the power of conceiving and bringing into execution plots hatched with such infernal power that only an assembly of demons could have succeeded with them—behold her! reduced to the ghost of her former self by the effects of that remorse which gnawed like a vulture at her heart, her reason disturbed until she became so unconscious of herself as to reveal her tremendous secret in her sleep. *Sleep*, did I say? It is rather a fever which mounts to her brain, which makes her drowsy, and only the physical suffering overmastering her spirit with the record of the evil of which it is the cause, controls and regulates her movements, and turns all her ideas astray. This is proved by her attendant's words to the Doctor :—

"Since his Majesty went into the field, I have seen her rise from her bed, thrown her nightgown upon her, unlock her closet, take forth paper, fold it, write upon it, read it, afterwards seal it, and again return to bed; yet all this while in a most fast sleep."

It cost me long and most anxious study to represent this artificial and duplex manifestation, melting the effects one into the other without falling into exaggeration at every change of manner, voice, or expression of my face. I came upon the scene looking like an automaton, and dragging my feet after me as though they were weighted with lead ; mechanically I placed my lamp upon the table, taking care that all my movements should be slow and deliberate, and thus indicate the numbness of my nerve power. My eyes were wide open, but fixed and glassy. They looked, and yet they saw nothing. I breathed hard and with difficulty. My whole appearance, in fact, showed a state of extreme nervous agitation produced by the disorganization of my brain. I endeavored by these distinct and visible effects to make the change in Lady Macbeth patent to all eyes, and to show that she was suffering from a mental rather than a physical malady, which had a terrible yet all-sufficient cause.

When I had placed the light upon the table I advanced to the front of the stage. I made as if I had discovered blood still upon my hands, and, in trying to wash it off, I used the attitude of one who holds a quantity of water in the hollow of his hand therewith to cleanse them. I was very careful in this movement, and repeated it in several places with slight variations. After this action I said :—

"Yet here's a spot! Out damned spot, I say!"

Then listening intently—

"One, two—why then 'tis time to do it."

And I continued, as though replying to some imaginary speaker—

"Hell is murky! Fie, my Lord, fie! a soldier, and afraid! What need we fear who knows it, when none can call our power to account."

Here, reverting to the real cause of my delirium, I cried :—

"Yet who would have thought the old man to have had so much blood in him!"

and, while I spoke, I made a movement with my hands as though I was struck at seeing the blood with which it seemed to me they were still stained. Then my delirium returned upon me—

"The Thane of Fife had a wife! Where is she now?"

I began, but my attention was once more attracted to my hands, and with an expression, half of anger, half of sorrow, I cried :—

"What! will these hands ne'er be clean?"

rubbing them as I spoke with convulsive energy.

Then, still in my delirium, and in a sharp, angry tone, I feigned to be whispering into the ear of Macbeth—

"No more o' that, my Lord, no more o' that! You mar all with this starting."

But once again my original idea possessed me. I slightly sniffed my hands, and pretending to recognize the smell of blood upon them, broke forth in my anguish—

"Here's the smell of the blood still; all the perfumes of Arabia will not sweeten this little hand. Oh! Oh! Oh!"

These exclamations were wrung from me as though a grasp of iron were laid upon my heart which would hardly allow me utterance, and I remained with my head thrown back, breathing with difficulty, as if overcome by a profound lethargy.

During the short dialogue between the lady-in-waiting and the doctor, I feigned that I was transported in my delirium to the scene of the murder of Duncan, and, as though the cause of my change of expression might be the sight of the King's apartment, I advanced cautiously, with my body bent forward towards the right-hand side of the stage, where, as I imagined, the assassination had taken place. I fancied I heard the hasty steps of my husband, and I stood in an attitude of expectation, and with straining eyes, apparently waiting his arrival to assure me that the dreadful deed was accomplished. Then, with a cry of joy, as though I saw him approach to announce the complete fulfilment of our plans, I exclaimed, in violent agitation :—

"Wash your hands!. Put on your nightgown. Look not so pale. I tell you yet again, Banquo's buried, he cannot come out of his grave."

Throughout this scene I was careful not to forget that I was a woman speaking in her disturbed sleep, therefore, between each sentence I uttered, I drew my breath in long, half-stifled gasps, and when I came to the words—

"To bed, to bed! there's knocking at the gate. Come, come, come! Give me your hand. What's done cannot be undone. To bed, to bed, to bed!"

I changed to a more coaxing and persuasive tone of voice, as though I would obtain ready compliance. Then, terrified by the knocking I fancied I heard at the castle gate, and fearful of a surprise, I showed a violent emotion, a sudden dismay. I imagined it was necessary to conceal ourselves promptly in our apartment, and turned towards it, inviting Macbeth to accompany me, speaking the last two words, "Come, come!" in imperative and furious tones ; after which, feigning to seize his hand, I showed that I would place him in safety in spite of himself, and urging him on with great difficulty I disappeared from the view of the audience, saying in a choking voice :—

"To bed, to bed, to bed!"

Here I end my analysis of a character which is one of the most remarkable that has ever been conceived by a human mind, and the study of which is rendered all the more difficult by the singular situations in which the imagination of the poet places Lady Macbeth.

But, as I am assured in my own mind that I have done the best that in me lay, to enter into the true character of this strange personage, I confide this analysis of my interpretation of it to the judgment of the critics, who, it seems to me, should at least appreciate the labor and study I have brought to bear upon it.

CHAPTER XII.

QUEEN ELIZABETH.

It is a task of the greatest difficulty to give any adequate idea of the real personality of Queen Elizabeth of England upon the stage, for in her regal dignity, haughtiness, transcendent abilities, great powers of dissimulation, consummate hypocrisy, and love of absolute authority were strangely combined with the weaknesses and frivolities of a woman who could condescend at times to actual vulgarity. Such a character would tax the powers of any actress, but more especially of one whose wide-spread fame had led the critics to expect great things from her.

Thus when, in 1854, I thought of adding to my *répertoire* the part of Queen Elizabeth in the drama of that name by my illustrious and much-lamented countryman, Paolo Giacometti, I felt that, as a preliminary step, it was necessary for me to devote all my powers to an exhaustive study of such historical notices of her as might serve to elucidate the character and disposition of this celebrated Queen.

The result of my investigations was to convince me that, although as a political personage and a Sovereign, Elizabeth was endowed with such great and eminent qualities as to render her famous throughout the civilized world, and especially endeared her to her own subjects, yet, as a woman, her

undoubted cruelty and hypocrisy, her violent prejudices, and her unreasonable fits of passion, all duly
authenticated by history, might well render her an
object of aversion rather than admiration. Indeed,
her character is so little in accord with the spirit of
the present day that the reader will easily understand
how utterly repugnant it was to my feelings to attempt the representation of such a rare and unique
personality as that of Queen Elizabeth.

Now it has always been a necessity of my nature
that a new part should not only contain some notable
difficulties to be overcome, but should also be one
with which I could feel myself in complete sympathy.
I was therefore strongly tempted to renounce my
project of assaying the *rôle* of the English Queen,
and my reluctance grew in proportion as I became
acquainted with her many acts of cruelty, especially
in relation to Mary Stuart. But my manager, who
was then director of the Royal Theatrical Company,
in the services of the King of Sardinia, waxed eloquent as he enumerated the many inconveniences
which would result from my refusal. For, while I
had been occupied with my researches, the preparations for putting the drama upon the stage had been
pushed on apace. Everything was therefore ready,
and the public were expecting the new play.

Under these circumstances, I felt I must endeavor
to evercome my own personal reluctance, and so,
although the character of Elizabeth was so uncon-
genial to me as to take from me all desire to interpret
it, I resolved to make an extra effort to enter into
the spirit of the part. And I had my reward, for I

believe I shall not err in saying that the public have always regarded this as one of the most elaborate and complete studies in my *répertoire.*

From the moment of my first appearance upon the stage in this character, I endeavored, by my bearing, gestures, and tone of voice, to convey to my audience that they were in the presence of a woman who was familiar with the management of difficult affairs of State, who had perfect confidence in her own judgment, and who was accustomed to have her decision received as final. In addition to this, I represented the Queen as a well-read and well-educated woman, perfectly aware of her own abilities and her unusual degree of culture, and especially proud of her extensive acquaintance with foreign languages, as is evident from her reply to the Polish Ambassador, who, when he was addressing her in the Latin tongue, made sundry indiscretions under the belief that the Queen would not understand him, and who was overwhelmed with amazement when she answered him in the same language. She afterwards boasted to her courtiers with ill-concealed pride : "I even brushed up my old Latin for him."—(Historical.)

I was also careful to show the audience by my manner at this early portion of the play that Elizabeth, in spite of the real inclination she then felt for the Earl of Essex, was determined by her scornful and haughty demeanor to place every one around her on a level far beneath her own, when she had grounds for believing that one of her subjects had dared to raise his ambition so high as to aspire to her hand.

In the first Act the scene is remarkable in which Giacometti, with one of those inspirations usual to him, imagined a very difficult contrast of action and at the same time a trait characteristic of this great Queen, offering besides an opportunity to the actress to give proof of her power.

Elizabeth is engaged in dictating two letters at the same time in alternate sentences, employing for the one the services of her secretary Davison, and for the other those of young Francis Bacon. The former is couched in a tone of deep irritation, and is addressed to the Earl of Leicester, who has written to inform her of the ovation he had received in Flanders, carrying his audacity so far as to ask her permission to accept the crown which has been offered him by Counts Egmont, Horn, and Flessing, in the name of the Low Countries. The Earl's communication has been made in terms much more befitting one monarch addressing another than a subject entreating a favor from his sovereign, and has roused Elizabeth's deep resentment.

The second missive is to Judge Popham, and has its origin in the following circumstances :—Although Bacon was well aware that Elizabeth objected very strongly to Shakespeare's latest play of Henry VIII., in which not only the Queen's father and mother, but herself also, as an infant, are brought upon ths stage, yet he had nevertheless, in order to extort her consent to its representation, ventured to entreat the Queen on bended knee to permit him to read some passages to her. With a very ill-grace she finally consented, and Bacon, animated by all the enthusiasm which an author might feel in reading his own work (and indeed there are people who believe that this drama was his) proceeded to declaim certain lines which foretold the grandeur, prosperity, and long life of Elizabeth, the poet also lauding to the skies the magnanimity and surpassing glory of the "Virgin Queen."

Bacon's stratagem fully succeeded. Hearing herself thus extolled, Elizabeth seized a pen and with her own hand wrote at the foot of the manuscript that it was her good pleasure for the drama of Henry VIII. to be represented within fifteen days at Windsor in the Court Theatre. But, hearing from Bacon that it was impossible to give effect so speedily to the Queen's wishes, Shakespeare himself being then in prison for debt, Elizabeth at once dictated to Bacon the letter to Judge Popham telling the latter that she had consented to the play being acted, and by way of reprimanding him for his want of acuteness in forbidding a piece which sang her own praises so loudly, she bade Bacon add that it was her good pleasure Popham himself should become liable for Shakespeare's debts, a full schedule of which would be sent to him by Sir Francis Bacon. The letter ended thus :— "I hope another time you will put on your spectacles in order the better to distinguish white from black."

I dictated these letters at the same time. In the one addressed to the Earl of Leicester, making use of the most severe expressions of anger, declaring that "crowns are not made for heads like yours—far less that of Belgium, which has already been refused by your Sovereign." I further ordered him to resign

immediately the command of the troops to Sir Walter
Raleigh, otherwise I would have him " taken prisoner
by a regiment of cavalry."

The dictation of this letter I alternated with that
to Popham, which was at once familiar, cold, authoritative, and sarcastic in expression.

In the second Act, there are some truly remarkable
scenes—and the author has found the way of deline-
ating them so well—collecting various passages in
the life of Elizabeth ; uniting them so skilfully with
each other ; making use of all the liberties of time
and space allowed on the stage, without, however,
injuring or changing in the slightest degree the regular course of the action, as to make the connection
appear both natural and interesting.

I especially liked this second Act, because it gave
me the opportunity for a little comedy of which I was
particularly fond at that time. Even later it was a
boon for me when through any circumstances I could
play *La Locomotiera* or *I Gelosi Fortunati.* When I
speak of comedy, I refer to the scene with the Earl
of Essex, in which, like an experienced coquette,
now she seems to understand and accept the love he
cherishes for her, compassionating his ill-concealed
jealousy of the Earl of Leicester, whom he believes
his fortunate rival ; now suddenly assuming the tone
of an offending sovereign and driving Essex from her
presence, when the latter, hearing the Queen boast—

" Into this royal heart no weak affection has ever entered,"

sarcastically rejoins, no longer able to restrain himself—

" If we except the Duke of Anjou and Admiral Seymour."

But when Essex, warned by the Queen's anger
that he had gone too far, threw himself at her feet
and implored her pardon ; I, while assuming all the
dignity of offended majesty, succeeded in conveying
to the audience, that in my heart, I rejoiced to see
these transports of jealousy. And though I exclaimed with apparent disdain—

" Dar'st thou then to love thy Queen ? "

I allowed him to seize my hand and endeavor to
imprint a kiss upon it. But I snatched my hand
away with an angry gesture before the Earl could
accomplish his purpose ; glancing at the same time
with secret admiration at the handsome knight still
kneeling before me. Love and pride struggled together for the mastery in my heart, until at last I
felt constrained to exclaim, in as playful a manner as
I could assume—

" Well ! Art saying thy prayers ? Rise ! rise ! "

While speaking these words, my hand, which I had
extended to indicate that I wished him to rise,
touched for an instant the Earl's bent head. Encouraged by this, he sprang to his feet, seized my hand in
his, and covered it with kisses. Then he pressed it
to his heart, exclaiming in passionate accents—

" Ah ! The daughter of Henry VIII. has pressed my hand."

Upon which, disengaging myself, I retreated, and
with affected modesty, remarked demurely—

" If so, it was unconsciously."

But, when I heard him murmur—

18

"What other woman could I love after having once seen
Elizabeth,"

I had much ado to hide the emotion that filled my
heart.   I gazed at him with a look, which, all too
plainly betrayed my feelings towards him ; and,
after some slight hesitation I drew a ring from my
finger and offered it to him with the solemn promise—

"If thou should'st one day lose thy Sovereign's favor or be
guilty of any crime, send me this ring, and I pledge thee my
Royal word thou shalt be pardon'd."

In the monologue which ends this scene, the
author still further develops and elaborates the character of the Queen.   But when love appears on the
point of mastering her indomitable pride, her determination to retain her absolute sovereignty comes to
her aid.   She beats down the tenderer sentiments
and womanly weakness with a strong hand.   Nay,
she can even mock at the very idea of yielding to
what her Parliament, the Puritans, and Lord Went-
worth have been long urging her to do; namely,
make choice of a husband.

"What!" [she exclaims. her anger rising afresh at the
thought]   "Divide my kingdom with another!   Be no longer
the sole ruler of everybody and everything !"

Her haughty spirit regains its self-control, and she is
ashamed of having been, even for a moment, surprised into feminine weakness.   While Elizabeth is
in this unpropitious state of mind, her secretary
Davison enters, bringing a letter from Mary Stuart,
as well as her death-warrant for the Queen's signature.
Elizabeth can hardly refrain from an exclamation of

pleasure at this unexpected interruption; but she tries to hide it by hypocritically assuming a mask of pity. She glances over the unhappy prisoner's letter with ill-concealed impatience, and gathering from it that the Queen of Scotland, believing her son James to have sided with her enemies, has declared the invincible Philip II., King of Spain, her successor to the throne, she is seized with an access of fury, and cries with a mocking smile—

"I will undertake to execute thy will for thee, and will send *thee* to the angels!"

Most cruel words, worthy only of a perverted mind.

In the scene of dissimulation between Elizabeth and James VI., who has come to entreat her to spare his mother's life, and who threatens her with his vengeance if she refuse to listen to his prayers, I endeavored, by the stern expression of my eyes, my set lips, and my rigid figure, to convey to the audience some idea of the tempest gathering within me. But when Davison entered and announced in a loud voice—

"Your Majesty, by this time the executioner has held up to the crowd the head of Mary Stuart!"

the storm which was rising in my breast subsided; in a moment a complete change came over me, an involuntary cry of joy escaped me, which was unnoticed in the general consternation caused by the terrible news.

In an instant I had recovered myself, and I broke out into furious invective against those who had so hastily carried out the sentence, and at the same time I caused my face to assume such an exaggerated expression of grief and utter consternation, that even James himself was constrained to exclaim—

"To Heaven I leave the task of judging if this be real or feigned!"

When I was left alone with my courtiers, I continued still to carry on the hollow mockery of grief. I declared this terrible event had decided me to renounce the throne and spend the rest of my days in penitence within the walls of a convent. At the unexpected arrival of Francis Drake, my thoughts instantly turned into another channel. He had been sent by the Queen sometime before to ravage the Spanish possessions in America, and endeavor to discover the designs of King Philip, but his prolonged absence had led to the belief that he must either have been taken prisoner or killed.

My face, my whole person underwent an instantaneous and total change. The death of Mary Stuart, my hypocritical intentions, my political feigning, all are forgotten in the feverish anxiety to know the result of the mission entrusted to Drake. Sir Francis informed me that a "mightier fleet than the world had yet seen, had already been gathered together by Spain, for the conquest of England; that this fleet when divided into two squadrons occupied a space of seven miles from one extremity to the other; that the most valiant captains in the world had been engaged to assist the Spaniards in their great enterprise, and that, in certain assurance of victory, the name of the *Invincible Armada* had been given to the assembled fleet."

When I heard this, I showed that I could restrain myself no longer. With flashing eyes and like a fiery charger pawing the ground at the clang of the trumpet, Elizabeth, eager for glory, and anticipating a brilliant victory, feels the blood of her forefathers thrill in her veins, while in imagination she is already transported to the field of battle. "At last, then, I have succeeded!" she cries in a voice of thunder. Therefore, when Mendoza, the Spanish Ambassador, appeared in my presence, and with proud mien and arrogant tone, declared war in the name of his master, Philip II., I thanked him in a tone of disdain. At once, like an experienced leader, with feverish ardor, I gave the necessary orders to prepare for war, and I distributed the different commands. My spirit rose to the occasion. Full of martial enthusiasm, I assured my lords that—

"Yet another sword will fight for England!"

"Which?" asked the Ambassador, mockingly.

"That of Henry VIII.,"

I answered proudly.

"And who will have the courage to wield it?"

he inquired, inexpressible scorn in his tones.

"Who! I!"

I answered, without a moment's hesitation, and springing towards the trophy of Henry VIII.'s weapons which decorated the hall of audience, I seized the large sword my father had once used, and which was once more to assure victory to England, I faced round on Mendoza and thundered out the words—

"Tell Philip that Elizabeth hurls the scabbard far from her! When these two nations, like gigantic athletes, shall meet on the ocean, the world itself will tremble. And after the encounter, one of the two—like the stone flung by a child into the water—will disappear among the blood-stained waves; either England or Spain—Elizabeth or Philip! I swear it by the King my father!"

I stood brandishing the sword in one hand, while I laid the other upon it, as in the act of taking an oath, and all present drawing theirs also, and touching mine with the points, repeated after me—

"We swear it."

The curtain falls on this "tableau."

With the exception of two historical incidents, the third Act does not contain many scenes for Elizabeth of great artistic difficulty. These incidents are the discovery of a plot for taking her life, of which Margaret Lamburn is proved to be the chief instigator, and the disgrace and punishment of Essex.

In the first of these, when Margaret is brought into my presence, I assumed a stern demeanor, and interrogated her in an angry voice, as though I had already decided to condemn her to death. But when I heard the resolute tone in which she answered me—when she boldly told me that she had sought to take my life in revenge for the death of Mary Stuart, her beloved mistress, and of her own husband, who had died of grief on account of the miserable end of his

Sovereign, I was deeply touched by her words, and asked her what punishment she herself would consider her strange confession deserved. She looked me full in the face, and answered proudly, that I ought to pardon her.

I cried in amazement—

"What! pardon thee; and what surety have I that thou wilt not again attempt my life."

To which Margaret answered—

"Madam, a boon which cannot be granted without so many precautions is no longer a favor, take thou then my life."

This arrogant speech, this temerity, and defiant courage, the like of which Elizabeth had never met with before during her reign from any *man*, still less from any woman, completely staggered her, and, after a moment's hesitation, she yielded to a sudden impulse of generosity, and, hastily, as though fearful she might repent, she cried—

"Go! get thee hence in peace! but lose no time!"

Throughout this scene, I considered I should best express the author's meaning, if I strove, by the intonation of my voice and the mobility of my features to emphasize the sudden transition from severity, to great and generous impulse, which was always so characteristic of this great Queen.

The other striking situation is found in the reception Elizabeth gives to the three conquerors of Cadiz, Lord Howard, Sir Francis Drake, and the Earl of Essex. I made it evident that I was animated by a desire to revenge myself upon Essex, whose secret passion for Lady Sarah I had discovered; and who had exceeded the powers conferred upon him, openly defying my commands. I therefore began my discourse by complimenting all three warriors, and thanking them in my own name, and that of England, for the splendid victory they had just gained over the Spanish fleet. I created Drake, Lord High Admiral; and Howard, Earl of Nottingham; but when I addressed Essex, who, like the others, knelt expectant at my feet, it was in a very different strain. I began by praising his bravery in battle, and then, in a soft and insinuating voice, as though I would prepare him to receive an adequate reward, I continued—

" We admire your valor, but since you have refused obedience to him, whom we have invested with supreme power over our forces by land and sea, and have rebelled against the mandates of your Queen, we shall defer *your* reward, until we receive from you proofs of obedience and submission. Rise ! "

I spoke these words in an austere, harsh voice, as though I desired each syllable to penetrate, like a poniard, into the heart of him I addressed, humiliating him before all the bystanders. The Earl remained for an instant, like one petrified; then, quickly recovering himself, he burst forth in no measured tones of complaint against the injustice done him; ending by reproaching me bitterly for having distinguished Lord Howard, who, as every one knew, had won the battle solely because a furious tempest had risen to aid him, and dashed the Spanish vessels upon the rocks. It was in vain I tried to silence the Earl. He continued his angry recriminations, and gradually increased my displeasure, until on hearing him boast that he also was of royal descent, and in that respect my equal, my indignation almost got the better of me. Still I managed to restrain it sufficiently to interfere between the two men, when Essex, scarcely knowing what he did, challenged Lord Howard to meet him in single combat.

" What ! "

exclaimed Essex in a sarcastic tone,

"can earls and dukes no longer fight in England without the special permission of the Queen ? "

The taunting words stung me to fury. I lost all control over myself, and flung my glove in the speaker's face. He in his turn, completely lost his head, and, exasperated by the insult he had received, deaf to every consideration of prudence, and totally forgetting the respect he owed his Sovereign, broke out into violent invective against her. He accuses her of having *blended her crown with the coronets of dukes and earls, and placed the Parliament of England on a level with the Divan of Mahomet, of having annulled all its privileges ;* and, as though this were not enough, he filled up the measure of his insults to overflowing by calling her :

" The Vestal of the West, who has more than once let the fire die out on the tripod of Jove ! "

All the by-play which should accompany the few words I have to speak during this culminating scene of the Act, as well as the tone of voice, are clearly indicated by the author, and it cost me no difficulty to understand and enter into the spirit of the situation. I was always most careful never to forget that I was a queen, even in the midst of my fury, and that this queen was Elizabeth of England.

Between the third and fourth Acts several years are supposed to elapse, during which, Essex, after being pardoned his egregious folly, regains his sovereign's favor; "and is sent by her as general to Ireland, invested with full powers to repress the tumults and revolts constantly arising there. But the incapacity of the new commander-in-chief soon became manifest. He was imprudent enough himself to raise the standard of revolt against his own queen, with the result that he was speedily arrested and condemned to the scaffold."

It is at this point of the story that the fourth Act begins. Elizabeth is beginning to show the weight of years. The grief of finding herself obliged to adopt stringent measures against the man so dear to her; the only man in fact she ever loved, has greatly conduced to break her haughty spirit. I therefore endeavored to show in my person and make-up the physical effects of age. (The queen is about sixty-eight at this time.) Yet, in spite of her bowed figure and wrinkled face, I rendered it evident that she still possessed the remains of that magnificent constitution and indomitable will which she never entirely lost until after the death of her favorite.

The fourth Act opens with the signature of Lord Essex's death warrant. Seeing that Lady Burleigh, who was in attendance at the time, was alarmed at the agitation Elizabeth betrayed, and feared it was caused by illness, I endeavored to reassure her and conceal its real origin by remarking :—

"Thou art already aware, Anna, that when I have to condemn any one to death, I suffer cruel and unspeakable agonies."

But in spite of myself, the bitter truth at last escaped my lips. I betrayed that I was suffering so intensely because I feared lest, either through pride or obstinacy, Essex might not send me the ring I had once, in a moment of tenderness, given to him ; with a promise of pardon whenever it should be presented to me. Lady Burleigh tried to comfort me by saying that doubtless the Earl was too sensible of his fault and too fearful of further irritating his sovereign to venture on claiming her promise. Then she offered to go herself to the Tower, as though entirely on her own impulse, and advise Essex to confide himself to the clemency and magnanimity of the Queen. Unseen by Lady Burleigh, I showed the audience what a relief this proposal was to me ; but, fearing that my dignity as a Sovereign must suffer if I yielded to the impulse of my heart, I harshly, though with evident effort, forbade Lady Burleigh to carry out her suggestion, saying :

"Anna—stay ! If he be as proud as Lucifer, let him go to him ! "

At this moment, Burleigh entering with the death-warrant of Lord Essex for the royal signature, Elizabeth cannot entirely suppress the painful emotion which overcomes her in spite of herself. She orders all her attendants to retire, and at the same time tells Burleigh to send her Davison, the Keeper of the Seals.

When alone and able to give full vent to the emotions that possessed me, with long and deep-drawn sighs, I spread out the fatal parchment on the table, gazing at it long and sadly, as though incredulous that only my signature was needed to send the one man I had ever truly loved to his death. I let the audience see the conflict that was raging within me. I tried to reassure myself and overcome my womanly weakness by dwelling on the fact that this man's execution was necessary to satisfy the demands of justice.

"Yes! he must die," [I murmured,] "as so many other conspirators have died,—Suffolk, Parry, Babington, Lopez,—as even a Queen of Scotland has died."

and at each broken sentence, I made a movement as though to dip my pen in the ink, and sign the fatal parchment, but I could not consummate the terrible deed. I tried to fortify myself with specious argument;

"Were I to pardon him, it would be but to confess my own weakness! I, weak! Never!"

and again I seized the pen and essayed to write the signature. But my courage once more abandoned me, and with a gesture of petulant anger at my own weakness, I dashed the pen to the ground. Then, for a moment, a strange hope arose in my agonized heart.

"But if, in the face of death, [I murmured,] the Earl's pride have deserted him! If, even now, he have intrusted the ring to some one! If!——"

Animated by the half-uttered thought, I vehemently
rang the bell, and inquired whether any message had
come for me from the Tower. Vain hope! None
had been received, and exhausted, I sank again on
my seat, exclaiming in my despair:

" Ah! pride, pride! To die thus with his life in his own hands." *

Then I began to complain bitterly to myself of
Lady Burleigh's conduct. She ought to have understood that for the first time in my long reign I had
wished to be disobeyed. In spite of my prohibition,
I should have rejoiced if she had gone to the Tower.
It was in vain I tried to convince myself that Essex
was a rebel, and as such deserving of punishment.
Then the apprehension of committing an injustice
made me hesitate again. Remorse began to torture
me. I tossed hither and thither on the waves of conscience. My imagination was so excited that I even
fancied I saw the spectre of Mary Stuart standing

---

* The author of the drama introduces this historical incident
to show what an important part this ring played in the death of
the Earl, and how, in a secondary degree, it also accelerated the
death of Elizabeth. Lally Tollendal has left it on record: " He
(the Earl) lost his head on the scaffold, and the grief the Queen
felt at being obliged to use such severity towards a man who
had been so dear to her, plunged her in a profound melancholy.
Two years afterwards, when Lady Nottingham confessed on her
death-bed that the ring had been intrusted to her care, but that,
overpersuaded by her husband, she had refrained from deliver-
ing it to the Queen, Elizabeth lost all control over herself, exclaiming, ' God may forgive you; I never can!' Henceforth
she refused food and remedies for her sickness, saying they
were no use to a dying woman."

before me in full noonday, just as she had stood every night since her execution to trouble my dreams, and make me start in terror from my bed. Returning to myself I blushed at my childish folly, and in the height of indignation and disappointment at not seeing the much-wished-for ring brought me—with the whole energy of my virile soul and my despised love—I thought of nothing more than the reasons of state, and the dignity of the crown, and sanctioned the decision of the judges. So once more I seized the pen, and hurriedly traced the fatal signature. My heart was utterly broken. Davison, sent by Lord Burleigh, entered at this moment to receive the warrant. His appearance startled me painfully, but I made a successful attempt to hide from him the misery I knew was written on my tell-tale face, and feeling I must bravely endure the sacrifice imposed on me by duty, I took up the parchment, and slowly, with a trembling hand, held it out towards the Keeper of the Seals. But as if grasping it a little longer in my hand seemed to me to add a few minutes to the life of Essex, I caused Davison, although humbly, to try and draw it by gentle force from my convulsive hold. Then he moved towards the door ; but a sudden impulse of feeling made me call him back in suppressed tones. He turned, as if expecting some further orders ; but, recalled to a sense of my own dignity, I merely told him, in as haughty a tone as I could assume, to be quick and see the sentence carried out.

When he was gone, and I was once more alone I gave free vent to my grief, bitterly accusing Essex of

being the cause of all my misery. The appearance
of the Countess of Nottingham, who arrived breathless to implore pardon for the Earl, only excited me
to greater fury, for in her I believed I saw my rival.
On hearing that her husband had forcibly taken from
her the ring, confided to her by Essex that she might
give it to me, I at first showed disbelief in her assertion, yet on her swearing by the soul of her mother
that her statement was true, I allowed myself to be
convinced. In the deepest agitation, I sent a page
with orders that a messenger, mounted on my fleetest
horse, should ride for his life to the Tower, and
intercept Davison before it was too late. I directed
that the warrant should be torn into a thousand
pieces, and promised a patent of nobility to whoever
should succeed in carrying out my wishes.

But before my messenger could well have started,
Lord Burleigh entered, followed by Bacon. They
came to announce, with mournful looks, that the sentence was already executed. For an instant I stood
as though petrified at their news ; then I dropped into
a chair, moaning in low tones—

" Dead! Dead! "

In a little while, however, I rose, and with blood-
shot eyes and trembling lips, began the magnificent
passage which Giacometti puts into Elizabeth's mouth
at the close of this Act :

"Dead ! But before sunset the fatal bell shall toll once more,"

. (alluding to the death of Nottingham, which she
meditated.) Pacing the stage in gathering excitement, I cried furiously—

" I must have within my hands the Earl of Nottingham's head ! "

Then, with a burst of desperate grief :

" My Robert is no more ! The only man I ever really loved, and I have killed him ! No one said a single word to appease my wrath; they all hated him, and yet not one of them was worthy to kiss the dust raised by his charger's hoof on a day of battle ! "

At this moment I became aware of the presence of Bacon, who was standing somewhat aside. I ordered him to come forward, and poured forth my wrath upon him, crying :

" And thou, base wretch, thou wast a nothing ; and if thou art something, to him alone thou owest it. To him thou owest the honors I have heaped on thee ! He who generously freed thee from the shame of thy debts might have counted on thee for his defence, and thou hast failed him ! It was thy sacred duty to contend for his life with me—ay, even with me. Thou should have pointed out to me Ireland subjugated, Cadiz in flames ! Thou shouldst have torn open his cuirass, counted out one by one his wounds, and offered them to me as a ransom for his life ! And thou, on the contrary, infamous wretch, hast preferred to guide the hand of his judges when they drew up the sentence, and mine when I signed it. Cursed be thou ! May Cain's curse light on thee ! "

The attendants drew near to calm my fury.

" Let all retire : I do command it ! "

I cried in imperious tones. But when they obeyed me and I was left alone, I—crushed with grief, shaken by such tremendous emotions, and not daring to lift my eyes to that Heaven whose wrath I dreaded —cast myself, face downwards, upon the ground, moaning :

" Here let me stay, alone ! Surrounded by a pool of blood— alone with my remorse—and with God ! "

Thus closes the fourth Act.

In the fifth Act, Elizabeth is approaching her end, and, according to history, although prostrated by failing strength, still her iron temperament manifested itself prodigiously at times, and the fire which circulated in her veins during her past years still sent forth a few sparks. Thus, when I came before the audience, I let them plainly see in my face and figure the ravages that time and disease had made. Yet I strove carefully to hide from my courtiers how much I was suffering. I entered, leaning on the arm of Burleigh—a bowed and decrepit old woman—still wearing, however, the robes and crown of State in which I had been present at the opening of Parliament. I tried, by my manner, to give the audience an impression of some one in the greatest nervous agitation, which had been caused by the excitement of the debate I had just been hearing ; but as I related the details to my attendants I manifested a clearness of intellect and strength of will, well calculated to surprise and deceive those who were listening to me. The careless arrangement of my hair, however, the wrinkles and furrows on my face, the slow movement of my hands, very plainly showed the audience that some secret sorrow had aged me, even more than the weight of years. Burleigh begged me to sit down and take some needful rest. I repulsed him, angrily exclaiming :

"No, no—motion is life. I have had too much rest of late. I thought I should have been stifled in my litter ! "

In truth, a strong impression had been produced

19

on my mind by the fact that when I returned to the
Palace from the House of Parliament, far fewer persons than usual had assembled outside to give me
greeting.　Yet I was resolute not to let my faithful
minister guess what a blow the apathy of my subjects
had been to me.　So I assumed a careless, indifferent air, which was anything but a true index to my
feelings, and, with a scrutinizing look at Burleigh,
said :

" Tell me, hast thou ordained that our loving subjects should
not congregate too densely on our way, and should not greet us
with shouts ? "

When Burleigh replied in the negative I frowned,
unperceived by him, and heaved a deep sigh.　Then
I remarked, with well-acted hypocrisy :

" No ! as I know that you, my good old Burleigh, deem me
in ill-health, and might have thought the sight of people crowding on my passage would tire me.　But I am not so ; and, if I
have been, *now* I am cured."

And in proof thereof I began to recount, with considerable vivacity, how the Parliament had been
defeated in its attempt to curtail the royal preroga-
tive.

I said all this with almost childish glee, adding :

" Well, what think you, my Lords ! "

in a tone of such entire satisfaction, that Burleigh,
who was before all things a courtier, hastened to applaud my argument.　Then I addressed Bacon, and
ordered him to inform William Shakespeare that it
was my good pleasure he should give another representation of *Henry VIII.* (because I delighted to

see myself figure in the play as an infant in my nurses' arms). I further gave orders for the preparation of a grand fête. Then I seated myself, and asked for news. I was told that it appeared certain that formidable Irish chief, the Earl of Tyrone, was safe under arrest; whereupon I exclaimed gayly to Burleigh:

"Aha! it seems to me that I have brushed away many flies from the Crown of England!"

Burleigh seized the opportunity to say—

"Of a surety, your successor will receive it brilliant and respected."

On hearing these words, I drew myself up, and gazed long and searchingly at him, for I had suspected for some time past he might be carrying on a secret correspondence with James VI. Burleigh, guessing what was in the Queen's mind, endeavored to explain away his words by observing—

"Before I die, I should like to see the succession determined on."

I affected to accept this plausible explanation, and, anxious to put an end to the farce, I replied—

"Let us hear now on whom this sagacious choice of thine falls!"

"On whom could it fall more appropriately than on the young King of Scotland,"

Burleigh answered diplomatically. At this reply my suppressed anger blazed forth, and I seized him by the arm, crying—

"Traitor! I awaited thee there!"

BURLEIGH.—"Burleigh traitor?"

ELIZABETH.—"Yes! for thou hast a secret correspondence with James."

BURLEIGH.—"No; but he alone, methinks, has it in his power to save England from civil war."

"Such too is my humble opinion,"

added Davison.

I turned upon them both with righteous indignation—

"Civil war! Eternal civil war! this is the phantasm with which ye compelled me to condemn to death, Suffolk, Babington, Mary, and Robert of Essex!"

But at mention of the last dear name, I broke down utterly, grief almost suffocated me. My eyes filled with tears, and, unable longer to refrain from weeping, I repeated the name of Robert amid my broken sobs. The by-standers hastened to me, imploring me to be calm, but their entreaties only made my anger blaze up once more, and I ordered them to leave me in peremptory tones, for their anxiety to console me increased my agitation. Exhausted with grief and physical sufferings, I had some difficulty in calming my irritation.

After a slight pause, having made certain that every one had left; no longer obliged to dissemble, body and mind appeared in all their sad reality—worn out. The remembrance that the death of Essex had been my own doing, gnaws my heart, remorse tears my soul, and, longing to throw myself on my couch, I dragged myself towards it with the greatest difficulty. As I staggered along with bent body, and bowed head, I lifted my trembling hands to my aching brow, and felt the crown which still rested there.

> "Ah! a heavy weight is on it,"

I moaned, with a weary air,

> "And yet for forty-four years I have worn it, and it seemed so light to me."

I lifted it slowly from my head, and gazed at it with deep emotion.

> "Who will wear it after me?"

I questioned myself, then, pushing it suddenly away from me, I added in a haughty tone—

> "I wish not to know."

But the springs of memory had been unloosed. I returned, in thought, once more to the years of my vanished glory, and began, in a voice that grew gradually weaker and weaker, bitterly to bewail the past.

> "No one loves me now—no one tells me I ride like Alexander, walk like Venus, sing and play like Orpheus. No! When I present myself to the public, they no longer greet me with cheers. This morning one would have thought that my litter was a bier. Am I then so very old? Certes, I have seen many fears pass away, but they have left no trace on me. Not a thread of silver mingles with my beautiful golden hair."

I smoothed my auburn locks with girlish self-complacency, and then, with an expressive gesture, I made the audience perceive that I wanted to assure myself of the truth of my words. I turned to the mirror that hung near, but scarcely had I seen myself reflected in it than I shrank away in disgust, perceiving the deep lines that furrowed my face, my dimmed eyes, my livid hollow cheeks. My breathing became labored, my eyes dark, my mind confused;

in terror I screamed for help. But a momentary return of pride made me hastily stuff my handkerchief into my mouth to stifle my cries. These sufferings increasing, my mind began to wander. All around me grew dark, out of the blackness I seemed to see pale shadows and bleeding spectres coming toward me. They drew nearer and nearer, they almost touched me. Severed heads seemed rolling about my feet. To escape them I curled myself up in a corner of my couch, and, sinking down helplessly among my pillows, I clasped my hands together, with inarticulate appeals to Heaven for mercy.

After a long time my senses seemed to return. Without opening my eyes I feebly called to Burleigh to come and help me. Hastening at the Queen's cries, he comes to her, followed by James VI., who had been waiting in the anteroom ; he helps her to rise without her recognizing him. Soon, standing up, I perceive James ; terrified, I call my guards with loud cries. All rush in and surround me. Gasping, in vain efforts to speak, I point inquiringly at James. Burleigh explained :

"The King of Scotland has journeyed to London to inquire for Your Majesty's health !"

"But," [I cried] "why bears he in his hand his mother's head? What will he do with it? Perchance dash it in my face! Look! Look!"

At these words, James approached me to show me he had nothing in his hands. I, alarmed, shrieking, take refuge in the arms of my faithful friends, covering my face with both hands, as if to repel contact with Mary's head. The reassurances of my courtiers, as well as of James VI. himself, calm me. Veiling my eyes with my hands, and with fearful hesitation, I looked through my fingers to see if James was not lying.

By degrees I took heart; I breathed more freely. A smile flitted across my pale lips; telling them all that it had been only a dream, I finished, saying:

"I am better! I am better."

At this point, Drake returned from his mission in Ireland. He announced the arrest of the dreaded Earl of Tyrone and, notwithstanding her physical weakness, and the terrible emotion through which she had just passed, Elizabeth uttered a cry of joy at the news. Her indomitable spirit blazed up once more. She was still sufficiently her old self to rejoice at the humiliation of one who had sought to rob her of her throne. She ordered Tyrone to instant execution, when Drake hastened to remind her that she would not probably have had her formidable enemy in her power had he not given himself up to justice, trusting in the clemency and magnanimity of the Queen. Touched by his words, and with a sudden impulse of generosity, I hesitated for a moment, consulting Burleigh with a significant look. He responded by a sign that I ought to pardon my prisoner. So I said to Drake, with great dignity:—

"'Tis well! Whoever has deemed me great shall ne'er have cause to think me less than my fame. He is pardoned."

But the Queen's last moments were drawing near. Her malady increased, her strength failed rapidly; Burleigh and his wife led her tottering back to her couch, place her upon it in an extremity of weakness. Elizabeth, feeling herself dying, consented at last to name her successor.

I gave James to understand, by a look, that my choice perforce fell upon him, and motioned him to kneel before me. Lady Burleigh handed me the crown, and with trembling fingers I was about to place it on his head, saying, unwillingly and with difficulty,

"James, kneel! I crown thee King!"

But I spoke the words with a visible effort, as though they were rent from my inmost heart. The crowd, gathering outside the palace, at a sign made by Davison from the balcony, set up a great shout of :—

"Long live James I., King of England!"

Their acclamations, however, irritated me almost past endurance. I cried in my pain and anger that my subjects were fickle and ungrateful. I tore the crown from James's head, and, placing it once more upon my own, held it there firmly with both hands, while I shrieked :—

"Ungrateful people, I yet live!"

But this supreme effort exhausted my small remaining strength. I sank back once more on my couch with the death-rattle in my throat, and with my last conscious breath committed to my successor's keeping

"The Bible and my father's sword."

Then began the final agony, rendered all the more terrible by my ever-present remembrance of the unfortunate Essex. I fancied I saw him stand before me. I stretched out my arms towards him, as though beseeching him to come and give me the kiss of forgiveness ; and after a brief struggle with death I sank to rest, and lay with glazed eyes, surrounded by my courtiers, who in awe-struck tones pronounced the words :—

"She is dead! Dead!"

Behold how I have endeavored to interpret this masterpiece of the lamented Giacometti. I have studied, as aforesaid, within the rigorous limits of history, that extraordinary character of a woman and a Queen.

For myself, the last scenes, which are, one may say, the epic of the drama, I went on developing with firmness the conviction that all the bitterness of those transitions, from dejection to energy, were the prelude of a very bitter adieu to a long past of power ; and all that I have studied to interpret and make understood is a recapitulation of the fascination slowly extinguishing itself and of the remorse increasing to gigantic proportions as death was drawing nigh.

THE END.

Famous Women Series.

MADAME DE STAËL.

By BELLA DUFFY.

One Volume. 16mo. Cloth. Price, $1.00.

It is a brilliant subject, and handled in a brilliant as well as an intelligent manner. — *The Independent.*

The biography of this remarkable woman is written in a spirit of candor and fairness that will at once commend it to the attention of those who are seeking the truth. The author is not so much in love with her subject as to lose sight of her faults; nor is she so blind to Madame de Staël's merits as to place confidence in the many cruel things that have been said of her by her enemies. The review of Madame de Staël's works, which closes this volume, exhibits rare critical insight; and the abstract of "Corinne" here given will be welcomed by those who have never had the patience to wade through this long but celebrated classic, which combines somewhat incongruously the qualities of a novel and an Italian guide-book. In answering the question, Why was not Madame de Staël a greater writer? her biographer admirably condenses a great deal of analytical comment into a very brief space. Madame de Staël was undoubtedly the most celebrated woman of her time, and this fact is never lost sight of in this carefully written record of her life. — *Saturday Evening Gazette.*

It treats of one of the most fascinating and remarkable women of history. The name of Madame de Staël is invested with every charm that brilliance of intellect, romance, and magnetic power to fascinate and compel the admiration of men can bestow. Not beautiful herself, she wielded a power which the most beautiful women envied her and could not rival. The story of her life should read like a novel, and is one of the best in this series of interesting books published by Roberts Brothers, Boston. — *Chicago Journal.*

We have Messrs. Roberts Brothers to thank for issuing a series of biographies upon which entire dependence may be placed, the volumes in the "Famous Women Series" being thus far invariably trustworthy and enjoyable. Certainly the life of Madame de Staël, which Miss Bella Duffy has just written for it, is as good as the best of its predecessors; of each of which, according to our reasoning, the same thing might appropriately be said. Miss Duffy has little to tell of her subject that has not already been told in longer biographies, it is true; but from a great variety of sources she has extracted enough material to make an excellent study of the great Frenchwoman in a small space, which has never been done before successfully, so far as we know. Considering the size of the book, one marvels at the completeness of the picture the author presents, not only of Madame de Staël herself, but of her friends, and of the stirring times in which she lived and which so deeply colored her whole life. Miss Duffy, though disposed to look at her faults rather leniently, is by no means forgetful of them; she simply does her all the justice that the facts in the case warrant, which is perhaps more than readers of the longer biographies before referred to expect. At the end of the volume is a chapter devoted to the writings of Madame de Staël, which is so admirable a bit of literary criticism that we advise the purchase of the book if only for its sake. — *The Capital, Washington.*

Sold by all booksellers. Mailed, post-paid, on receipt of price, by the publishers,

ROBERTS BROTHERS, Boston.

Famous Women Series.

SUSANNA WESLEY.

By ELIZA CLARKE.

ONE VOLUME. 16mo. CLOTH. PRICE, $1.00.

The "Famous Women Series," published at a dollar the volume by Roberts Brothers, now comprises George Eliot, Emily Brontë, George Sand, Mary Lamb, Margaret Fuller, Maria Edgeworth, Elizabeth Fry, the Countess of Albany, Mary Wollstonecraft, Harriet Martineau, Rachel, Madame Roland, and Susanna Wesley. The next volume will be Madame de Staël. The world has not gone into any ecstasies over these volumes. They are not discussed in the theatre or hotel lobbies, and even fashionable society knows very little about them. Yet there is a goodly company of quiet people that delight in this series. And well they may; for there are few biographical series more attractive, more modest, and more profitable than these "Famous Women." If one wanted to send a birthday or Christmas gift to a woman one honors, — whether she is twenty or sixty years old need not matter, — it would not be easy to select a better set than these volumes. To be sure, Americans do not figure prominently in the series, a certain preference being given to Englishwomen and Frenchwomen; but that does not diminish the intrinsic merit of each volume. One likes to add, also, that nearly the whole set has been written from a purely historical or matter-of-fact point of view, there being very little in the way of special pleading or one-sidedness. This applies especially to the mother of the Wesleys. Mankind has treated the whole Wesley family as if it was the special, not to say exclusive, property of the Methodists. But there is no fee-simple in good men or women, and all mankind may well lay a certain claim to all those who have in any way excelled or rendered important service to mankind at large. Eliza Clarke's life of Susanna Wesley tells us truly that she was "a lady of ancient lineage, a woman of intellect, a keen politician," and profoundly religious, as well as a shrewd observer of men, things, and society at large. . . . Her life is that of a gifted, high-minded, and prudent woman. It is told in a straightforward manner, and it should be read far beyond the lines of the Methodist denomination. There must have been many women in Colonial New England who resembled Susanna Wesley; for she was a typical character, both in worldly matters and in her spiritual life. — *The Beacon.*

Mrs. Wesley was the mother of nineteen children, among whom were John, the founder, and Charles, the sweet singer, of Methodism. Her husband was a poor country rector, who eked out by writing verses the slender stipend his clerical office brought him. Mrs. Wesley was a woman of gentle birth, intense religious convictions, strong character, and singular devotion to her children. This biography is well written, and is eminently readable, as well as historically valuable. — *Cambridge Tribune.*

Sold by all booksellers. Mailed, post-paid, on receipt of the price, by the publishers,

ROBERTS BROTHERS, Boston.

Famous Women Series.

MRS. SIDDONS.

By NINA H. KENNARD.

One Volume. 16mo. Cloth. Price, $1.00.

The latest contribution to the "Famous Women Series" gives the life of Mrs. Siddons, carefully and appreciatively compiled by Nina H. Kennard. Previous lives of Mrs. Siddons have failed to present the many-sided character of the great tragic queen, representing her more exclusively in her dramatic capacity. Mrs. Kennard presents the main facts in the lives previously written by Campbell and Boaden, as well as the portion of the great actress's history appearing in Percy Fitzgerald's "Lives of the Kembles;" and beyond any other biographer gives the more tender and domestic side of her nature, particularly as shown in her hitherto unpublished letters. The story of the early dramatic endeavors of the little Sarah Kemble proves not the least interesting part of the narrative, and it is with a distinct human interest that her varying progress is followed until she gains the summit of popular favor and success. The picture of her greatest public triumphs receives tender and artistic touches in the view we are given of the idol of brilliant and intellectual London sitting down with her husband and father to a frugal home supper on retiring from the glare of the footlights. — *Commonwealth.*

We think the author shows good judgment in devoting comparatively little space to criticism of Mrs. Siddons's dramatic methods, and giving special attention to her personal traits and history. Hers was an extremely interesting life, remarkable no less for its private virtues than for its public triumphs. Her struggle to gain the place her genius deserved was heroic in its persistence and dignity. Her relations with the authors, wits, and notables of her day give occasion for much entertaining and interesting anecdotical literature. Herself free from humor, she was herself often the occasion of fun in others. The stories of her tragic manner in private life are many and ludicrous. . . . The book abounds in anecdotes, bits of criticism, and pictures of the stage and of society in a very interesting transitional period. — *Christian Union.*

A fitting addition to this so well and so favorably known series is the life of the wonderful actress, Sarah Siddons, by Mrs. Nina Kennard. To most of the present generation the great woman is only a name, though she lived until 1831; but the present volume, with its vivid account of her life, its struggles, triumphs, and closing years, will give to such a picture that is most lifelike. A particularly pleasant feature of the book is the way in which the author quotes so copiously from Mrs. Siddons's correspondence. These extracts from letters written to friends, and with no thought of their ever appearing in print, give the most spontaneous expressions of feeling on the part of the writer, as well as her own account of many events of her life. They furnish, therefore, better data upon which to base an opinion of her real personality and character than anything else could possibly give. The volume is interesting from beginning to end, and one rises from its perusal with the warmest admiration for Sarah Siddons because of her great genius, her real goodness, and her true womanliness, shown in the relations of daughter, wife, and mother. Modern actresses, amateur or professional, with avowed intentions of "elevating the stage," should study this noble woman's example; for in this direction she accomplished more, probably, than any other one person has ever done, and at greater odds. — *N. E. Journal of Education.*

Sold by all booksellers. Mailed, post-paid, on receipt of price, by the publishers,

ROBERTS BROTHERS, Boston.

𝔉𝔞𝔪𝔬𝔲𝔰 𝔚𝔬𝔪𝔢𝔫 𝔖𝔢𝔯𝔦𝔢𝔰.

MARGARET OF ANGOULÊME,

QUEEN OF NAVARRE.

By A. MARY F. ROBINSON.

One Volume. 16mo. Cloth. Price, $1.00.

The latest addition to the excellent "Famous Women Series" is a sketch of the Queen of Navarre, one of the most deservedly famous women of the sixteenth century. In political influence she is fitly compared to Queen Elizabeth of England and Margaret of Austria; and as to her services to religion, she has been referred to as "the divinity of the great religious movement of her time, and the upholder of the mere natural rights of humanity in an age that only respected opinions." The story of this remarkable woman is here told briefly, and with a discrimination that does credit to the biographer. — *Times-Star, Cincinnati.*

Margaret of Angoulême furnishes a noble subject, which has been ably treated. Miss Robinson's sketch proves thorough research and a clear conception of her work, possessing a perfect knowledge of the characters and events connected with that period. She is in sympathy with every movement, and explicit in detail, being strictly confined to facts which may be authentically received. . . . This excellent biography is a source of enjoyment from the first page to the last, and should be read by every student and lover of history. It abounds in instructive and enjoyable reading, furnishing a valuable addition to this popular series. — *Utica Press.*

One of the most readable volumes thus far in the "Famous Women Series" has just been published by Roberts Brothers. It is Mary F. Robinson's "Life of Margaret of Angoulême, Queen of Navarre." Judging from the fifty different authorities that the writer has consulted, it is evident that she has taken great pains to sympathize with the spirit of the era which she describes. Only a warm imagination, stimulated by an intimate knowledge of details, will help an author to make his reader realize that the past was as present to those who lived in it as the present is to us. Miss Robinson has compiled a popular history, that has the easy flow and lifelike picturesqueness which it is so often the aim of the novelist to display. Such books as this, carefully and even artistically written as they are, help to fill up vacant nooks in the minds of those who have read large histories in which personal biography can hold but a small place; while at the same time they give the non-historical reader a good deal of information which is, or ought to be, more interesting than many a fiction. Nor does Miss Robinson estimate the influence of Margaret of Angoulême wrongly when she traces the salvation of a nation to her mercy and magnanimity. — *N. Y. Telegram.*

It is reasonable and impartial in its views, and yet clear in its judgments. The immense importance of Queen Margaret's influence on the beginnings of modern thoughts in France is clearly set forth, but without exaggeration or undue emphasis. Miss Robinson is especially happy in her portrayal of Margaret's complex character, which under her hand becomes both human and consistent; and the volume, although small, is a valuable addition to the history of France in the sixteenth century. — *Boston Courier.*

Sold by all booksellers. Mailed, post-paid, on receipt of price, by the publishers,

ROBERTS BROTHERS, Boston.

Famous Women Series.

◆

MADAME ROLAND.

By MATHILDE BLIND,

AUTHOR OF "GEORGE ELIOT'S LIFE."

One volume. 16mo. Cloth. Price, $1.00.

———— ◆ ————

"Of all the interesting biographies published in the Famous Women Series, Mathilde Blind's life of Mme. Roland is by far the most fascinating. . . . But no one can read Mme. Roland's thrilling story, and no one can study the character of this noble, heroic woman without feeling certain that it is good for the world to have every incident of her life brought again before the public eye. Among the famous women who have been enjoying a new birth through this set of short biographies, no single one has been worthy of the adjective *great* until we come to Mme. Roland. . . .

"We see a brilliant intellectual women in Mme. Roland; we see a dutiful daughter and devoted wife; we see a woman going forth bravely to place her neck under the guillotine, — a woman who had been known as the 'Soul of the Girondins;' and we see a woman struggling with and not being overcome by an intense and passionate love. Has history a more heroic picture to present us with? Is there any woman more deserving of the adjective 'great'?

"Mathilde Blind has had rich materials from which to draw for Mme. Roland's biography. She writes graphically, and describes some of the terrible scenes in the French Revolution with great picturesqueness. The writer's sympathy with Mme. Roland and her enthusiasm is very contagious; and we follow her record almost breathlessly, and with intense feeling turn over the last few pages of this little volume. No one can doubt that this life was worth the writing, and even earnest students of the French Revolution will be glad to refresh their memories of Lamartine's 'History of the Girondins,' and again have brought vividly before them the terrible tragedy of Mme. Roland's life and death." — *Boston Evening Transcript.*

"The thrilling story of Madame Roland's genius, nobility, self-sacrifice, and death loses nothing in its retelling here. The material has been collected and arranged in an unbroken and skilfully narrated sketch, each picturesque or exciting incident being brought out into a strong light. The book is one of the best in an excellent series." — *Christian Union.*

———— ◆ ————

For sale by all booksellers. Mailed, post-paid, on receipt of price by the publishers,

𝔉𝔞𝔪𝔬𝔲𝔰 𝔚𝔬𝔪𝔢𝔫 𝔖𝔢𝔯𝔦𝔢𝔰.

HARRIET MARTINEAU.

By Mrs. F. FENWICK MILLER.

16mo. Cloth. Price $1.00.

"The almost uniform excellence of the 'Famous Women' series is well sustained in Mrs. Fenwick Miller's life of Harriet Martineau, the latest addition to this little library of biography. Indeed, we are disposed to rank it as the best of the lot. The subject is an entertaining one, and Mrs. Miller has done her work admirably. Miss Martineau was a remarkable woman, in a century that has not been deficient in notable characters. Her native genius, and her perseverance in developing it ; her trials and afflictions, and the determination with which she rose superior to them ; her conscientious adherence to principle, and the important place which her writings hold in the political and educational literature of her day, —all combine to make the story of her life one of exceptional interest. . . . With the exception, possibly, of George Eliot, Harriet Martineau was the greatest of English women. She was a poet and a novelist, but not as such did she make good her title to distinction. Much more noteworthy were her achievements in other lines of thought, not usually essayed by women. She was eminent as a political economist, a theologian, a journalist, and a historian. . . . But to attempt a mere outline of her life and works is out of the question in our limited space. Her biography should be read by all in search of entertainment." — *Professor Woods in Saturday Mirror.*

"The present volume has already shared the fate of several of the recent biographies of the distinguished dead, and has been well advertised by the public contradiction of more or less important points in the relation by the living friends of the dead genius. One of Mrs. Miller's chief concerns in writing this life seems to have been to redeem the character of Harriet Martineau from the appearance of hardness and unamiability with which her own autobiography impresses the reader. . . . Mrs. Miller, however, succeeds in this volume in showing us an altogether different side to her character, —a home-loving, neighborly, bright-natured, tender-hearted, witty, lovable, and altogether womanly woman, as well as the clear thinker, the philosophical reasoner, and comprehensive writer whom we already knew." — *The Index.*

"Already ten volumes in this library are published ; namely, George Eliot, Emily Brontë, George Sand, Mary Lamb, Margaret Fuller, Maria Edgeworth, Elizabeth Fry, The Countess of Albany, Mary Wollstonecraft, and the present volume. Surely a galaxy of wit and wealth of no mean order ! Miss M. will rank with any of them in womanliness or gifts or grace. At home or abroad, in public or private. She was noble and true, and her life stands confessed a success. True, she was literary, but she was a home lover and home builder. She never lost the higher aims and ends of life, no matter how flattering her success. This whole series ought to be read by the young ladies of to-day. More of such biography would prove highly beneficial." — *Troy Telegram.*

Our publications are for sale by all booksellers, or will be mailed, post-paid, on receipt of price.

ROBERTS BROTHERS, Boston.

Famous Women Series.

RACHEL.

By Mrs. NINA H. KENNARD.

One Volume. 16mo. Cloth. Price, $1.00.

"*Rachel*, by Nina H. Kennard, is an interesting sketch of the famous woman whose passion and genius won for her an almost unrivalled fame as an actress. The story of Rachel's career is of the most brilliant success in art and of the most pathetic failure in character. Her faults, many and grievous, are overlooked in this volume, and the better aspects of her nature and history are recorded." — *Hartford Courant*.

"The book is well planned, has been carefully constructed, and is pleasantly written." — *The Critic*.

"The life of Mlle. Élisa Rachel Félix has never been adequately told, and the appearance of her biography in the 'Famous Women Series' of Messrs. Roberts Brothers will be welcomed. . . . Yet we must be glad the book is written, and welcome it to a place among the minor biographies; and because there is nothing else so good, the volume is indispensable to library and study." — *Boston Evening Traveller*.

"Another life of the great actress Rachel has been written. It forms part of the 'Famous Women Series,' which that firm is now bringing out, and which already includes eleven volumes. Mrs. Kennard deals with her subject much more amiably than one or two of the other biographers have done. She has none of those vindictive feelings which are so obvious in Madame B.'s narrative of the great tragedienne. On the contrary, she wants to be fair, and she probably is as fair as the materials which came into her possession enabled her to be. The endeavor has been made to show us Rachel as she really was, by relying to a great extent upon her letters. . . . A good many stories that we are familiar with are repeated, and some are contradicted. From first to last, however, the sympathy of the author is ardent, whether she recounts the misery of Rachel's childhood, or the splendid altitude to which she climbed when her name echoed through the world and the great ones of the earth vied in doing her homage. On this account Mrs. Kennard's book is a welcome addition to the pre-existing biographies of one of the greatest actresses the world ever saw." — *N. Y. Evening Telegram*.

Sold everywhere. Mailed postpaid, by the Publishers,

ROBERTS BROTHERS, Boston.

Famous Women Series.

———◆———

MARY WOLLSTONECRAFT.

BY

ELIZABETH ROBINS PENNELL.

One volume. 16mo. Cloth. Price $1.00.

———◆———

"So far as it has been published, and it has now reached its ninth volume, the Famous Women Series is rather better on the whole than the English Men of Letters Series. One had but to recall the names and characteristics of some of the women with whom it deals, — literary women, like Maria Edgeworth, Margaret Fuller, Mary Lamb, Emily Brontë, George Eliot, and George Sand; women of the world (not to mention the other parties in that well-known Scriptural firm), like the naughty but fascinating Countess of Albany; and women of philanthropy, of which the only example given here so far is Mrs. Elizabeth Fry, — one has but to compare the intellectual qualities of the majority of English men of letters to perceive that the former are the most difficult to handle, and that a series of which they are the heroines is, if successful, a remarkable collection of biographies. We thought so as we read Miss Blind's study of George Sand, and Vernon Lee's study of the Countess of Albany, and we think so now that we have read Mrs. Elizabeth Robins Pennell's study of Mary Wollstonecraft, who, with all her faults, was an honor to her sex. She was not so considered while she lived, except by those who knew her well, nor for years after her death; but she is so considered now, even by the granddaughters of the good ladies who so bitterly condemned her when the century was new. She was notable for the sacrifices that she made for her worthless father and her weak, inefficient sisters, for her dogged persistence and untiring industry, and for her independence and her courage. The soul of goodness was in her, though she would be herself and go on her own way; and if she loved not wisely, according to the world's creed, she loved too well for her own happiness, and paid the penalty of suffering. What she might have been if she had not met Capt. Gilbert Imlay, who was a scoundrel, and William Godwin, who was a philosopher, can only be conjectured. She was a force in literature and in the enfranchisement of her sisterhood, and as such was worthy of the remembrance which she will long retain through Mrs. Pennell's able memoir." — *R. H. Stoddard, in the Mail and Express.*

———◆———

Sold by all booksellers. Mailed, post-paid, on receipt of price by the publishers,

ROBERTS BROTHERS,

BOSTON

FAMOUS WOMEN SERIES.

THE COUNTESS OF ALBANY.

BY VERNON LEE.

One volume. 16mo. Cloth. Price $1.00.

"It is no disparagement to the many excellent previous sketches to say that 'The Countess of Albany,' by Vernon Lee, is decidedly the cleverest of the series of biographies of ' Famous Women,' published in this country by Roberts Brothers, Boston. In the present instance there is a freer subject, a little farther removed from contemporary events, and sufficiently out of the way of prejudice to admit of a lucid handling. Moreover, there is a trained hand at the work, and a mind not only familiar with and in sympathy with the character under discussion, but also at home with the ruling forces of the eighteenth century, which were the forces that made the Countess of Albany what she was. The biography is really dual, tracing the life of Alfieri, for twenty-five years the heart and soul companion of the Countess, quite as carefully as it traces that of the fixed subject of the sketch." — *Philadelphia Times.*

"To be unable altogether to acquiesce in Vernon Lee's portrait of Louise of Stolberg does not militate against our sense of the excellence of her work. Her pictures of eighteenth-century Italy are definite and brilliant. They are instinct with a quality that is akin to magic." — *London Academy.*

"In the records of famous women preserved in the interesting series which has been devoted to such noble characters as Margaret Fuller, Elizabeth Fry, and George Eliot, the life of the Countess of Albany holds a unique place. Louise of Albany, or Louise R., as she liked to sign herself, possessed a character famed, not for domestic virtues, nor even for peculiar wisdom and creative power, but rather notorious for an easy-going indifference to conventionality and a worldly wisdom and cynicism. Her life, which is a singular exponent of the false ideas prevalent upon the subject of love and marriage in the eighteenth century, is told by Vernon Lee in a vivid and discriminating manner. The biography is one of the most fascinating, if the most sorrowful, of the series." — *Boston Journal.*

"She is the first really historical character who has appeared on the literary horizon of this particular series, her predecessors having been limited to purely literary women. This brilliant little biography is strongly written. Unlike preceding writers — German, French, and English — on the same subject, the author does not hastily pass over the details of the Platonic relations that existed between the Countess and the celebrated Italian poet ' Alfieri.' In this biography the details of that passionate friendship are given with a fidelity to truth, and a knowledge of its nature, that is based upon the strictest and most conscientious investigation, and access to means heretofore unattainable to other biographers. The history of this friendship is not only exceedingly interesting, but it presents a fascinating psychological study to those who are interested in the metaphysical aspect of human nature. The book is almost as much of a biography of ' Alfieri ' as it is of the wife of the Pretender, who expected to become the Queen of England." — *Hartford Times.*

Sold by all booksellers. Mailed, postpaid, on receipt of the price, by the publishers,

ROBERTS BROTHERS, Boston.

Famous Women Series.

— • —

ELIZABETH FRY.

By Mrs. E. R. PITMAN.

One vol. 16mo. Cloth. Price $1.00.

———— • ————

"In the records of famous women there are few more noble examples of Christian womanhood and philanthropic enthusiasm than the life of Elizabeth Fry presents. Her character was beautifully rounded and complete, and if she had not won fame through her public benefactions, she would have been no less esteemed and remembered by all who knew her because of her domestic virtues, her sweet womanly charms, and the wisdom, purity, and love which marked her conduct as wife, mother, and friend. She came of that sound old Quaker stock which has bred so many eminent men and women. The time came when her home functions could no longer satisfy the yearnings of a heart filled with the tenderest pity for all who suffered; and her work was not far to seek. The prisons of England, nay, of all Europe, were in a deplorable condition. In Newgate, dirt, disease, starvation, depravity, drunkenness, &c., prevailed. All who surveyed the situation regarded it as hopeless; all but Mrs. Fry. She saw here the opening she had been awaiting. Into this seething mass she bravely entered, Bible in hand, and love and pity in her eyes and upon her lips. If any one should ask which of all the famous women recorded in this series did the most practical good in her day and generation, the answer must be, Elizabeth Fry." — *New York Tribune.*

"Mrs. Pitman has written a very interesting and appreciative sketch of the life, character, and eminent services in the causes of humanity of one of England's most famous philanthropists. She was known as the prison philanthropist, and probably no laborer in the cause of prison reform ever won a larger share of success, and certainly none ever received a larger meed of reverential love. No one can read this volume without feelings of admiration for the noble woman who devoted her life to befriend sinful and suffering humanity." — *Chicago Evening Journal.*

"The story of her splendid and successful philanthropy is admirably told by her biographer, and every reader should find in the tale a breath of inspiration. Not every woman can become an Elizabeth Fry, but no one can fail to be impressed with the thought that no woman, however great her talent and ambition, can fail to find opportunity to do a noble work in life without neglecting her own feminine duties, without ceasing to dignify all the distinctive virtues of her sex, without fretting and crying aloud over the restrictions placed on woman's field of work." — *Eclectic Monthly.*

————— ◇ —————

Our publications are for sale by all booksellers, or will be sent post-paid on receipt of advertised price.

ROBERTS BROTHERS, Boston.

Famous Women Series.

MARGARET FULLER.

By JULIA WARD HOWE.

One volume. 16mo. Cloth. Price $1.00.

" A memoir of the woman who first in New England took a position of moral and intellectual leadership, by the woman who wrote the Battle Hymn of the Republic, is a literary event of no common or transient interest. The Famous Women Series will have no worthier subject and no more illustrious biographer. Nor will the reader be disappointed, — for the narrative is deeply interesting and full of inspiration." — *Woman's Journal.*

"Mrs. Julia Ward Howe's biography of *Margaret Fuller*, in the Famous Women Series of Messrs. Roberts Brothers, is a work which has been looked for with curiosity. It will not disappoint expectation. She has made a brilliant and an interesting book. Her study of Margaret Fuller's character is thoroughly sympathetic ; her relation of her life is done in a graphic and at times a fascinating manner. It is the case of one woman of strong individuality depicting the points which made another one of the most marked characters of her day. It is always agreeable to follow Mrs. Howe in this ; for while we see marks of her own mind constantly, there is no inartistic protrusion of her personality. The book is always readable, and the relation of the death-scene is thrillingly impressive." — *Saturday Gazette.*

"Mrs. Julia Ward Howe has retold the story of Margaret Fuller's life and career in a very interesting manner. This remarkable woman was happy in having James Freeman Clarke, Ralph Waldo Emerson, and William Henry Channing, all of whom had been intimate with her and had felt the spell of her extraordinary personal influence, for her biographers. It is needless to say, of course, that nothing could be better than these reminiscences in their way." — *New York World.*

"The selection of Mrs. Howe as the writer of this biography was a happy thought on the part of the editor of the series ; for, aside from the natural appreciation she would have for Margaret Fuller, comes her knowledge of all the influences that had their effect on Margaret Fuller's life. She tells the story of Margaret Fuller's interesting life from all sources and from her own knowledge, not hesitating to use plenty of quotations when she felt that others, or even Margaret Fuller herself, had done the work better." — *Miss Gilder, in Philadelphia Press.*

Sold by all booksellers. Mailed, post-paid, on receipt of the price, by the publishers,

ROBERTS BROTHERS,
BOSTON, MASS.

Famous Women Series.

·

MARIA EDGEWORTH.

By HELEN ZIMMERN.

One volume. 16mo. Cloth. Price $1.00.

·

"This little volume shows good literary workmanship. It does not weary the reader with vague theories; nor does it give over much expression to the enthusiasm — not to say baseless encomium — for which too many female biographers have accustomed us to look. It is a simple and discriminative sketch of one of the most clever and lovable of the class at whom Carlyle sneered as 'scribbling women.' . . . Of Maria Edgeworth, the woman, one cannot easily say too much in praise. That home life, so loving, so wise, and so helpful, was beautiful to its end. Miss Zimmern has treated it with delicate appreciation. Her book is refined in conception and tasteful in execution, — all, in short, the cynic might say, that we expect a woman's book to be." — *New York Tribune.*

"It was high time that we should possess an adequate biography of this ornament and general benefactor of her time. And so we hail with uncommon pleasure the volume just published in the Roberts Brothers' series of Famous Women, of which it is the sixth. We have only words of praise for the manner in which Miss Zimmern has written her life of Maria Edgeworth. It exhibits sound judgment, critical analysis, and clear characterization. . . . The style of the volume is pure, limpid, and strong, as we might expect from a well-trained English writer." — *Margaret J. Preston, in the Home Journal.*

"We can heartily recommend this life of Maria Edgeworth, not only because it is singularly readable in itself, but because it makes familiar to readers of the present age a notable figure in English literary history, with whose lineaments we suspect most readers, especially of the present generation, are less familiar than they ought to be." — *Eclectic.*

"This biography contains several letters and papers by Miss Edgeworth that have not before been made public, notably some charming letters written during the latter part of her life to Dr. Holland and Mr. and Mrs. Ticknor. The author had access to a life of Miss Edgeworth written by her step-mother, as well as to a large collection of her private letters, and has therefore been able to bring forward many facts in her life which have not been noted by other writers. The book is written in a pleasant vein, and is altogether a delightful one to read." — *Utica Herald.*

·

Sold by all booksellers. Mailed, post-paid, by the publishers,

ROBERTS BROTHERS,

Boston, Mass.

FAMOUS WOMEN SERIES.

GEORGE SAND.

By BERTHA THOMAS.

One volume. 16mo. Cloth. Price, $1.00.

"Miss Thomas has accomplished a difficult task with as much good sense as good feeling. She presents the main facts of George Sand's life, extenuating nothing, and setting naught down in malice, but wisely leaving her readers to form their own conclusions. Everybody knows that it was not such a life as the women of England and America are accustomed to live, and as the worst of men are glad to have them live. . . . Whatever may be said against it, its result on George Sand was not what it would have been upon an English or American woman of genius." — *New York Mail and Express.*

"This is a volume of the 'Famous Women Series,' which was begun so well with George Eliot and Emily Brontë. The book is a review and critical analysis of George Sand's life and work, by no means a detailed biography. Amantine Lucile Aurore Dupin, the maiden, or Mme. Dudevant, the married woman, is forgotten in the renown of the pseudonym George Sand.

"Altogether, George Sand, with all her excesses and defects, is a representative woman, one of the names of the nineteenth century. She was great among the greatest, the friend and compeer of the finest intellects, and Miss Thomas's essay will be a useful and agreeable introduction to a more extended study of her life and works." — *Knickerbocker.*

"The biography of this famous woman, by Miss Thomas, is the only one in existence. Those who have awaited it with pleasurable anticipation, but with some trepidation as to the treatment of the erratic side of her character, cannot fail to be pleased with the skill by which it is done. It is the best production on George Sand that has yet been published. The author modestly refers to it as a sketch, which it undoubtedly is, but a sketch that gives a just and discriminating analysis of George Sand's life, tastes, occupations, and of the motives and impulses which prompted her unconventional actions, that were misunderstood by a narrow public. The difficulties encountered by the writer in describing this remarkable character are shown in the first line of the opening chapter, which says, 'In naming George Sand we name something more exceptional than even a great genius.' That tells the whole story. Misconstruction, condemnation, and isolation are the penalties enforced upon the great leaders in the realm of advanced thought, by the bigoted people of their time. The thinkers soar beyond the common herd, whose soul-wings are not strong enough to fly aloft to clearer atmospheres, and consequently they censure or ridicule what they are powerless to reach. George Sand, even to a greater extent than her contemporary, George Eliot, was a victim to ignorant social prejudices, but even the conservative world was forced to recognize the matchless genius of these two extraordinary women, each widely different in her character and method of thought and writing. : . . She has told much that is good which has been untold, and just what will interest the reader, and no more, in the same easy, entertaining style that characterizes all of these unpretentious biographies." — *Hartford Times.*

Sold everywhere. Mailed, post-paid, on receipt of price, by the publishers,

ROBERTS BROTHERS, Boston.

FAMOUS WOMEN SERIES.

—•—

EMILY BRONTË.

By A. MARY F. ROBINSON.

One vol. 16mo. Cloth. Price, $1.00.

" Miss Robinson has written a fascinating biography. . . . Emily Brontë is interesting, not because she wrote 'Wuthering Heights,' but because of her brave, baffled, human life, so lonely, so full of pain, but with a great hope shining beyond all the darkness, and a passionate defiance in bearing more than the burdens that were laid upon her. The story of the three sisters is infinitely sad, but it is the ennobling sadness that belongs to large natures cramped and striving for freedom to heroic, almost desperate, work, with little or no result. The author of this intensely interesting, sympathetic, and eloquent biography, is a young lady and a poet, to whom a place is given in a recent anthology of living English poets, which is supposed to contain only the best poems of the best writers." — *Boston Daily Advertiser.*

" Miss Robinson had many excellent qualifications for the task she has performed in this little volume, among which may be named, an enthusiastic interest in her subject and a real sympathy with Emily Brontë's sad and heroic life. 'To represent her as she was,' says Miss Robinson, 'would be her noblest and most fitting monument.' . . . Emily Brontë here becomes well known to us and, in one sense, this should be praise enough for any biography." — *New York Times.*

" The biographer who finds such material before him as the lives and characters of the Brontë family need have no anxiety as to the interest of his work. Characters not only strong but so uniquely strong, genius so supreme, misfortunes so overwhelming, set in its scenery so forlornly picturesque, could not fail to attract all readers, if told even in the most prosaic language. When we add to this, that Miss Robinson has told their story *not* in prosaic language, but with a literary style exhibiting all the qualities essential to good biography, our readers will understand that this life of Emily Brontë is not only as interesting as a novel, but a great deal more interesting than most novels. As it presents most vividly a general picture of the family, there seems hardly a reason for giving it Emily's name alone, except perhaps for the masterly chapters on ' Wuthering Heights,' which the reader will find a grateful condensation of the best in that powerful but somewhat forbidding story. We know of no point in the Brontë history — their genius, their surroundings, their faults, their happiness, their misery, their love and friendships, their peculiarities, their power, their gentleness, their patience, their pride, — which Miss Robinson has not touched upon with conscientiousness and sympathy." — *The Critic.*

" ' Emily Brontë ' is the second of the ' Famous Women Series,' which Roberts Brothers, Boston, propose to publish, and of which ' George Eliot ' was the initial volume. Not the least remarkable of a very remarkable family, the personage whose life is here written, possesses a peculiar interest to all who are at all familiar with the sad and singular history of herself and her sister Charlotte. That the author, Miss A. Mary F. Robinson, has done her work with minute fidelity to facts as well as affectionate devotion to the subject of her sketch, is plainly to be seen all through the book." — *Washington Post.*

———

Sold by all Booksellers, or mailed, post-paid, on receipt of price, by the Publishers,

ROBERTS BROTHERS, Boston.